# Other Doors

by

G. L. Helm

Published by Rogue Phoenix Press


Names, characters and incidents depicted in this book are products of the author's imagination or are used fictitiously. Any resemblance to actual events, locales, organizations, or persons, living or dead, is entirely coincidental and beyond the intent of the author or the publisher.



ISBN: 978-1-62420-024-3

**Credits**

Cover Artist: Christine Young

Editor: Brian Young

**Printed in the United States of America**

# PART ONE

# THE VOYAGER

*"Seek Peace, and pursue it."*
Psalms 34:14

*"Blessed are the Peacemakers, for they shall be called the children of God."*
Matthew 5:9

## Chapter One

Ben Fordham opened his eyes and didn't like what he saw. There seemed to be a damp slimy stone wall a couple of yards in front of him and he knew that wasn't right. A flickery yellow light from somewhere out of his line of sight made the slimy ooze reflect back like the trail a snail leaves on a sidewalk. A steady sound of dripping water came from somewhere. He had awakened in some pretty strange places over the last several weeks, but this was the worst. His head felt like it was being squeezed in a vice and his stomach felt as slimy and gross as the wall looked, but he didn't see any spiders or snakes--real or alcoholic--and he was thankful for that.

Life had not done well by Benjamin Fordham recently. It had never done all that well by him, but of late it had been more cruel than usual. Over the last several months he had lost his wife, his job, and a small piece of his skull. The job and the piece of his skull he felt he could live without, although having the left front side of his skull just above the hairline crunched with a framing hammer had come pretty close to taking his life.

Ben squeezed his eyes shut so hard he began to see phosphene spots then opened them again. He was disappointed to discover that the nasty looking wall was still there. There was also a musty mildewed smell he hadn't noticed at first.

*This is some nightmare.* He was familiar with nightmares of such a place. In those he was always chained up waiting for something horrible to come and get him. He tried to comfort himself with the thought that he would wake up pretty soon, but somehow his mind just wasn't buying it. He had dreamed like this since he was a kid, especially after having gotten in the middle of some fight and been read the riot act by his father. That usually came after his mother had patched him up so he wouldn't bleed on the rug.

Ben tried to turn his head to ease the pain in his neck, but found he could not move. The vice squeezing his head wasn't all hangover. Something else was there. Something real.

*OK Ben. Time to wake up. This is entirely too real.*

A drop of cold water dripped down the back of his neck. The shock of it made him jump and the thought that the water was similar to what he could see oozing down the other wall made his stomach rebel. He gagged, but nothing came up.

The jumping away from the cold drip told him something else too. This wasn't a nightmare. He was chained up in some sort of dungeon with slimy wet walls, just like from his nightmares.

Panic grabbed his insides and he thrashed against his restraints like a trapped wild animal. Only the tightness of his bonds saved him from hurting himself. Sturdy leather bands held his thick wrists and broad forearms to the chair arms.

There were straps across his chest, around his forehead, across his shins, and around his ankles. He could move his eyes and hump his hips up and down, but that was all.

In his childhood nightmares the next thing would have been the heavy tread of booted feet, which was usually the end of the dream, but when the sound of measured steps laid themselves over the rhythmic drip, this time he didn't wake up. The dungeon lightened suddenly as two men carrying torches came from behind Ben. They bore themselves like soldiers, but they were like no soldiers Ben had ever seen before. They wore round bronze helmets with stiff cheek flaps. The metal reflected the red light of the torches, as did the leather and bronze chest armor. It all glowed with polishing. Soft leather tunics were beneath the armor. It showed at the armholes and between the stiff leather palings which hung like skirts from the soldiers' waists. There was nothing in the least feminine looking about the skirts, and they were made even less feminine by the expanse of hairy leg showing between their bottoms and the tops of the bound leather shin armor. Both soldiers had short swords and daggers belted to their waists. The grips of the weapons were polished with use. The flickering light of the torches and the close fit of the helmets' cheek-guards made it hard to see the soldiers' faces. They might not have been human at all.

The two soldiers stopped in front of Ben, leaving room for a third to step between them. This soldier was obviously of higher rank for his helmet was decorated with a red brush crest, and his chest armor, more bronze than leather, was chased with silver.

Ben's panic was frozen in him. He opened his mouth to scream, but no sound came out.

The ranking soldier bent over and began untying the straps that held Ben to the chair. The strap that held his head was last to be loosed, and when it fell away, the soldier took half a step back and said, "Stand," in a voice so commanding Ben felt it pry him out of the chair. His legs shook with disuse, fear, and hangover. His head spun causing his vision to fade out. He started to sit back down, but the soldier barked, "Remain standing!" and Ben managed to pull himself together enough to remain on his feet.

The soldier pointed past Fordham's shoulder and said, "Go."

Ben turned his head and saw a pointed arch door opening with red orange torches flaming in holders at each side of it. More light came through the opening. He turned back to the soldier and started to protest, but the words never made it out of his mouth. The soldier backhanded him across the face. There was no malice in the blow. It was simply a means to an end. "Go," the soldier said again.

With no more attempts at protest Ben, dazed and on the edge of madness, turned and walked toward the door.

Four more soldiers waited in the passage. Two carried torches and wore short swords and daggers. The other two carried thick hafted spears with gleaming sharp heads rather than swords. The spearmen fell in at each side of their prisoner and the torchbearers took up positions before and behind. The ranking soldier commanded, "Forward," and the detail stepped smartly ahead.

Ben's stomach bubbled and turned. He felt as though

some filthy acid was leaking into him, and he was afraid he would suddenly vomit or lose control of his bowels. He didn't. He marched ahead on quivering legs.

The passageway spiraled upward. There were no windows and no other doors, only solid walls made of rough dressed stone and an earthen floor compacted by marching feet. The mildew smell seemed to lessen and Ben hoped they were coming out of the dank chamber. A moment later he regretted his desire. The passage ended in another pointed arch doorway with eye stabbingly bright daylight pouring through it. Without slowing, the detail marched out the door which was more like a mine audit than a door.

Ben squinted against the glare of the afternoon sun and raised his right arm to block the brightness. The heat of the day smote him like a club and a stinking sweat mixed of fear and booze squeezed out of his pores. The heat, the fear, and the left over booze made him feel faint. He was thirsty too, with the cottony, phlegmy thirst of the morning after.

A short way outside the door a troop of perhaps fifty soldiers waited. They stood down from their horses but snapped to attention when the ranking soldier with the escort detail came toward them. Ben was marched to a horse and stood looking at it for a moment.

"Mount," the commander ordered. All swung into their saddles except Ben who stood looking at the horse. There was a saddle of sorts on its back, but there were no stirrups, no way to climb up. Not that it would have mattered much since Ben hardly knew which end of a horse was which.

"Mount," the commander ordered again, more firmly.

Ben stepped a little closer to the horse and grabbed a handful of mane like he had seen the others do and tried to swing himself up as they had, but it didn't work. He fell on his rear end and the jar of the fall was too much for his touchy stomach. He gagged and brought up some greenish bile.

The fall and the gagging irritated the commander. "Mount or I will have you tossed over the saddle like a sack of grain."

Ben stood and tried the up-swing mount again with no more luck than the first try.

"Enough," the commander said. "You two, put him on. Belly down so we don't lose him."

"Wait a minute," Ben said and received another clout across the mouth.

The two troopers stepped down from their horses and picked Ben up like he was a child though he was six feet four inches tall and had weighed two forty before he began taking most of his meals out of a bottle. They dumped him ungently across the saddle and tied his wrists and ankles together under the belly of the horse. The jostling and bashing made him heave some more and his head felt as though an ax was cleaving his skull right down the middle. Tears filled his eyes.

All this abuse should have made Ben collapse into a debilitating case of the screaming meemies, but it didn't. He was still more than half convinced this was all a long running and particularly vivid nightmare. He had dreamt of the stone chamber since he was a child, though the dream had never gone this far before.

Ben squeezed his eyes shut again, trying to clear the

tears from them. When he opened them, he shook his head a little. His eyes fell upon the inside of his left forearm. A tattoo was there which had never been there before. It covered his arm from wrist to the bend of his elbow and went most of the way around his arm. It was a sun burst pattern, very intricate and colorful, and each of the sun burst's rays held pictures. The bottom-most ray, the one nearest the bend of his elbow, had a sheaf of wheat in it. The sheaf was yellow-brown and dry and so real Ben could almost smell the bran dust of the field, but there was something wrong with the sheaf. It drooped over because it was broken at the point where the straw tie went round it.

*This is wrong. It shouldn't be a broken sheaf. It should be a hand holding a tattoo stylus…"*

Then it hit him like a jolt of electricity. This tattoo was called a Voyager's Mark and the last time he had seen one it had d been on the forearm of a short, squat, dark skinned, little man named Mardian. Mardian was a tattoo artist. His Voyager's Mark was the one with the hand holding the stylus.

Suddenly it all came clear. Ben remembered everything and the terror of it seized his heart. He screamed.

## Chapter Two

Ben Fordham had never quite fit in the world into which he had been born. Somehow, out there in the place where souls exist before they are born, he had stood in the wrong line and ended up on Terra rather than whereever he was supposed to have gone, or at least that was the way he always felt.

His parents felt it too. They began looking askance at him when he was a baby and cried every time any violence or fighting came on the television. They found the only way to stop him from crying and screaming was to turn the set off or change the channel to something nonviolent. This even extended to violent sports like football and basketball. When humans purposefully set out to harm one another for whatever end, Ben Fordham protested loud and long, or worse yet, he tried to break it up. That didn't mean he went around the country breaking up football games, but he did avoid them like the plague. The same with any other violent pastime, but there were some violent things he couldn't avoid especially in the part of Los Angeles where he grew up. Fights; adult fights, kid fights, gang fights, any kind of fights--and Ben was always in the middle of them trying to break them up. He had started making like a super-hero when he was a child, jumping into fights to stop them. The fourth or fifth time he came home with his nose bloodied from sticking it into someone else's battle his father began to really look at him funny.

"It wasn't your fight, Ben?" his father asked then answered his own question. "No, of course it wasn't. What was I thinking? It wasn't your fight. So why the hell did you get in the middle of it?"

"I had to stop them," Ben answered. "They were hurting each other and it made me sick."

"So you jumped in and let them pound on you a little?"

"They didn't mean to hit me. I just got in the way."

Ben's father looked up to the heavens, shook his head in disbelief, and then looked down at his son. "So stay the hell out of the way!" he cried. "Let 'em fight! It's none of your business!"

Ben shrugged and looked at the ground. "I can't," he said.

"Whadda ya mean you can't? Just turn your ass around and walk away!"

"I just can't do that, Dad."

Ben's father shook his head in wonder and disgust. "Well, at least for God sakes stay out of fights where they got guns or knives," he pleaded.

Ben and his father had variations of this same conversation repeatedly, usually while his mother was patching him up or when he came out of the emergency room after being stitched back together. Ben's parents hoped the boy would learn better as his life went along; that he would get hardened to the violence in America and become more normal, but it didn't happen. Ben spent the first twenty-five years of his life jumping into brawls and taking plenty of lumps for it. It gained him nothing, or almost nothing. It did gain him the love and admiration of a young woman named Maggie Winters.

Maggie was beautiful. She had the classic beauty of a Lladro porcelain figurine. She was tall and slim with waist length hair black as the depths of Carlsbad Caverns with the lights off. She knew Ben from high school and admired his "ideals." She also admired his six foot four inch frame, his broad, thick muscled shoulders, and his green eyes.

Ben tried to explain to Maggie that his stopping fights had nothing to do with ideals. He had told his parents that violence made him sick and he wasn't speaking figuratively. He meant it in a very literal sense. Being in the presence of violence was like having boiling water poured down his throat. It scalded his heart and made him fight against the pain of it by trying to stop the violence. When he told Maggie this, she smiled and nodded her understanding but continued to love him for his ideals. She loved and admired him so much that when he asked her to marry him a year after they graduated from college, she said yes.

Ben Fordham had studied history and philosophy in college, trying to find the reason he was like he was, but he did not find any explanation, and, because of his chosen fields of study, he found no employment when he graduated. He tried to find a job in a school or research firm, but failed. He had worked in the building trades in the summers between college years so he went back to that when the Halls of Academe failed to roll out the red carpet for him. His strong body and quick mind helped him do well there, though it was a strange kind of job for a man of his particular peaceful bent. The innate violence of driving nails and the strong, but sometimes violent men who did the work kept him on the edge of nervous exhaustion much of the time. He did learn to control his urges to step into the middle of violent situations to some degree, but sometimes he simply could not help himself so he continued to come home with the occasional black eye or bloody nose, but Maggie just chalked it up to his "ideals" and let it go. She loved and admired him, but she began to worry more and more about him the longer she was married to him. Eventually the worry began to wear on her.

One Tuesday in February Ben went to a job in west L.A. He strapped on his nail pouches and started nailing studwork together. Nearby a plumber was soldering copper pipes together by a method called "sweating." This meant using a bottled gas torch to heat the pipes and the solder, but the plumber was not the most brilliant man on the job sight, nor the most skilled sweater of pipes. He allowed the torch flame to stay in one place too long and set the wooden studwork through which the pipes ran on fire.

Nearby--entirely too nearby--was a can of "juice." Juice is kerosene with paraffin wax melted into it which carpenters sometimes pour over nails to make them drive into wood more easily. Building inspectors do not like it when carpenters use juiced nails and they tend to down check any work they find which has been juiced.

Also, juice is dangerous when it is used near flames.

The can of juice exploded like a bomb, throwing flaming juice all over the piles of yet to be used studs and already used studs, and all over the not-so-bright plumber.

Ben saw the plumber's clothes catch fire and he flew off the scaffold where he had been working. Ignoring the flames he picked up the plumber and carried him to safety then threw the plumber to the floor and rolled him around to smother the flames.

The plumber was not hurt much, nor was Ben and the plumber was wonderfully grateful. He shook Ben by the hand and hugged him like they were brothers, but the man who was the building contractor was not a happy man. His building had great black fire scars and a building inspector discovered the proximate cause of the fire was a can of juice. The inspector immediately shut the building site down pending a complete reinspection. The contractor strode to where the plumber was hugging Ben and began screaming and cursing.

"You dumb sonofabitch, you just cost me my license!" he screamed.

"Hey, man," the plumber answered back. "You shouldn't have been using juiced nails!"

This was a mistake. The contractor's face turned purple with rage and he grabbed a framing hammer out of his tool belt. "You sonofabitch!" he screamed and went after the plumber with mayhem in his eyes.

Ben Fordham, peacemaker, stepped between the two and caught the framing hammer full on the upper left side of his forehead just above the hair line.

~ * ~

"You were unbelievably lucky," the doctor told Ben when he woke up in the hospital. "That hammer should have killed you. If you didn't have such a hard head, it would have. As it was we drilled a hole and pulled the splinters of bone out of your brain then replaced the piece of your skull with a steel plate. If you can walk and scratch your rear end with your right hand and remember you own name most of the time, you will have come away having beaten the odds like winning the lottery."

"Thanks Doc," Ben said. His speech was a little slurred, but understandable.

"Next time get the hell out of the way," the doctor said, grinning at his own joke.

Ben didn't grin back. He thought about how his father was going to give him the same lecture when he found out about this.

The physical therapy was surprisingly simple. There was not as much damage to the brain as the doctors thought and the stainless steel plate healed over very well with no infection or other complications. Not so the relationship between Ben and his parents or Maggie and Ben. His parents came to visit during his hospital stay, and he stayed with them during the "at home," portion of his recovery. He couldn't stay at his own home because Maggie worked and the doctors said it was better he shouldn't be alone for a while yet. His mother coddled him and kissed his forehead; his father started out to do his usual lecture, but gave it up after the first sentence. It wasn't like Ben hadn't heard it all before.

Maggie, on the other hand, was unusually quiet, and she had a frightened look in her eyes when she looked at her husband. The few times she talked it was to tell Ben he had to let some of his "ideals" lapse before they got him killed.

"Maggie," he explained again, "it has nothing to do with ideals. I wish it were ideals. I'd drop them like hot rocks if I could, but I can't. I could no more have *not* tried to stop Gingrich from braining Narski than I could fly. When I am exposed to violence, I have to try to stop it. It is like a sickness. I can't help it."

Maggie didn't say anything to that; only looked at her husband a little more strangely than ever before.

Six weeks after the incident the doctors said Ben could go home to his wife. He walked out of the hospital from his final doctor visit, hopped into a cab, and went home to the apartment in which he and Maggie lived. Ben had told Maggie he would probably be able to stay home with her and he expected to be greeted with open arms. Perhaps there would even be a small party, but there wasn't. Instead he found a note taped to a string and hanging in the middle of the kitchen door right at eye level so he couldn't miss it. He pulled the note down and read it. It said, "Your damned ideals are going to get you killed. I'd rather be divorced than widowed. Good bye."

~ * ~

A month later Ben found himself sitting in a bar on Ninth Street in Los Angeles called the Golden Gopher. A loyal Minnesota fan had once owned the place and named it after his favorite team, but the Gopher had fallen on hard times. It wasn't completely disreputable like some of the bars over around Fifth and Los Angeles Streets, but it wasn't far from it.

Ben had been steadily drunk since he found the note from Maggie. He showed up at the Union Hall sozzled a couple of times and was told the Carpenters and Joiners Union didn't send drunks out to jobs and to stay the hell away until he got himself together. That was ok with Ben. He really didn't care about jobs or anything else without Maggie. All he wanted to do was crawl into a hole of forgetfulness, and a bottle of Jack Daniels was the closest he could come.

Sitting next to Ben at the bar was a little fellow with a wide mouth which would have been more at home on a frog. The little guy had sat down a while before and struck up a conversation, or at least his half of one. Ben mostly ignored the flutey, squeaky voice, but couldn't avoid a grunt or nod every now and then. He didn't want to offend the little guy because there was a chance he might decide to buy Ben a drink.

"Have you ever considered body art?" the little guy asked after a while. He spoke with a slight accent Ben couldn't identify.

"Body Art?" Ben asked.

"Yes. The vulgar call it tattooing."

"Oh, tattoos. Naw. I never thought much about it. Sorta thought about it in college because it was the hip thing to do, but my mother would have had a fit…you know?"

The little guy nodded and sighed. "Sad. Body art has

become the province of hooligans for the most part, and I refuse to be a party to such things."

"Oh yeah? What does that mean?"

"It means I will not tattoo anyone disreputable," he said firmly.

"You a tattooer, or what ever you call it?"

The little guy stuck out his hand. "Permit me to introduce myself. I am Mardian, premiere body artist."

Ben shook the outstretched hand and gave his own name as he looked over the man more closely. This Mardian was short and compact and round, with slicked back hair which peaked at the top of his broad forehead. He was wearing a bone gray turtleneck shirt which covered him from lower lip to wrist. It made him look as though he didn't have a neck.

"You got tattoos under your shirt?" Ben asked.

"Yes, many."

"Oh yeah? How come you got 'em all covered up? They ugly or something?"

"No, they are not ugly! They are beautiful! They were done by the second best tattoo artist in the world."

"Second best? Why not the best?"

"Because I am the best, and it is very difficult to work on one's self."

Ben nodded. "Guess that's true, especially on your back." He laughed.

"Yes, indeed," Mardian agreed, smiling. He noticed Ben twisting his empty shot glass.

"May I buy you another drink, Mr. Fordham?"

Ben smiled. "Thought you'd never ask, and you

might as well call me Ben if we're gonna be drinking buddies."

"Of course, Ben," Mardian said and signaled the bartender.

When the drinks were poured and tasted Ben asked, "So, how come you keep your tattoos all covered up if you're so proud of them?"

"I only show my art to special people. Like a collector of great paintings."

"Ah," said Ben, grinning. "So instead of asking the girl if she wants to see your etchings you ask her if she wants to see your body art. Clever."

"Not exactly what I meant, but yes."

They nodded to one another and sipped their drinks quietly for a time.

"I have been looking at your forearms, Ben," Mardian said eventually.

Ben shot a glance at his companion that had a little sparks of suspicion in it. *This guy is trying to pick me up*. "What about them?" he asked.

"They are very broad and solid looking. Your whole body is, for that matter."

Ben's suspicions grew. He was wearing jeans and tennies and a tank top, none of them particularly clean or stylish, but the shirt did show off his muscular arms and broad chest. "Are you one of those kind of guys, Mardian?"

The other frowned in puzzlement for a moment then understanding dawned. "Oh, no, no," he said, not particularly taken aback by the accusation. "I am no homosexual. I was merely admiring the expanse of your forearms like a painter would examine and admire blank canvas. I was thinking how wonderful a design I might place there." He nodded at Ben's left arm.

"Oh, yeah?"

"Yes. Perhaps some variation of this one," he said, and began pulling up his left sleeve.

The tattoo was breath taking. It was like nothing Ben had ever seen before. It seemed to glow with some inner light, and it pulled the eye deep into itself. It was a sunburst and each of its rays contained a picture of surpassing beauty which seemed to shift and change before his eyes. There were mythic animals and symbols and portraits. One was of a person all dressed in white wearing a heavy veil. Ben got the feeling if the veil were removed the person beneath would radiate like the sun.

"That's amazing," Ben breathed. "I've never seen anything so beautiful."

"Thank you. It is my own work. The only one of my tattoos that is."

"Really? Man, it must have been a hell of a job doing it all upside down like that."

"It was a challenge."

"How did you get such bright colors? I've never seen such bright colors. They are usually just red and blue and black, aren't they?"

"There are more now, but even so, I do not use commercial inks. I mix my own from ancient formulas."

"Wow."

"Yes, indeed. It is called a Voyager's Mark. Would you like one?"

"Huh?" Ben said, thinking he had misunderstood.

"A Voyager's Mark. Would you like one?" Mardian asked again.

Ben looked from the tattoo to Mardian's eyes and realized the little man was serious. "Ah, look man," he began. "That is a beautiful thing, and I'd really like to have one, but hell, it would cost a fortune! I couldn't even afford the price of another drink, much less a work of art like that."

Mardian looked horrified and lifted both of his hands palms toward Ben. "No, no! You misunderstand. I would not charge for a Voyager's Mark. I would do it for the sheer joy of creation. As for the price of a drink--" he waved the barkeep over. "Please, sir, give us each another of these." He pointed to the glasses.

The barkeep shambled to the other end of the bar and brought back a bottle. He poured and Mardian shelled out money then said, "Please leave the bottle nearby. We may have need of it again."

The barkeep shrugged and set the bottle on the ledge under the mirror behind him.

Mardian and Ben drank a couple more and continued to talk. "Will mine be like that one?" Ben asked after a time.

"Not quite. It will have your personal mark here." He pointed to the top center ray just below the bend of his elbow. In his tattoo the ray contained a hand holding a needle sharp tattoo stylus of the sort which had not been used in the U.S. since the advent of the electric tattoo needle. The symbol was repeated in the bottom center ray near the bend of the wrist. Ben asked why.

"It is my signature mark," Mardian explained. "You

will have one like it in the same place."

"Ah," Ben said. His tongue was getting thick and his eyes were not focusing properly any more.

The barkeep poured again and the two men drank.

After another drink or two Mardian suggested they go to his studio where his equipment and a bottle of "exquisite" Napoleon Brandy resided.

Ben agreed. He found it necessary to lean on the little tattoo artist as they left the Golden Gopher.

## Chapter Three

A trooper was holding Ben's head up by the hair and slapping him repeatedly. "Shut up," the trooper said calmly. "You been screaming for hours. You're making the horses jumpy. Shut up."

Ben's mind came back from the dark hole it had fallen into and he shut up.

"Better," said the trooper. "Don't make so much noise, you hear? Scream some more and I'll bat you some more. You understand me?"

Ben tried to nod his head, but the trooper still had him by the hair so it was a short jerky thing, but it was understood. The trooper nodded his head in answer and let go of Ben's hair. "All you boys make a lot of holler when you get here," he said with no particular malice. He pulled off his helmet and the padded cap beneath it and wiped his brow with his forearm. His head was round and close shorn. His hair was black with a few flecks of gray. His arms were thick and covered with dark hair. His hands were large and hard. He needed a shave.

"How come you make so much holler?" he asked. "This ain't such a bad place. You ain't even hurt much."

Ben held his head up enough to look at the trooper, but he didn't answer him.

Another trooper standing beside his horse looked on with disgust. "He's like all the rest Borj. Either he don't understand or he's too shit-scared to talk."

Borj grunted. "Guess so," he said and turned away.

"Can I have some water?" Ben asked. Between stomach acid and screaming, his abused voice was scratchy and almost inaudible, but the trooper called Borj heard him and turned back. He studied Ben for a moment then shrugged.

"Go 'head Borj. I'll watch 'im. Not that he looks like he going anywhere."

Borj looked at the trooper then back at Ben and shrugged again. He walked out of Ben's line of sight and Ben thought he was destined to go thirsty, but Borj came back in a few minutes with his helmet full of water. It was blood warm and tasted coppery, but it was almost the best tasting stuff he had ever drunk. "Thanks," he said. It was automatic. He didn't exactly mean it, though he was grateful for the water.

Borj frowned at the prisoner for a moment then dumped the rest of the water over Ben's head. It felt good. The only bad thing about it was it brought home the fact this was a real thing, not a dream. He almost slipped off into the screaming meemies again, but muscle memory or Borj's large, hard, hand stopped him.

The troop commander sang out "Mount," and Borj clapped his cap and helmet back on his head and stepped out of Ben's sight. In a few moments the troop moved out and

Ben began to regret the water he had drunk, but not enough to wish he hadn't drunk it.

Ben tried to look around a little as they clopped along through the rugged brown hills, but hanging head down across a saddle was not the most conducive way to look at the scenery. Mostly he saw horse legs and dust, but he did see some scrubby brush which reminded him of greasewood from the California desert. It didn't surprise him. The feel of the afternoon sun beating on his back felt like the desert. To add to his already considerable misery, he could feel the sun crisping his bare shoulders. He was going to be sunburned to the bone pretty soon.

Evening came at last. The troop pulled into a grove of oak trees which grew in a small bowl shaped valley. There was a pond in the valley's center. Borj and the other trooper hauled Ben off the horse and dumped him under a tree. They didn't seem very concerned he would try to escape. They didn't re-tie his hands or feet. Ben found out why soon enough. Besides the fact he didn't know which way was home, his hands and feet were all but useless. They had been tied so tight there was no feeling in them. They were like blocks of wood. He couldn't stand, but he did manage to scoot himself around enough to lean against the trunk of the tree rather than simply lying in the dirt.

Ben tried to move his fingers and toes to get the blood flowing, but it was tough. He worried about gangrene setting in and was relieved when he felt the prickly tingle of returning feeling. He began to reconsider the relief after the tingling became a burning ache which made him clench his teeth in an effort not to cry out with the pain.

The troopers moved around their camp, setting up for the night. They started fires and began cooking something. Ben couldn't tell what it was, but after a bit the aroma of it drifted toward him. It smelled pretty good--onions and meat and maybe potatoes. Ben found he *was* hungry. He hadn't eaten anything for--he didn't know how long he had been here (where ever here was), but he knew he hadn't eaten anything the day he met Mardian, only drunk some juice and then some booze.

The pain of returning circulation was almost gone, and it was near dark in the oak grove when Borj came to check on him. "Scoot up tighter to the tree," Borj said. "I gotta bind you again."

"Come on Borj, have a heart will you? I just got the feeling back in my hands and feet. I'm not gonna try to run. Where would I go? I don't even know where the hell I am."

"Captain said bind you, so I gotta bind you."

"Ah man…am I gonna get something to eat or at least some more water?"

Borj scratched his scruffy chin and looked at his prisoner. "Dunnknow," he said at last.

"Well, can't ya go ask or something?"

Borj continued to look at Ben for a time then said, "Yeah, all right, but first scoot back against the tree."

Ben started to protest, but Borj just waggled his hand as if to push the prisoner back against the tree so Ben scooted back. Borj tied a cord around Ben's chest and around the tree trunk. He didn't make it too tight, but he did put the knot out of reach. He didn't tie Ben's hands.

Back at the fire Borj hunkered down as though he

had no intention of going to ask. He talked to his friend Sko who hunkered on the other side of the fire. "You hear him Sko? He wants to eat. Any of 'em ever ask to eat before?"

Sko shrugged. "Dunnknow. You gonna feed him?"

Borj kept looking at the fire, thinking. Then he took off his helmet leaving the padded cap on and used a wood ladle to dip something from the pot on the fire into the helmet. He carried it unhurriedly to where Ben was tied and stood over him. After a moment he shifted the helmet to his left hand and drew his dagger with his right. He squatted and poked the point of the dagger under Fordham's chin. "Eat quick. You make funny when I untie you, I'll slice you a good one. Understand?"

Ben could hardly open his mouth with the dagger point under his chin, but he managed to say, "Right. Nothing funny."

Borj poked him a little harder just to make sure they understood one another, but the poke wasn't hard enough to break the skin. He put the dagger across his knee and bent to untie the knot. If Ben had been anyone other than himself, he might have made a grab for the dagger handle which was only an inch from his hand, but Ben didn't do anything except take the helmet from Borj when his arms were free.

The helmet contained a sort of semi-liquid stuff with chunks of something indefinable in it, but it smelled good. There was no spoon, but Ben didn't let that stop him. He dug in with his hands. The stuff turned out to be some kind of meat stew with chunks of potato and carrot and onion. It had a slightly musty taste to it, but that didn't even slow him down. He wiped every drop he could out of the helmet then licked his fingers.

"Could I have some water now?" he asked, handing the helmet to Borj.

The soldier stood, walked to the pond, dipped the helmet in and came back. He squatted again and handed the helmet to Ben who drank deeply. When he lowered the helmet from his mouth, he studied his captor. This was a professional soldier and no doubt about it. Anyone with eyes could have seen it even without the military trappings. "Where is this, Borj?" He asked. "And where are you taking me?"

Borj ignored the first question and said, "You are going to Lau."

"Where's that?"

"Not a where, a who. She's high priestess of Lady Tarsa."

"Tarsa? Who's Tarsa?"

Borj shook his head in disbelief anybody could be so ignorant. "Lady Tarsa is Goddess of Dark, who else? Who else would have Priestess? You done?"

Ben drank the rest of the water then handed the helmet back. Borj took it and clapped it on his head. "Scoot up tight to the tree," he said.

"Ah Borj…" Ben began.

Calmly and without malice Borj backhanded him across the mouth. "Scoot up tight to the tree," he said patiently.

Ben shook his head to clear out the twinkley lights and said, "But I want to know where I am, damn it! Who the hell are you, and what the hell am I doing here?"

Borj backhanded him again and said, "Scoot back to the tree before I run out of patience."

Ben's lower lip was split and the blood was running down his chin. He had bitten his tongue and it was bleeding and swelling. He scooted back tighter to the tree.

"I still want to know where I am," he said through as Borj tied him, hands and feet included this time.

"Shut up and sleep," Borj said. "You got a pretty hard day tomorrow."

"Doing what?"

Borj drew his hand back and lifted his thick eyebrows quizzically. "You gonna shut up or am I gonna smack you some more?"

"All right, all right," Ben said cringing back despite himself.

Borj walked back to his fire.

The camp quieted as the fires died down and troopers rolled themselves into cloaks and blankets. Ben tried to find a comfortable position, but there was no such thing as comfort tied to a tree. Soon the desert night began to grow cold and his tank top did nothing to keep in his body heat. He shivered until he could feel his bones rattle and the cold made him need to urinate so badly it was painful. At last he gave up trying to be civilized and wet his pants. Soon the wet grew cold and made him more miserable than before. *Here I am. Victim of some cosmic error--two cosmic errors. Still taking lumps and gaining nothing. Course this could still be a nightmare, or I could still be drunk and having DTs in some alley somewhere, or maybe I'm nuts,* but he couldn't convince himself of any of those. He ran his swollen tongue over his swollen mouth and was convinced this was about as real as it got. The final proof came when his tongue flicked over his bottom front teeth and discovered one of them was chipped leaving a sharp point sticking up.

Ben looked up through the tangled leaves of the oak tree to which he was tied and asked, "Hey God, what did I ever do to deserve this?" He got no answer and after a little he cried himself to sleep.

~ * ~

Ben woke when Borj kicked him--not too hard--in the ribs. The rest of the troop had been up for a while. They were all fed, watered, and saddled up waiting only to have their prisoner put on a horse.

Ben tried to ask for some water, but between his banged up mouth and Borj's hurry he didn't get any. Borj untied the rope from round the tree but not from Ben's hands and feet. He simply picked Ben up and slung him over a thick shoulder. Ben was impressed. Borj was a little shorter than himself but with heavily muscled arms and a barrel shaped torso which made him appear strong. Ben had not thought how strong until Borj picked him up with only a slight grunt and carried him to the horse.

"Can I ride sitting up today," Ben asked before Borj could throw him over the saddle.

Borj considered it and looked at the captain who was glaring impatiently at them and didn't even answer, just flopped Ben over the saddle and added the hand and feet tie beneath the horse's belly.

The troop started off at a jog and the bouncing hurt Ben from his abused mouth to his tied ankles, but what hurt most was the pounding of the saddle against his belly. It was like being hit repeatedly with a board and there was no position he could gain which did not hurt. At last the pain was too much. His vision grayed over and he fainted. He came too when Borj and Sko pulled him off the horse and dumped a couple of helmets full of water over him. "You alive?" Borj asked.

Ben shook his head, trying to clear the cobwebs out. "I won't be much longer if I have to hang over that saddle again."

They looked him over for a couple of moments then Borj untied his feet. Without much effort they picked him up and stuck him astride the horse.

"Try to run and it's my ass," Borj said.

"And you won't make it far anyway," Sko added.

Ben nodded. He had no intention of trying to run. He had no idea where he could run too.

In the afternoon the troop topped a rise and looked down into a broad valley. The far edge of it was so distant it was lost in a blue haze. Below them, perhaps five miles from the edge of the height where they rested, was a large walled city. It looked ancient to Ben, like an illustration from some ancient civilizations text.

The city was set upon a flat topped hill which did not look like a natural mesa. it was more like the ruin topped tells of the Fertile Crescent civilizations, but there was nothing of the ruin about this city. It was a thriving place with smoke rising in columns through the still air and streams of people coming and going from the visible gates. Outside the gates were patch work farm fields. Mostly these stretched out toward the west, the side opposite the heights. Not far from the trail the soldiers were traveling Ben could see several piles of tailings from mines, but he could not guess what kind of mines they were. Smoke rose from smelters nearby.

Something about the whole scene was familiar to Ben. He had seen this city before, but could not quite remember where. Perhaps it was in his dreams…then he remembered. Yes in dreams, but more recently he had seen it in the tattoo on his left forearm. He looked at it now and cursed Mardian with all his might.

It took several more hours for the troop to wind down from the heights and afternoon was settling toward evening as they passed through the gates of the city. The walls were ten plus yards thick and built of hewn stone blocks taller and broader than the height of a man. Within the walls the streets were narrow and crooked with many odd angled turns. The houses were built of mud brick plastered with gesso and roofed with half round burned tile.

The evening streets were still jammed with people. The crowd flowed and eddied like a river and impeded the progress of the troop. No one paid much attention to them. The flow parted reluctantly to let them through and closed behind them as though they had never been there. After an hour of pushing through crowds the troop stopped. A few people paused to watch Borj haul Ben off his horse then shrugged it off and went about their business without a second thought.

Ben could hardly stand. His legs were weak from

disuse and renewed fear. The troop had stopped before something which could only be a temple. There was nothing of beauty about the building. It was massive and hulking with ten squat looking columns holding up the front façade. Each column was carved into a horrific demon, which made Ben's already shaky legs even shakier.

The troop formed up around Ben with the captain at the head of the detail. Borj and Sko frog-marched their prisoner up the steps onto the colonnade. He was like a marionette danced along by puppeteers across the colonnade and into the temple. Inside the gigantic building were more columns. These were of highly polished black stone. They supported a soot blackened wood beam ceiling which was carved with mystic symbols--pentagrams, vortex whorls, death's heads, and crossed bones. The floor was gray limestone blocks polished by thousands of feet.

Across the broad expanse of temple, opposite the entrance was a stone cube as large as a two-story house. It was worked with gold chased pentagrams on its sides and Ben thought he could remember this block and its decorations in the tattoo on his arm, but he was too frightened to try to look. He could not take his eyes off the stone cube, and as they approached it, a feeling of dread rose up in him and threatened to make him lose control of his bowels.

The stone cube was not solid as he had first thought but was a stone building within the temple. It was the precinct of the altar and so was set apart from the rest of the temple. At the entrance of the altar precinct the troop stopped and parted so the captain, Borj, Sko, and Ben could continue in.

The altar served as a pedestal for a ten-foot tall alabaster statue of a woman. The face of the idol was beautiful beyond description, but the icy cruelty of it made the beauty seem a mistake. Two horns projected from the head, one on each side above the ears.

When the four reached the altar, they knelt and turned their eyes down. Ben glanced up, but the captain who knelt behind the other three roughly forced his head back down.

Minutes passed. Ben's abused muscles were beginning to cramp when a contralto voice said, "You may look up."

There was no softness, no kindness in the voice though it belonged to the most beautiful woman Ben had ever seen. She might have been the model for the statue upon the altar even to the horns, but they were the only inhuman things about her. Her hair was blue-black and flowed down her shoulders and back. Her eyes were golden brown and they pinned Ben to the floor like a bug under glass.

Ben's stomach churned and quivered with fear, and he shook as though he was freezing, but he managed to say, "You are Lau."

The woman's eyes flashed. "A very special one for Lady Tarsa this time, Captain. The others you brought me were so terrified they could only blubber and scream."

"Why am I here?" Ben demanded, but the demand lost any power it might have had to the quake in his voice.

Lau favored him with a freezing smile. "Inquisitive, aren't you?" she said and turned from him to the captain. "Prepare him. We go to the Valley of Voices tomorrow."

"Yes, Mistress," the captain answered.

"Damage him no more than necessary. Lady Tarsa will not be pleased if so lively a one as this does not arrive still lively."

"Hey, wait a minute," Ben began

No one got upset with his noise. Lau lifted her hand and that was the last thing Ben remembered before being batted across the back of the head with something hard.

## Chapter Four

The saw-toothed mountains surrounding the Valley of Voices were stained red by the last rays of the sinking sun. It was a desolate and forbidding place. The mountains were pierced by thousands of caves and hollows and a wind blowing through them made the hollows moan and scream like the voices of a million damned souls. The sound made Ben shake even more than before. It was like having his already raw nerves scrapped with steel wool.

Ben had been bathed, shaved, and generally pampered once he woke from the rap on the head, and he began to think perhaps this wasn't going to be such a bad place after all. He was dressed in a fine linen robe and served food and drink by a bevy of beautiful women. He didn't eat much because his mouth was still sore and, pampering aside, he had an ongoing feeling of foreboding which made his stomach nervous.

When he finished with his meal, four of the servant girls returned him to the bathhouse. They massaged him with warm sweet smelling oils then bathed him again. They soaped and scrubbed him in ways he would have found--stimulating, under other circumstances, but try as they might, they could not arouse him.

"I would appreciate it if you would tell me why you are doing all this," Ben said as they dried him with fluffy bath sheets as big as blankets.

They only giggled and smiled at him.

After the bath they anointed him with a musky perfume and tried to feed him again, but he couldn't eat. At last they put him to bed and warmed it by climbing in with him. It was like a porno fantasy with four delicious young women all trying to outdo one another to please him, but it was no use. There was a lump of chilly premonition in his stomach which would not allow him to enjoy anything the houris did. When they gave up trying, Ben waited until he thought they were asleep and tried to get up. All four women were instantly awake and they were no longer houris. They had become guards quite strong enough to control him at will.

In the morning they bathed and anointed him again, but they were no longer playful. They were hard eyed and cold. They dressed him in a silken breechclout and escorted him into a closet sized room which turned out to be a cage with gold decorated ebony bars. The cage was only a little taller than he was and so narrow he could only squat if he grew tired of standing.

Moments after the cage was secured, long wooden handles were slipped through metal rings near the bottom of it and twenty sweating male bearers lifted it. Lau, the priestess, joined them along with some women dressed in the same toga-like dresses, a couple of calves, and some men who played pipes, trumpets, and drums. The procession marched out of the city and across the valley to the sound of music, but when they reached the Valley of Voices, the horns and flutes, unable to compete with the wailings of the valley, stopped playing. The drum kept up a steady throb more felt in the bones than heard with the ears.

At the center of the valley was another altar that looked like the one in the temple. It did not look out of place in the desolation of the valley and sight of it made Ben's knees buckle. Only the narrowness of the cage kept him from falling down. The procession approached the altar, stopped, and set the cage down. "What's going on here?" Ben protested weakly. No one answered.

He was taken from his cage without much trouble though he tried to resist by holding on to the bars. Two powerful cage bearers pulled him out like pulling a snail out of its shell and carried him to the altar. They held him while two of the servant maids locked his wrists and ankles into bronze brackets riveted to the front of the altar. He stood with arms spread and slightly above his head and legs apart like the Da Vinci sketch of the perfectly proportioned male figure.

As the twilight thickened, two calves were brought forward and Lau cut their throats. Two temple maidens caught some of the streaming blood in a huge silver basin. The company lit torches and chanted a tuneless dirge, which fitted with the moan and scream of the valley.

When the carcasses were drained, the maidens

brought the basin toward Ben. Lau followed and lifted her arms up toward the statue upon the altar. The maidens lifted the reeking basin toward Ben's mouth and the brassy-sweet stink of the blood made him gag. He turned his head away thinking they were going to try to make him drink from the basin, but they didn't. They only brought it close to his face and took it away. Lau touched a finger to the blood and daubed a drop of it on Ben's chin then the bowl was moved back and each of the company came forward to taste of the bowl. Watching them made Ben gag.

Lau was last to drink and when she finished, she once more lifted her arms to the altar and said, "All have tasted the sacred blood that they may be strong to serve. Mother Tarsa, receive this offering and bless us with thy dark bounty," A gong sounded.

Ben heard the words and the gong and knew his life was finished, but he struggled against the metal brackets all the same. Flesh peeled from his wrists and ankles and blood began to run down his forearms, but the brackets held firm. After a little, the calm of complete hopelessness engulfed him, and he stopped struggling. He closed his eyes and waited for Lau to slit his throat as though he were a calf.

The valley fell silent. Even the voices of the wind were silent. Expectant. A tingling static charge was in the air.

"Mother Tarsa comes," Lau whispered. "Let us away."

Ben opened his eyes when he heard that and for a

moment hope sprang up again, but it faded quickly as he watched the torch lit company quick march back the way they had come, leaving him chained to the altar. Wind once more caused the Valley of Voices to moan and cry.

"Oh, God!" He cried. "Why is this happening to me?"

As if in answer to his prayer, a big red bearded man appeared before him. "Can you walk?" the man asked.

Ben did not understand at first and could only stare at the man.

Red-beard drew back his hand and smacked Ben hard across the face. "Can you walk?" he shouted again, an inch away from Ben's face.

Brought back to reality by the blow Ben said, "I think so…I think so. Just get me loose!"

Two other men were already working at that. They cut the lock rivets with hammer and chisel. In a moment he was free.

"Hurry!" Red-beard shouted over the rising scream of the wind. The earth was quivering beneath their feet and there was a sudden bone rattling cold in the air.

Ben stepped away from the altar, glanced back, and his guts turned to water. From the other end of the valley a greasy black cloud seemed to flow over the mountains and toward the altar. It blotted out the stars as though swallowing them. "Come!" The men who had freed him shouted and took off at a dead run despite the shaking of the earth. The sound of rushing wind was ear shattering, though Ben could feel no wind. Razor slash cold increased second by second. Ben raced after his saviors.

The men glanced back to be sure Ben was keeping up. Terror was pumping adrenaline into him like a fire hose. He overtook them as they looked back and kept running blindly along the straight line they had established.

Darkness thickened around them. Chill stabbed at his aching muscles and laboring lungs, but they did not slow. The edge of the valley rose up before them like a wall in the gloom. It looked like a dead end to Ben, but he didn't stop running. Almost at the wall he saw a red glow from a crack in the mountain. It looked wide enough for a man to enter, but he turned and gasped, "There?"

"Yes!" they answered and waved him on. "Go! Do not stop for anything!"

The crack gave into a tunnel dimly lit by a flickering torch. Ben was sweating and wheezing like an asthmatic, but he pounded on, pumping his weary legs as hard as he could, but by the time he had passed three or four of the torches down the tunnel, he was finished. Even the terror behind him could not have carried him any farther. He had no breath left and lactic acid burned in his leg muscles. Knowing it was probably his doom, he slowed to a shambling walk. The cold of the valley did not seem to have followed him. Here it seemed only as cool as caverns usually are.

His breath was almost back to normal when the three rescuers caught up with him. Seeing them Ben felt the icy cloud from the valley seize his heart again and he started to run, but the men shouted, "No! It's all right. The wards are set. Tarsa cannot follow us here."

Ben stopped and turned back. "Wards? What's that?"

"God signs. When they are set, Tarsa cannot pass," the red bearded one said.

"Isn't this Tarsa a goddess or something?"

"Yes, but she cannot pass my Lord Aris' wards--"

"Nor can he pass hers," another added.

Ben looked from face to face seeking more explanation, but he got none. "I don't understand," he said.

"It doesn't matter. All will be explained later," Red-beard said. "For now let us get on to the camp."

The others agreed and Ben's body, quivering with adrenal reaction and weariness, made him decide later was soon enough for explanations.

The camp was deeper into the mountain. It was a large, torch lit chamber with a flat sandy floor. Many people were there waiting and they excitedly surrounded the four when they came in, pounding their backs and congratulating the rescuers and ogling Ben as though he were some strange animal. A young woman pushed through the crowd and shouted for attention with an authority that reached them all. "Is all well?" she asked.

"All is well, Rema," the red bearded one answered, "but it was a near thing. The chill was well and truly upon us, but we made it past the wards only a little the worse for it."

"Speak for yourself, Rothean," said another of the rescuers, a short knotty muscled fellow with wiry black hair and beard. "I felt Tarsa bite my ass in the last few steps."

Everyone laughed. Their relief at having their men

back safe was apparent.

Rema said, "No doubt Mother Tarsa will have indigestion from her snack, Marrad." Everyone laughed again. "Other than your chewed fundament is anyone else hurt?"

The four, including Ben, shook their heads, but the read bearded one called Rothean said, "I think you had best look him over Rema. He is more hurt than he knows."

Rema, tall and lithe as a sapling with sparkling golden eyes, glowing tan face, and brown hair cut almost crew cut short, took Ben's hand and led him nearer to a torch. She first looked into his eyes then looked at his still bloody wrists and ankles. After a little, she took his hand and led him to a fire near one wall of the chamber. Beside the fire sat a large leather box. Rema told him to sit, opened the box, and drew forth and uncovered a small ceramic pot. The smell of aloe and honeysuckle rose from it. She daubed some of the ointment on his wrists and ankles. It burned like hot coals for a moment but then felt cool and soothing. After a moment she turned her attention to the tattoo, smoothing it with gentle hands.

Ben said, "All I need now is hepatitis from that toad-mouthed son-of-a-bitch's needle." He shook his head

"I do not know this *hepits* you speak of, but the Voyager's Mark heals well. Has there been fever?"

Ben thought a moment but could not be sure. "I've been bounced around so much in the last few days I really don't know."

Rema nodded. "I understand, but I think there has not been. Your eyes are fairly clear," she laid her hand upon his forehead then upon the back of his neck. "There is no fever now."

"Hope you're right."

Rema turned and dipped a bowl of broth from a pot which had been steaming on the fire and held it out to Ben.

"I'm not really hungry."

"This is not food. It is curative and relaxing."

Ben took the bowl and sniffed at it. The steam smelled mediciney and he wrinkled his nose. "Will it put me to sleep? I don't want to go to sleep yet. I want some answers first."

Rema laughed, a gentle bubbly sound that almost called Ben's mind away from his worries for a moment. "It will not make you sleep Voyager, only help to relax the knots in your muscles.

He eyed the bowl and sniffed at it again then lifted it to his mouth.

"Sip slowly. It is hot."

The taste was bitter, but with a meaty back taste unlike anything he had ever tasted before. It was good, and after a few sips he felt the warmth of it radiating out from his middle. It did seem to begin untying the knots and he sighed and leaned back against the cavern wall, but instantly sprang upright again. He still wore only the embroidered breechcloth and his naked back had come in contact with the chilly stone. "Damn! That's cold!" he said.

Rema and many others laughed at him, but she jumped to her feet and brought a rough woven blanket to Ben. She draped it over his shoulders with a graceful movement. The swell of her breasts and the sway of her hips caught Ben's attention. She was not as beautiful as the houris who had been his captors nor as overtly sexual, but there was a magnetism about her like Maggie's...

The thought of Maggie stabbed at his heart and he felt ashamed. He had not thought of her once in the last days, and now he was assessing the beauty of another woman compared to her. He was disgusted with himself.

In the wavering firelight Rema saw Ben's face change. "Is something wrong, Voyager?" she asked.

"I was thinking of my wife."

Rema nodded sadly. "I am sorry."

"Me too," he said and rubbed his eyes to stop the stinging in them. "I could use a drink."

"I will bring water," Rema said and started to rise.

"Not water. Whiskey or brandy or some such."

"Ah," she said.

"Don't have such things?"

"Oh, yes. We have brandies of several kinds, but you do not need them."

"Yes I do. Believe me, I really do,"

Rema gazed at him for a time, her eyes professionally attentive. "You have abused your body with strong drink for some time, have you not?"

Ben's eyebrows drew down. "How did you know?"

She shrugged. "The color of the flesh beneath your skin; the tiny blood vessels in your eyes; the feel of your flesh; the smell of you."

He blinked at her a moment. "If you can see all that, you know I really need a drink."

"It will not bring you back to your world or to your

wife, nor will it help you any other way."

"It will help me to forget."

She shook her head. "Have you forgotten anything from this abuse?"

He breathed deeply and let it waver out. "No," he said at last.

"What you need is rest."

Ben looked into her golden eyes for a time then nodded. "Yeah. Rest. But first some answers."

"Yes, answers." She turned away and called. "Rothean, come here."

Red-beard rose from his fire and the one called Marrad rose with him. They came to Rema's fire and squatted down. "How are you feeling now, Voyager?" he asked.

For the first time Ben noticed all his rescuers wore swords. He glanced around the cave and in the dim light could see other weapons stacked here and there. Long swords, heavy spears meant for jabbing not throwing, javelins, long bows, and round shields. It was a very warlike gathering and it made him uncomfortable. "I guess I'll live," he answered at last. "May I ask some questions?"

All three nodded.

"Who are you?" Ben asked.

"I am Rothean," said the red beard and stuck out his hand. Ben shook it and when Marrad introduced himself and stuck out his hand Ben shook that one too.

"Actually I meant all of you together."

Rothean grinned crookedly. "We are your benefactors, Voyager."

"Na!" Rema said, wagging her finger at the others.

"Do not tease. He has had enough. Answer seriously or not at all."

The two men studied her for the length of a breath then nodded. "We are servants of Lord Aris, God of Light and Order," Rothean said. Marrad nodded agreement.

Ben let that sink in for a moment and, though he still did not understand it, he asked, "Why did you save me?"

"To maintain the balance."

"Balance? What balance? And what do I have to do with it?"

"The balance between light and dark. Between order and chaos. Lord Aris bids us foil Mother Tarsa anytime we can for the sake of the balance," Rothean said.

"And we certainly did that today when we snatched you right from under Mother Tarsa's very clutch," Marrad said, grinning.

"Umh," Rothean grunted. "And with our success the job became harder. I doubt any more Voyagers will be brought to the valley. Lau has delayed longer and longer each time before departing, but she cannot delay longer without being caught up in the chill."

Rema arched an eyebrow. "Lau is happy to serve, but she has no wish to visit the Home."

"I do not blame her at all," Marrad agreed. "Mother Tarsa is said to be more beautiful than her statues and more cruel than her priestesses. She does not care whom she devours so long as she devours, and when all is devoured she would devour herself. She wishes nothingness."

"What does that have to do with me?" Ben demanded and tapped his chest with two fingers. Sparks jumped from his hand like sparks struck from flint by steel. All eyes in the cavern snapped around to the four beside Rema's fire. All had felt the surge of power released by Ben's anger.

"There is much power in you, Voyager," Rothean said in a hushed voice. Heads all around the cavern chamber nodded in awed agreement and a murmur of questions arose.

Ben looked at his hand. "That has never happened before," he said then looked back at the other three. "What do you mean power? What power?"

Marrad's eyes got a faraway look then he turned to Rothean. "If such power could be tapped, it might be a very useful weapon."

"No!" Ben shouted. "No!"

Again all eyes in the chamber turned to Rema's fire and the agitated buzz rose to a higher pitch.

After a moment Ben realized he was causing a stir and said, "I'm sorry. I know I owe you people my life, but--" he stopped for a second, drew a deep breath and then said, "I cannot help you. I can't be used as a weapon, no matter what. I don't think I could even if I wanted to be. I'm not made that way. All my life I have tried to stop people from hurting one another. I can't help it. I could never be a weapon. I'm sorry."

Rothean scratched at his beard and shook his head sorrowfully. "You will not fare well here, Voyager. Weapons and war are the way of the world. The Over-God made it thus. We maintain the balance by war, and in the maintaining many are wounded and many die. More than healers like Rema can help."

Ben looked to Rema, who nodded her agreement.

Ben's head was whirling with all this. His sense of reality was beginning to tear loose from his bones. Gods of chaos and order? Over-Gods? Unending war? "I don't understand any of this," he cried. "What am I doing here? Where is here?"

They looked at him helplessly. "You are here because the gods willed it."

"Gods? How dare they! How dare they bring me here against my will? I don't serve any gods. I don't believe in any gods!" Ben's voice grew louder and more harried. He was on the edge of insanity, and as he denied his fate and lifted his fists toward the ceiling, power released by his anger and despair crackled from him.

There was a gasp of fear from those in the cavern chamber; fear of the power of this voyager; fear that this voyager was becoming a howling madman like those other voyagers who had come before only this time the madman wielded great power.

Rema's heart went out to her patient despite the crackling power. She could feel his fear and his despair. They wrung her heart and after a moment she reached out and took hold of Ben's up stretched wrists. "Stop it!" she said softly. "Do not do this. You will harm yourself with such despair. Come back now. Come back to me."

Ben turned his wild eyes down to her and her empathy drew the madness from him. He felt it draining away like dirty bath water.

"You must rest now, Voyager," she said gently. "Tomorrow you will meet Lord Aris. Perhaps he can answer more of your questions and help you to understand. For now be calm. Rest."

Ben let her pull his arms down. "Lord Aris? I'll see him tomorrow?"

"Yes. Tomorrow," she said. "Now you must rest. Sleep. Tomorrow is soon enough."

"No. I want to see this Aris! I want to see him now!" He sounded like a spoiled child even to himself. "I must see him. I'll go insane if I don't get some answers. Or wake up. This could still be some kind of booze nightmare!"

Rema scooted closer to him and put her arm around his shoulders. With her other hand she stroked his forehead like a mother comforting her child. "This is no dream, Voyager. We will not be gone when you awake. Lord Aris will come tomorrow and answer all."

Her smooth hand and calm voice eased Ben's anxiety enough to allow him a tenuous hold on sanity. "All right. I'll sleep and wait a little longer." He glanced down at the beautiful glowing Voyager's Mark on his arm. "Did this bring me here?" he asked.

They nodded.

"But why? Why did Mardian send me here?"

"Tomorrow," Rema said. "Now come and lie down."

Ben looked into her golden eyes for a moment and gave in.

Rema led him to a pallet in a darker corner of the chamber and when he lay down, she covered him with an animal skin robe. She sat beside him and held his hand until the exhaustion he had been holding off over came him and he slept.

## Chapter Five

Ben woke to a gentle shaking of his shoulder and Rema's quiet voice saying, "Lord Aris comes. You must prepare yourself."

"Prepare?" he asked. "I'm ready now." He sat up. The creak and pull of his muscles and the fire at his wrists and ankles told him he was not quite as ready as he thought.

Rema noticed. She noticed everything about her patients. "You are in pain," she said. It was not a question.

Ben grimaced. "A little."

She gingerly examined his wrists and ankles and nodded. "They are healing well, but the power of the ointment has worn off. I will put more on."

Ben was surprised there were no red lines of blood poisoning creeping from his wounds toward his heart. "They feel pretty fiery," he said doubtfully. "You sure they are all right?"

Rema daubed more of the ointment onto the hurts. "They feel fiery," she said, "because the power in you is trying to leak out through the breaks in your flesh.

Ben was even more doubtful, but the ointment was again anesthetizing the pain so he let it go.

"Now, for the stiffness and pain in your muscles," she said after a moment. She rose and helped Ben to his feet. He felt a hundred years old and not a particularly healthy hundred, but for the first time in a long time he had no hang over and that was something new. For the past several weeks, hangovers had been constantly with him. He usually cured them with "the hair of the dog."

Rema led him across the bustling cavern camp. The servants of Aris were packing for a move with the efficiency of long practice. Ben filed the scene away in his head but said nothing.

They went out through a diagonal crack in the wall of the cavern and into another chamber which was filled with the gurgle and chuckle of flowing water. The chamber was warm and steamy and there was a smell of sulfur. Rema pointed toward a pool, which had webs of steam crawling across its surface. "Go into the pool," she said. "Be careful though. It is very hot. From this side it is less hot, but as you move that way it grows hotter. Go as far as you can to the hot side. It will soak the hurt from your muscles."

Ben nodded and moved toward the pool.

"Voyager," Rema stopped him. "Give me the breechcloth. I will bring other clothes." She held out her hand. Ben looked toward the pool then back at her. He considered simply stepping into the murky, steamy water before taking off the cloth but then shrugged mentally and skinned out of it.

Rema did not seem to notice his nakedness. She took the silken rag and left.

Ben eased into the cool end of the pool and moved

toward the hot side until he could hardly endure it. It was only a little deeper than his knees so he eased himself into a sitting position. The hot sulfurey water reached to just beneath his chin like a Japanese bath, and he had no more than settled himself when he felt the aches in his body lessen.

Rema returned in a few moments bringing clothes like those worn by Rothean, Marrad, and the others; a knee length, tightly woven tunic with short sleeves, a soft leather strip to use as a tie belt to cinch in the waist of the tunic, and sandals with wrap around thongs to weave up the calf. She also brought a piece of cloth to be used as a towel. She dropped everything in a pile and came to squat beside the pool. “You cannot stay too long,” she said, smiling. “Your muscles will be like wet rags and you may have need of them later.”

Ben smiled in return and glanced down at the long smooth length of thigh Rema exposed to him. He lifted his eyes a bit and found he could see the dark triangle at the top of those thighs. He blushed hotter than the sulfur pool at the sight and his body began to react in other ways.

Rema noticed the direction of his eyes and blushed too. She dropped her knees to the sand and smoothed her skirt.

“I’m sorry,” Ben stammered.

“No, I am sorry, Voyager. I didn’t think.”

They sat in silence for a time, uncomfortably aware they were now man and woman, not doctor and patient. Ben, looking for something to fill the thunderous silence said, “How is it I can understand the language here? I know it isn’t English, but I haven’t had any trouble understanding, even the first day."

"The Voyager's Mark."

"Ah, of course."

"You had best come out now," she said. "Lord Aris will soon be here."

He nodded and started to stand then stopped. His body reaction to his glimpse of Rema's womanhood had not disappeared. "Could you turn around or something?" he asked.

Rema, who had seen a thousand naked bodies, male and female, in her calling as healer, blushed a deep crimson, stood, and turned her back as her patient stepped out of the pool. She picked up the towel and handed it back to Ben without turning around. This effected him more than if she had just turned and given it to him. His body reacted by sending more blood to his semi-tumescent manhood, and he felt like crawling back into the pool and slipping under the water never to re-surface again.

"I'm sorry," he stammered again.

"I am sorry too," Rema said, but there was a gentle laugh in her voice, "and glad in another way. If your male reaction is still so quick, the rest of your body is probably fairly healthy."

Ben found himself grinning at her words.

"Now hurry and dress. Lord Aris will be here soon."

Rothean met them at Rema's fire. He had a bowl of gruel dipped and extended it to Ben as he squatted beside the fire. Ben and Rema were both careful to put their knees down so the short skirt of their tunics did not allow a repeat of the earlier problem.

Rothean noticed the tension between them and guessed the cause. It made him smile, but he said nothing.

"Is Lord Aris here yet?" Ben asked.

"Soon," Rothean said. "For now, eat and collect your thoughts."

Ben did as he was told but not quietly. "Is there anything I should do when I meet Lord Aris?" he asked.

"I do not understand," Rothean said.

"Should I bow or get down on my knees or something?"

"No. Lord Aris demands no obeisance, but you may find it easier to look at the ground until he darkens your eyes. Some, if they have too sensitive eyes, find they must turn their backs to my Lord's brightness until their eyes are darkened. Lord Aris only allows us into his presence when he is heavily veiled from head to foot, but the brightness is still great."

A shock of recognition ran through Ben. He looked down at his Voyager's Mark and found the veiled figure there. It seemed to emit eye-searing light such as Rothean described.

Rothean, seeing Ben's attention to the tattoo said, "All the world is represented in the Mark."

The intricacy of the tattoo was daunting, but more than that. It seemed to change from moment to moment. Ben could see the brilliance of Lord Aris, the light swallowing darkness of Lady Tarsa, and the marks, which represented him and Mardian and more. There was much of the tattoo which he could not truly see. It was as though portions of it were covered with impenetrable mist, but whatever he needed to see always had cleared when he needed to see it.

"Finish your breakfast, Voyager," Rothean said. "Lord Aris waits."

Rothean, carrying a torch, led the way down a rounded corridor. The walls showed signs of having been worked with tools and there were several sharp bends. As the two walked, the passage grew lighter and lighter. Soon the torch was useless and Rothean stuck it into a socket drilled into the wall. They walked on, rounding two more sharp bends. The light was bright as day now.

Rothean stopped. "From here you go on alone."

Ben glanced at his guide, suddenly not so anxious to confront Lord Aris. "Alone?" he asked with a tremble in his voice.

There was no contempt in Rothean when he said, "Do not be afraid, Voyager. Lord Aris is not like Lady Tarsa."

"Uh huh," Ben grunted, remembering the quick departure of the servants of Lady Tarsa from the presence of their goddess.

As though reading his thoughts, Rothean said, "Lord Aris has no need to see me, and I have other things to attend too. I will see you later. Keep straight ahead. You cannot go wrong; there are no other passages. Remember to look down, and you might also want to shield your eyes with your hands when you first enter."

"That won't offend Lord Aris?"

"He understands our weakness. It will not offend him."

Ben swallowed hard, took a deep breath, and said, "All right." He turned toward the light and walked forward.

Two bends farther the light became as bright as desert noon and after two bends more it was like staring into an arc welder. Ben turned his eyes toward the ground, shielding them with his hands, and continued forward.

"You have arrived, Ben Fordham," a pleasant baritone voice said. "Come forward three steps and do not look up until I tell you."

Ben did as he was told and when he stopped, he felt the touch of a hand on his temple. Instantly the glare was reduced to the strength of strong morning light. "You may look up now," Lord Aris said.

Ben looked up and around. He was in a conical chamber which was not a natural part of the cavern. Lord Aris, covered from head to foot with a thick veil, sat upon a stone block in the center of the chamber. Other stone blocks were around the place where the God of Light sat. "Please sit down, Ben Fordham."

It dawned on Ben that until now no one had called him by his name. He had been called *Voyager* or not addressed by any name at all.

Lord Aris examined Ben thoughtfully for a long time. "They said you were filled with a power they did not understand," the god said at last. "I see it and I do not understand it either."

"Don't understand?" Ben said. "But you're a god. How can you not understand something?"

Still looking at Ben speculatively, Aris answered. "First, though I am a god, you are an out-world being; therefore I am not your god. Nor am I the Over-God. Perhaps he is omniscient; I am not. Nor do I wish to be. I have my hands quite full enough maintaining the balance."

"Then you can't send me back?" Ben asked, already knowing but still dreading the answer.

"No, Ben Fordham, I cannot. Perhaps the Over-God could, but I do not know."

A flash of the screaming hysterics of Ben's first hours in this world returned like a nagging bellyache. He had developed a hope, based on nothing at all, that Aris might bring this whole nightmare to an end. Now that fragile creation was crushed. He almost cried.

After a little Ben said, "Rothean and the others said there had been others like me. Where are they?"

"Dead," the God of Light said.

"Dead? But they can't all be dead. Your people rescued me. They must have rescued others."

"My servants have rescued many others from Tarsa's altars, but most have been raving mad. All died soon after they were rescued, and I must assume those whom Tarsa reached before we did are dead also since I have not seen them."

*Dead*, Ben thought. Which *means I will probably die*--suddenly what the God of Light had said got through Ben's self pity. "What do you mean you haven't seen them? How could you see them? Tarsa got them, didn't she?"

"I might have seen them at the Home were they still alive."

"The Home? Where Tarsa would have taken me if Rothean and the others hadn't--"

"Yes."

"Why would you go there?"

"It is my dwelling. Tarsa and I are wed."

"Wed? You mean like married?" Ben's voice squeaked with unbelief.

Aris shrugged. "We are the balance," he said.

"Balance?"

"We are two sides of the world. She rules all things dark while I rule all things light. We must be wed. Without one or the other the world could not exist. All things exist by the existence of their opposites," Aris said. "Without life there is no death--without death, no life. Lady Tarsa and I are equal and opposite."

"I don't understand," Ben said, staving off the nausea caused by his sanity trying to tear loose from his control with questions about this world into which he had been shanghaied. "What about the third god? This Over-God? How can there be a balance with three gods."

"Not three. Only two."

"What about this Over-God? You, Tarsa, and the Over-God. That's three."

"Three do not rule. Only two rule. My power and the power of Tarsa rule on the world only, and our power is balanced. Above us is the Over-God. The creator. He does not exercise his power except as he has established how our power is to be exercised. He returns at the end of each age to judge if the balance has been maintained. If the balance is tipped too far, he will bring his creation to an end."

"Just like that? Blink and it is all gone?"

"Yes."

"What about all the people? Do they just go blink too?"

Lord Aris did not answer for a moment but then said, "I do not know. I have never asked."

"Never asked? All of them can be gone in a blink and you haven't asked?" This did not seem very god-like behavior to Ben. "How many people on this world? Thousands? Millions? What kind of god are you that you don't care enough to ask what happens to them?"

"You are wrong," Aris said. "I care. It is why I strive to maintain the balance. It is the only thing I can do. The rest is in the hands of the Over-God."

"And Tarsa tries to unbalance everything?"

"Yes."

"Wouldn't unbalancing everything destroy her as well as you and the world?"

"Yes. That is why she wishes it. She is the goddess of ending. I am the god of continuing. Balance."

Ben shook his head. "Your home must be a noisy place," he said with bitter sarcasm. "What with you and the wife fighting all the time."

Aris noted the tone and considered how to answer. This being was very different from those who had come before him. Those had either been unable to maintain sanity or to cope with the abuse of being brought to a new world. Fordham, while not totally stable, seemed to be coping and even fighting back. Such a one might become a considerable weapon if he continued to live, but Rothean and the others had reported his reluctance to be a weapon.

"Sometimes," the God of Light answered. "Actually, we seldom contend one with the other. There would be little point. We are the scales in the balance. Only our servants are weighed. We can have no direct effect on the balance. If we did, Mother Tarsa could unbalance the world simply by swallowing up all, but the Over-God has decreed that such is not possible."

"Then why did Lau and the others run away so fast?"

With some irony Aris said, "While Tarsa cannot directly swallow them up, her aspects are not to be disregarded. She is horrifying and dread attends her, so even those who serve her avoid her."

Ben allowed this to sink in for a moment. "Why would anyone serve her if she is so horrible?"

Aris shrugged. "Gain. Power. Because the Over-God has created in humans some contrary nature which can love death or life or both at the same time."

Ben rolled this explanation over in his mind. Aris waited patiently as though he, a god, had nothing more to do than wait upon the questions of one displaced person.

"So then, why doesn't she just have Mardian send her a whole bunch of other-worlders?" Ben asked.

"Because it would take tens of thousands to truly effect the balance. It is much more effective to continue in the normal way with our servants contending for power."

"Then why am I here? If I don't effect the balance. why did Mardian kidnap me?" Ben demanded, his voice full of resentment.

"I told you. To effect the balance a little, but also because Tarsa gains some sort of joy from it."

Ben's mouth opened, but he found nothing more to say so he closed it and just sat thinking for a bit. At last he asked, "What does Mardian get out of it?"

Aris seemed surprised by the question. "Why gain, of course."

"Gain? You mean like money?"

"Yes."

Ben shook his head. "How does he collect? I'm here and he is there."

"He will come to collect his price and return to your world.

Ben's ears pricked up. "He can come and go between worlds?"

"Yes."

"How?"

"By means of a Voyager's Mark."

"Then I could--"

"No," Aris shook his head. "Your Voyager's Mark is for this world. You would need another mark, one for your own world, to go back."

"So where can I get one?"

"Not here…" Aris began then stopped short and was silent for a moment. The god still did not know whether Fordham would continue to live and stay sane, but if he did, Aris still might find a way to tap into the power the out-worlder possessed, but a little time and thought might remedy such ignorance, so "…Probably not here," he finished thoughtfully.

Ben's mind spun like a compass in a magnetic field. "What do you mean, *probably not*?"

"Mardian is not a creature of this world. His power is like your power--outside the normal--therefore I do not think you will find one who has such power and can use it here, but perhaps you may."

"How? Where?" Ben asked eagerly.

"As I see it," Aris began, pointedly not answering Ben's question, "You are left with three possible courses. You may serve me and help to maintain the balance. You may return to Lau and serve Lady Tarsa--"

A chill ran through Ben.

"--Or you may strike out on your own as a wanderer."

Ben suddenly had the feeling the God of Light was being less than truthful with him. The god might not be lying outright, but Ben felt there was more so he grew cautious. "Suppose I do strike out on my own? Where would I want to wander too?"

Aris did not smile though he was pleased. "The life of a wanderer is not an easy one. You would be in danger from everyone, but especially from Tarsa. Her servants patrol the roads around her strong holds and make excursions into the territories of my strength. Those who serve me might be less inclined to harm you, but a stranger is always suspect and generally shunned."

Ben waited for the rest. He knew there was more, but when Aris did not go on he said, "There is more, isn't there. There is more than just wandering around dodging everyone. Where would I wander too? Where might I find someone to give me a Voyager's Mark to get me home?"

Aris hesitated just enough to see that Ben was well and truly hooked before he said, "There is a store house of knowledge. It is called the Valley of Seers."

Ben tried not to hope, feeling hope was a plague at the moment, but he could not keep the hunger out of his voice when he said, "What is the Valley of Seers?"

"It is a valley of madmen--"

"Madmen," Ben cried. "What use is that?"

Aris took no notice of the protest and went on. "--Madmen who have been touched by the Over-God in special ways. They have no power as such, but some have great knowledge. After a fashion they are like you. They are out of place in this world though they were born into it. They do not serve Tarsa or me but only the Over-God."

"Can they help me get home?"

"Perhaps, but you must reach them to find out, and the knowledge is sometimes in a garbled form which is difficult to understand. They do have knowledge though and if you do unravel it, perhaps it can help."

Ben suddenly could not keep hope under control. It flamed up despite all he could do. "In my world," he said still fighting not to hope, "in the old times insanity was considered being touched by the gods. That idea is long gone because we discovered it was really just a kind of sickness. It is probably the same here."

"That is perhaps true," Aris agreed.

"You don't give many straight answers do you?" Ben said, still fighting not to hope, which made the question come out as bitterness.

Aris disregarded the bitterness and said, "I do not know how gods on your world are, but as for me, I am sorry you were brought here. My heart is wrung by your despair, and I would ease it if I could, but it is not in my power. I have told you all I know that might help you. It is not much and may not help at all, but it is all I can do."

Ben ran his eyes over the veiled face. He felt Aris was speaking the truth, but not necessarily the whole truth; nevertheless, he realized he had no choice but to believe this shining god.

"I will send Rema with you, Voyager," Aris continued. "She knows the Valley of Seers and can guide you. Her empathy with all living things may be of more use to you than anything else in his world."

Ben's heart leapt at this. Rema. But he put the thought aside with a pang of guilt. His wife Maggie used to make his heart leap in his chest the same way. "Won't that affect the balance?" he asked.

Aris shrugged. "Yes, but not much and, in her way, Rema will still be serving me. She preserves human life which serves me." He rose. "I do not know if I will be able to help you further, but I will try. Call on me in time of need and I will exercise all the power at my disposal."

Ben stood. "Thank you, Lord Aris," he said. "I'll try not to call on you, but it is comforting to know you're there all the same."

"Rothean waits for you. He will lead you to the beginning of your path. Farewell, Voyager," the god said and was gone.

The disappearance of the brightness of Aris left a crashing darkness in the cavern and seconds passed before the flicker of a torch pushed it back a little. It was Rothean. He stood staring at Ben with a strange look, which might have been fear, on his face.

"What is it, Rothean?"

"You glowed."

"Glowed?"

"Light. Brighter than my torch. You were brighter than my torch."

"You mean like Lord Aris' light?"

"No," Rothean shook his head. "No, different. Soft and blue like the sparks which came from your fingers last night."

"Everything was black when Aris left until you came in with a torch."

Rothean lowered the torch and looked into Ben's eyes, but apparently he found no explanation for he shook his head and continued to stare for a while longer before he said, "Come. Rema waits. There is food and day will soon be here."

"You already know what is happening?"

"Yes."

Rothean shrugged his thick shoulders and turned toward the passage assuming Ben would follow.

## Chapter Six

Rothean led them out of the cavern just as the sun topped the ridges. The exit was a small hole. Ben did not think his broad shoulders were going to pass through, but they did--barely. His hands and knees were scrapped raw from the crawl down the last part of the exit tunnel. The pain of them added to the pain of his sore wrists and ankles.

Rothean did not let them linger near the exit, but started down the mountainside at a sliding, tumbling lope with Rema and Ben behind him. Cascades of scree rolled into the canyon below.

Ben had more chance to look around than he had hanging head down over a saddle, but what he saw only confirmed what he had guessed at before. The area was much like southern California, not many trees and most of those the prickly leafed pin oaks. The mountains were as saw-toothed as they had looked from the Valley of Voices, but here sparse brown plants and clumps of rich colored wild flowers grew. Rothean did not give him much time for sightseeing. At the bottom of the moraine Rothean charged into the thick, stickery brush of the canyon floor without slowing down. There was no apparent path, but the barrier yielded slowly to his assault.

"How long will it take us to get to this Valley?" Ben panted.

"The journey is difficult," Rema answered. "I cannot know. If the paths were smooth, if there were no patrols, if we were sure there would be no injuries, we might make the journey in a few weeks.

"But no guarantees, right?"

She nodded.

Ben had been panting like a broken bellows and sweating rivers. He had been in good condition, but weeks of boozing and the abuse of the last few days had ended that. Still, he hung in like grim death and refused to ask Rothean to slow down.

Rema saw her patient was laboring to keep up, but did not say anything at first. Soon, however, it was clear he could not keep up much longer so she called out, "We must stop 'Thean."

Rothean looked back then glanced at the heavens. Already the blue of the sky was washed out with rising heat. The day was going to be desert hot.

"A couple more hours and we will reach Rayhan's spring. There will be shade and cool water there."

"He cannot go farther at this pace," she said flatly and stopped.

The big red head shot her a disapproving glance, but it did not seem to bother her. Ben was grateful. If she had not stopped, he would have had to ask himself, and he did not want to appear weak before them. Besides, Rothean might not have stopped.

They squatted in the tangle of brush. Ben put his head between his knees and breathed deeply, trying to clear out the exploding purple and green lights. The air was dusty and smelled of wild sage. He could taste the bitterness of it in the air as he gasped through his open mouth.

"Breath slowly," Rema said. "Hold each breath two heart beats before you release it."

Ben did as he was told and soon the ache in his chest began to ease. Sweat still poured off him in rivers. It stung his eyes and when it touched his lips, the taste of it was a mixture of salt and old booze.

Rothean, squatting a little ahead, was as immobile as a stone. He might always have been there, and he might remain another ten thousand years without moving.

"Why are we in such a hurry?" Ben asked once his breathing slowed.

"Traveling in the open like this can be dangerous. There are patrols everywhere and they especially watch cave entrances if they know where they are. That one," she tossed her head back the way they had come, "can be seen from far away so we get as far from it as fast as possible."

The news made the flesh of Ben's neck crawl. "Was anyone watching the hole?"

Rema shrugged.

Ben was on the edge of exhaustion already, but the news they might be watched prodded him. Better to be gasping for air and drowning in sweat than to be taken like a rabbit sitting in the brush. "Let's go," he said.

"We can wait a little longer, until you are rested," she said, putting her hand on his arm.

Ben shook the hand off and stood. Rothean noticed and was up and moving in a second. He eased his pace a little until they came out of the thick brush onto a narrow path then his pace increased, and Ben was once again hard pressed to keep up.

Two hours of non-stop push brought the little party to a small stream which bubbled out of a crack in the canyon wall. They stopped and sat down to rest in the shade of a water oak which angled out of the canyon wall. The stream flowed over the roots of the tree.

Rema settled herself beside the tree and leaned back, taking deep breaths. Ben settled near her. He was almost too weary to drink, though his mouth and throat burned with thirst. Rothean knelt by the roots of the oak and scooped water to his mouth with his left hand. His right hand lay across his lap, fingers dangling near the grip of his sword. His senses were as alert as those of a wild animal.

"Where are we headed?" Ben asked after a few minutes rest.

"Rayhan," Rothean said, not letting his awareness of the surrounding area slip at all.

"Is it much farther?"

"A bit farther," Rothean answered. His glance paused for a second on Ben and he grinned. "Tonight you will be able to sleep on pointed stones and find them soft."

Ben could not spare the energy to laugh. "You're right. And I'll probably have to be pried loose from those stones I'll be so stiff."

Rothean laughed. "Rema is strong. She can pry you up, but you won't have to sleep on the ground tonight.

Rayhan is not much, but there is an inn with beds."

"Glad to hear it. Rema won't have to pry so hard. Bed or not I'm not so sure she could do it alone, but I guess you can always help her."

"At some other time perhaps, but not tomorrow," he said. "I leave you at Rayhan."

"What, tonight?"

Rothean nodded which made drips of perspiration flick off his long red hair. It had darkened with the dampness.

"Why not wait until tomorrow at least?"

"I have not seen my family for months. I am anxious. Besides, it is cooler traveling by night."

"Is it far to your family?"

"Achema, north of here, a day or so. If there is no trouble, I should be there by tomorrow morning." Ben noticed Rothean's eyes never stopped moving. They roamed the clearing around the spring and over the dense brush and did not rest anywhere for more than a moment. The travelers' backs were against an almost vertical cliff and it made his watching easier. It would be difficult for anyone to trap the three because of that and the heavy brush. Even a small group of men coming from the brush would make a clatter which could be heard for miles and the travelers could fade into the same brush in moments if need be.

"You have children, Rothean?"

"Three," he said with pride. "Two sons and a daughter."

"Are they still small?"

He nodded. "The eldest is six summers. And you? Do you have children?"

"No, and I am glad. It would have been horrible to have left family behind."

"You are alone on your world too?" Rothean's eyes did not stop moving.

"More or less. My parents are there, and I was married, but she left me weeks before I ran into Mardian."

"Then why are you anxious to return? You have no one to return too except your parents, and they are old, yes?"

Ben was surprised by the coldness of the question, but tried not to let it show. "Yes, but not so old I wouldn't want to see them again. Besides they might need me someday. And the other place is home. This isn't."

Rothean smiled and scratched his beard. "True," he said. "Home is home, no matter what."

They fell silent then. Rothean continued to watch for enemies and Ben thought of Home and Maggie. That part of his life was over and he knew it. Even if he got home, it would still be over, but it did not make him like it any more.

"Drink again, Voyager," Rothean said. "Deeply. We must move on soon and it is growing hotter."

Rema heard and stood. She took a leather water bag which had been on a thong over her shoulder and dropped it into the stream then knelt beside it and drank. After a little she pulled the now filled and dripping water bag from the stream and corked it. Ben noticed Rothean had a bag too and wondered why he didn't have one. He asked Rema.

"We had no extra ones in the cave," she answered. "We will buy one at Rayhan."

"I don't have any money."

"It is provided. Lord Aris commanded me to look

after you and I will," she said, smiling.

Ben felt the smile in the pit of his stomach then felt bad about the feeling.

Rothean led off down the path, which ran beside the trickling stream. Other small streams joined the trickle and soon it had become a considerable brook. The pace was brisk and Ben sweated buckets, but he kept up.

Soon salt wedges crusted the fronts and backs of all three travelers' tunics. The sun crept up higher and grew hotter. Small sounds from the edges of the stream began to disappear as the day grew hotter. After an hour Ben found himself straining to hear something besides the roar of the blood in his ears, the sigh of his breath, and the soft splash of the stream, but there was nothing. His concentration was so intense that when the two men leapt from the brush beside the stream, his heart lurched with startlement which turned to real fear in a moment.

The two threatened with drawn swords. They were dressed in rags and they looked hungry, but their weapons were well cared for and sharp. They bracketed Rothean and were on him before the three travelers could draw breath.

Rothean's sword was out of its scabbard so fast as to be only a blur. It was like part of his arm. The fighters engaged in a blink and the clang and hiss of weaponry and the grunts of effort filled the blistering air for a few seconds then the attackers broke off and retreated a step.

"Let us pass, fools," Rothean said through clenched teeth. "I want none of your blood!"

The three looked at one another for a moment then the shortest bandit screamed,

"We want yours!" as the two charged.

Rothean flicked the nearer of the two swords away with his own and whirled low, kicking out at the second attacker. There was a stomach turning pop-crunch as the bandit's knee dislocated. That one went down screaming.

Ben was so surprised he could only stand with his mouth open at first, but a fiery blue aura grew bright around him. The sound of the dislocated knee made his heart rage and the aura flame. All sense fled from him and he charged into the middle of the fight shouting, "Stop! Stop!"

Four sets of eyes snapped to him like iron to a magnet, including the eyes of the bandit with the dislocated knee though he was writhing on the ground in agony.

Ben's eyes flayed the three combatants. The rage on his face and the blazing cobalt blue aura terrified them. "Put up your swords," he commanded.

The combatants stared at this azure flaming madman with mouths hanging open and all the world hung suspended for an instant. "Put up your swords!" He commanded again. "There will be no killing here today!"

Rothean sheathed his sword in a movement too fast to follow with the eye. The bandit still standing was a heart beat behind Rothean in returning his sword to its scabbard. The man on the ground could not so easily reach his weapon as it had been knocked away in the scramble, but now he dragged himself toward it though his knee tortured him with each movement.

Rema, who was slightly behind the four men, stepped forward to help the injured bandit. That one would not stop squirming until Rema handed him the fallen sword and the weapon was replaced in its scabbard.

Ben Fordham's presence made everything else in the world seem insignificant. The four had no thought of anything save this powerful presence. Ben, still ablaze with blue fire demanded, "Why did you attack us?" His voice was irresistible. The bandit still standing began to stammer. "I…We…" he stopped and fell to his knees then put his face in the dust. "Your forgiveness, Lord," he mumbled into the dirt. "Your forgiveness. We knew not what we were doing. We were hungry and poor and knew no other way."

Ben looked down at the bent trembling back and said, "Forgiveness is not mine to give. Forgive yourself and never lift your hand against another person for the rest of your life."

"Yes, Lord," the bandit said still not looking up.

"I'm no Lord," Ben snapped, his anger still boiling. His aura blazed brighter. "I'm only Ben Fordham. Stand up! Don't bow to me. Stand up!"

The bandit continued to grovel until Ben stooped to lift him to his feet. The man tried to jerk away from the blazing touch, but Ben seized his arm and hauled him to his feet as though he were a small child.

Awe and fear evaporated from the bandit when he looked into Ben's eyes, and a crushing sorrow came over him. Tears flowed down the bandit's leathery, bearded face.

Ben, whose strength had seemed limitless a moment before, was suddenly exhausted, overcome with bone aching weariness so severe he could not continue to stand. He slumped to the ground and put his head in his hands. All eyes remained on him as the aura faded and when it was gone Rema knelt beside him and asked, "Are you well, my Lord?"

Ben lifted his head and the aura flared again, but weaker. "I told you I am not a Lord. Not yours or anyone else's," he growled and was sorry an instant later, for he saw how the words cut Rema. The aura extinguished itself.

"I'm sorry, Rema," he said, his voice breathy with weariness. "I'm very tired. And I am not anybody's Lord. I'm sorry."

Rema stroked his hair back from his forehead. "Rest," she said. "Just rest for a little while."

Ben nodded his head a fraction.

Rema examined Fordham. She surely could see he was nearly used up.

"We cannot stay here," Rothean said. "There might be more like these around and I do not think--" he did not finish.

"There are no others," the uninjured bandit volunteered. "We were here only because we were too weak to join another band. We were hiding. This is not a very traveled way. We were surprised to see you coming."

Rothean looked over the bandit and could probably see he was telling the truth. "Rayhan is not far. We can reach it before dark even if I must carry the Voyager."

"If he can go on," Rema said, casting a worried glance at the slumped figure a few feet away. "And what about him?" She lifted her chin in the direction of the injured bandit who clutched his ruined knee and groaned softly. The other knelt beside him.

"His partner can deal with him," Rothean said with some bitterness, and stood. He went to Ben's side and squatted down. "Ben Fordham?" he said and waited to see if there was any reaction.

Ben lifted his head a little so Rothean went on. "The day runs quickly. If we would be at Rayhan before dark we must go. I will carry you if need be."

Ben's eyes met Rothean's. "Carry me?" he asked, not comprehending at first. Then he shook his head. "No, I can walk. Carry him. He can't. We can't leave him here."

Rothean looked toward the injured bandit with distaste, but he did not protest. He stood and went back to Rema. "Can you get him in shape to move?"

Rema looked from Rothean to the bandit then toward Ben. His green eyes caught hers, and she saw the plea in them before they closed. She said, "I will see."

An hour later the dislocated knee had been returned to its proper alignment and splinted. Rema woke Ben from what was more like a coma than sleep and got him on his feet. Rothean picked up the injured bandit with the help of the other bandit and placed the man over his shoulders in a fireman's carry and the five marched off downstream toward Rayhan.

## Chapter Seven

Ben Fordham opened his eyes and could not believe what he saw. Lying beside him, only inches away was the beautiful face of the woman he had seen in his dreams. Her face was peaceful--relaxed. Her eyes were closed and the gently sensuous curves of her lips were held in a Mona Lisa smile which caused his heart to melt.

The some of it came back to him--Mardian, the Voyager's Mark, and Lady Tarsa. He did not really know where he was, but decided this must be the inn at Rayhan. He squeezed his eyes tight shut, hoping when he opened them he would be back home but it didn't work this time either.

Ben lay still so as not to disturb Rema and some memory of the previous day came back to him. He vaguely remembered stumbling down the path beside the stream being supported by Rema and the little robber, but that was about all except the most crushing weariness he had ever experienced. That seemed to be gone now, leaving only some stiff muscles and a slight headache.

Ben wondered what time it was. The gray light filtering through the slit window of the room did not tell him much; it could have been morning or evening light. He eased himself into a sitting position still trying not to wake Rema, but her golden eyes flicked open and she smiled. "How are you?" She asked.

"I'm still here," he answered with a little acid in the words. She frowned, not understanding, so he said, "I'm all right." Her frown cleared and that made him feel better for some reason. "Is this Rayhan?"

"Yes. We got here just before dark, day before yesterday."

"Day before…What happened to yesterday?"

"You slept through it."

Ben thought about it a little then asked, "The others? Rothean? The bandits?"

"Rothean is gone. Yesterday morning."

"I thought he was going to go on the night we got here."

"He was too tired. He carried the injured bandit--Morin is his name--all the way here."

Ben was indignant. "The other guy should have helped him!" he said.

"He couldn't. It was all the two of us could do to carry you, so 'Thean carried Morin, and Othway and I carried you."

Ben listened with his mouth hanging open. He remembered none of what she described. The last thing he remembered was starting out from the sight of the ambush. "Where are the bandits?"

"Below. Morin will stay here until his leg heals and Othway will go with us."

"What? Why? We don't need anybody else do we?

You know the way don't you?"

"I tried to tell Othway that, and that he should stay here with his friend, but he'll have none of it. He swears you are his Lord and he will go with you no matter what."

"His *Lord,"* Ben groaned. "How did I get to be his *Lord*?"

Rema ran her eyes over Ben's face. "You don't remember what you did?"

"Of course I remember!" he said, frowning and tilting his head impatiently. "I told them to stop fighting and they did. So what? How does that make me anybody's *Lord*?"

Rema continued to stare at him with worried eyes. "My Lor…" she stopped, swallowed, and started again. "Ben Fordham, you did not *tell* them to stop, you *commanded* them to stop with such force they could do nothing but stop."

Ben shook his head in confusion and said "Huh?"

"When you told them to stop thunder rolled though there was no cloud in the sky, and lightning crackled around you. When you spoke such power flowed out of you, it wrung their hearts to weeping with sorrow at ever having thought to do hurt to one another."

Ben blinked at her and began shaking his head in denial. "No. No! I just told them to stop and they stopped," he said, but in the back of his mind he heard his father's voice saying, *"It wasn't your fight? Then why did you get into it?"*

Rema took his hand and studied his eyes, deep lines of concentration furrowing her brows. "Please, my Lord," she begged. "Please stay with me here. Do not let your mind go away." She threw her arms around his neck and crushed him to her. "I was so afraid last night when you cried out in your sleep!"

Ben put his arms around her in return, but it was only body reaction at first. After a little he said, "I'm all right. It's all right, Rema. Don't be afraid. Please don't be afraid."

Rema pulled back to examine his eyes again and finding no more madness there, sighed with relief. She let him go and sat back. "Last night you were fevered and you raved. You spoke to your father and your wife and thrashed about. You cried and would not stop until I held you."

"Dreams," he said, remembering. "Nightmares. Real beauties--" he broke off with a feeling of déjà vu. *I've had these nightmares before. Dreams of this place. Of this world.* Then the feeling was gone.

"What time is it?" he asked. "I mean is it morning or evening?"

"Morning," she answered, puzzled at the sudden change.

"Then we can go on," he said and started to rise.

"You need more rest, my Lor…Ben Fordham. You were fevered and shaking with chill last night."

"I'm all right now. Nothing the matter a cup of coffee and a couple of eggs wouldn't cure," he said with a false heartiness Rema saw right through.

"Why is there so much hurry?" She asked with exasperated concern. "The Valley of Seer's has been in the same place for as long as forever. It will not move if it takes us a year or ten years to reach it."

Ben could feel her worry. He reached out and tenderly stroked her cheek. "I know, but I want to go home," he said, knowing it was not completely true. He wanted to go home, but there were other reasons to reach the Valley of Seer's--reasons he did not understand, only felt, were connected with his dreams.

Rema felt Ben's troubled spirit in his touch. To wait another day would be better, but there was urgency in him which would not be denied. "Let me look at your wrists again," she said.

Ben extended his wrists.

"Do they still hurt?"

"No."

"And the Voyager's Mark? Is it still sore?"

He glanced down at the tattoo. It was still beautiful and the internal light of it still drew the eye. "Do you know what any of this means, Rema?"

She shrugged. "Some," she answered. "That is Lord Aris," she said, pointing. "And that is Lady Tarsa. That the Valley of Voices. I think that is Mardian's Mark, and this," she touched the broken sheaf mark just below Mardian's, "this must be your mark, and this is the Valley of Seer's."

A cold hand clutched Ben's heart. A field of golden ripe wheat represented the Valley of Seer's.

~ * ~

Rothean had said Rayhan wasn't much and he was not wrong. It was an assemblage of a dozen ramshackle adobe buildings in a grove of scabby looking sycamore trees. It had grown up around the inn which existed only because of the ferry crossing the river Rayhan. The river, which had grown from the spring where the travelers had rested, was not deep, but it was wide and the bottom was soft and shifting which made the ferry necessary.

The proprietor of the inn was a short round man with long greasy hair and a beard to match. The common room of his inn was dark and smoky and smelled of ancient cooking. Rema gave the man enough money to pay for the injured bandit's keep for a couple of weeks. The bandit, Morin, promised to work off the rest of the cost when his leg was healed. "See you don't start working him before that leg is healed," she said handing over the coins.

"I am no servant of Tarsa, to try to work a sick man," the innkeeper protested. "I will wait until he is able. I have some charity in my heart."

Rema was not convinced but said nothing further. She was not sure who she pitied more, the innkeeper who would try to wring blood from a stone, or the bandit who was the stone to be wrung. She turned to the table where Ben and the other bandit sat. Ben's head was in his hands and utter despair fairly dripped from him. He had been trying for the last half-hour to convince Othway he, Ben Fordham, was no Lord, and Othway should stay with his friend in Rayhan. It had been a dismal failure.

"Are you well, Ben Fordham?" Rema asked.

He looked at her and shook his head in disgust. "Let's go," he said and stood. "Let's just go. There is no reasoning with the man."

Rema felt like laughing for the first time in three days, but she held it in and strode out of the inn. Ben followed her and Othway trailed them, head down and shoulders hunched like a scolded puppy.

~ * ~

The day was hot, but not as blistering as the day of the ambush. Rema and Ben walked side by side and Othway trailed them. Ben ignored him, hoping he would take the hint and go back, but after a couple of hours Ben couldn't ignore the bandit any longer.

"If we can't get rid of you, you might as well walk up here with us," Ben called, and Othway hustled up to join them, grinning from ear to ear.

The bandit was shorter than Ben by more than a head, but in other ways he was not small. He was well muscled and had slightly long arms and legs well suited to traveling on foot. His eyes were deep brown, almost black, and his hair and beard were blue black as a crow's feather. "Thank you, my Lord," he said as he came up to them.

Ben held up a forbidding hand. "No. Look, I don't care what else you want to call me, but don't call me *my Lord.* All right?"

"Yes, my Lord," Othway said.

Ben glanced at Rema, seeking help, but she shrugged. He took a deep breath and tried another tack. "Othway, why do you call me My Lord?"

"Because you are my Lord," the bandit answered.

Ben studied the man's face. There was no levity there, though Othway was smiling. "If I truly am your *Lord,* will you go away if I command you to go away?"

The smile disappeared from the bandit's face. "Please, my Lord. Do not command me to go away. I beg you."

Ben's eyebrows drew down. "Why not?"

"If you command, I must obey."

Ben shook his head, trying to understand. "I did command you back in Rayhan--"

"No, my Lord, you did not. You asked and you reasoned. You tried to convince. You did not command."

Ben looked to Rema for help once again, but found her nodding agreement with what Othway was saying. "Ah, I see," he said. The thought to simply command Othway to leave crossed his mind then, but just as he could taste the words on his tongue he stopped. Instead he asked, "Why do you want to stay with me?"

Othway shrugged. "You may have need of me," he said. "And I have nowhere else to go."

"You could have stayed with your partner, but if you didn't want to, you could have just gone home."

"I have no home, my Lord. Except with you."

"I don't understand."

Othway hesitated and looked at the ground as though he really did not want to explain, as though he was ashamed for some reason, but after a moment he said, "I come from a people who live by raiding and looting, but my band, our band, grew too large and pickings became too small so Morin and I struck out on our own. I am ashamed to say we would have slit all your throats for the little you had, but then you commanded us to peace. You commanded us, commanded me, to put up my sword and I did. I am changed forever. You are my Lord now. You are my home. I will never draw sword again to kill a man."

Confused and torn between pity for Othway and frustration at finding himself responsible for another life, Ben shook his head and turned away. Rema and the bandit trailed after him. They walked in silence as Ben turned what he had just heard over in his mind. After a while he asked, "You said you would never ever kill a man again, right?"

"Yes, my Lord."

"You mean because you are with me? Is that why you want to stay with me? To make sure you never kill again?"

"Oh no, my Lord. With you or without you I will never kill another person. Never."

Ben did not know how to feel about that. On the one hand an end to violence made him feel good, but on the other hand, he felt rather like he had de-clawed a tiger then sent it out to starve because it could no longer fend for itself.

"How about your partner?" Ben asked.

"Morin?"

"Yes, Morin. Was he effected the same way?"

"Yes. But for his leg he would be here too."

"Rothean was changed too, Ben Fordham," Rema said.

Inside his head Ben could hear his father's voice. *Why did you do that? It wasn't your fight!*

*I couldn't help it!* Ben answered the thought. *It is my nature! I didn't mean too!*

But meaning to or not, he had somehow changed the nature of four people by his command, and it made him responsible.

~ * ~

The desert wind grew cold as darkness thickened. The travelers moved off the road into a gully protected from the wind to camp. During the afternoon Othway knocked over a rabbit with a well thrown rock and Ben looked askance at him, not understanding how it was possible for the bandit to kill a rabbit and skin it without a qualm but swear he would never again kill a man. Ben felt the difference between a man and a rabbit himself, but could not satisfactorily explain it to himself. He had wondered many times why he could eat meat back on his own world, but never came up with a satisfactory answer there either. And it wasn't as though he was one who didn't know the meat he ate had once been alive. He knew the rabbit had been alive. He had seen it alive and was cheered and happy when Othway knocked it off. He was also made hungry by the smell of it roasting. Puzzling, he thought, along with a few thousand other puzzling things which ran around his brain as he gnawed stringy roast rabbit then rolled up in a heavy animal skin robe to sleep, but puzzling or not it did not keep him from sleeping.

Sometime during the night Ben woke. Othway and Rema were jammed tight against either side of him for warmth. He looked up at the icy glimmer of the stars and felt the disturbing closeness of Rema. Maggie flickered through his mind but didn't stay long. She was pushed out by hurt, abandonment, and anger--and by Rema's thigh, which had somehow pushed out of her bedroll, and into his. It lay across his legs and the warmth of it caused a tickle at the base of his testicles and a coppery taste to come into his mouth. His hands fairly itched to stroke the soft inside of it, and the earlier glimpse of her womanhood played through his mind over and over like a video loop. It had been a long time since Maggie.

I wonder if I could command her? Ben thought, but shoved the thought away with all his might. It was tempting though.

Night wind rattled and moaned through the brush and it almost sounded like mocking laughter. Ben was still awake, listening and suffering with temptation and desire when the dawn came.

~ * ~

They traveled three days along the road. On the morning of the fourth day they turned north, cutting across country.

"Why are we leaving the road?" Ben, used to more civilized places where people traveled by roads, asked.

"We must go north."

"Too bad. Walking along the road wasn't bad. A lot easier than brush jumping like we started out from the cave."

Rema shrugged. "We could have stayed on the road, but turning north here saves days, and there is a path. Walking it will not be hard. Besides, Tarsa's servants patrol the roads this side of the Tyand Mountains. The other side of the mountains we will not have to be so wary and in Bakar we can get horses."

"Ah," Ben said. He liked the idea of not having to worry about Tarsa's servants, but wasn't so sure he liked the idea of horses. He didn't know much about them and had only ridden once--voluntarily. He didn't count the time spent slung over a saddle like cargo as riding. "It would be nice if we could hop a bus," he said.

Rema and Othway looked at him with puzzled expressions. "Hop a what, Ben Fordham?" Rema asked.

"A bus."

"What is Bus?" Othway asked.

"It's a … thing," Ben said then thought how little that explained and tried to come up with something better. He failed. "I can't tell you what it is."

"Is it secret knowledge?" Rema asked. "Like some potions and herbs?"

"No, it's just--" he shook his head in frustration. "I can see the thing I mean in my mind, but I don't know how to explain it. There is no such thing here or anything like it. A bus is a thing like a wagon, only it isn't pulled by animals. It moves by itself sort of, and people can ride it from place to place."

The other two looked confused and skeptical.

"Never mind," Ben said. "Just lead on toward Bakar."

## Chapter Eight

Ten days into the mountains the wind brought a curious noise which sounded disturbingly like the rattle and clank of armor. Rema scrambled up a high ridge and carefully turned her head side to side to home in on where the sound was coming from. She stopped turning with her face back in the direction from which they had come, and after a moment she motioned for Othway and Ben to come up beside her. Belly down, with heads barely above the ridge, the peered down their back trail. A yellowish cloud stained the heat washed blue of the sky. "What is it?" Ben asked, remembering another horror which came in a cloud.

"Dust," Othway answered.

"Troops," Rema said, a puzzled frown on her face. "Many troops to raise so much dust."

"Tarsa?" Ben asked.

Rema, not taking her eyes off the smear of dust said, "Probably."

A tingle of fear shot through Ben. "I thought you said Tarsa's people stick to the roads."

"Usually they do."

"Are they after us?"

Rema licked the corner of her mouth with the tip of her tongue then shrugged, still not taking her eyes off their back trail. After a few more minutes she said, "Come," and scooted down the ridgeback to the path. She squatted in the shade of a greasewood bush and the others squatted too.

"What now?" Ben asked, trying not to show the fear that had started a small flame burning in his middle.

"We might hide out until they pass," Rema said, thinking out loud.

"If they are truly after us, won't they be tracking us or something?"

"Why would they be tracking us with such an army?" Othway said.

Rema nodded her agreement. "They would be tracking us with a smaller, quieter force."

"Maybe it isn't Tarsa," Ben said hopefully. The others gave him such looks he felt stupid, but he added, "Well, what if it isn't?"

"Our safest choice is to assume it is," Rema explained patiently.

Knowing Rema was right did not make Ben any happier. "So what do we do then?"

"Run for Bakar," she answered.

Othway nodded his agreement and after a moment Ben did too.

"Then let's go," She said and set off at a brisker pace than they had been keeping.

Ben was in better shape now than when he left the cavern, but his body was still paying for the weeks of booze before he was kidnapped and the abuse since his arrival. In moments he was breathing hard and drenched in sweat, but when Rema asked if he needed to rest. He shook his head, not wasting any breath on words. She eased up a little, nevertheless and started watching Ben more closely. When he looked as though he was ready to drop, she called a halt. He protested that he was fine, but Othway, standing behind him, shook his head. "We can go faster longer if we do not kill our selves now," she said.

Relief passed over Ben's face, but he quickly covered it with a nod and a mumbled, "All right."

They sat in the shade of a scrub cedar, drank deeply from their water skins and ate some dried fruit. "Shouldn't we get off the path?" Ben asked when his breathing had returned to normal. "Wouldn't it make us harder to track?"

"If they are tracking us, but we can move faster on the trail, and I do not think they are tracking us.

"Why else would they be behind us?"

"That is the question going round and round in my head," Rema said, hitting the stopper of her water skin to seal it tight. She stood. Othway did likewise then turned to pull Ben to his feet. They started up the trail without an answer.

They traveled hard taking only short breaks until it was too dark to continue. Because they were hot and sweaty the cold of the desert chilled them to the bone, but they dared not light a fire. Wrapped in a sleeping robe, but still shaking with the cold Ben asked, "How much farther to Bakar?"

"Two more days," Rema said.

"Can we stay ahead of them?"

Rema shrugged. "Depends if they are infantry or cavalry. Cavalry will be harder, but I don't think they will come much farther. Bakar has been a stronghold of Lord Aris for many years. It is very well defended, and I do not think they will chance coming much closer to it."

"Unless they think I am valuable enough to chance it," Ben said. The other two did not answer.

They continued to travel fast and hungry for the next two days, coming to a lookout post above Bakar in the late afternoon of the second day. Much to Rema's surprise the troops had continued to follow them, but when she mentioned it to the lookouts manning the post they were not surprised. "There have been rumblings," they said. "Rumor has it Lady Tarsa intends something momentous."

"Surely she will not try Bakar," Rema said, not sounding as convinced as she had a few days before.

"I almost hope they do," one of the lookouts said. "We will grind them to bits."

He laughed and his partner joined him. Rema, Othway and Ben did not.

Bakar was actually two cities set in a horseshoe shaped valley bounded by steep craggy cliffs on its inland side but open to the sea at the west end. The port of Bakar rested there sprawling out from a series of piled stone and sand breakwaters. Wooden plank piers extended from the breakwaters and a half dozen ships were tied to the piers. They were shallow drafted, wide beamed craft with single masts which reminded Ben of the ships of ancient Phoenicia he had seen in pictures.

"There are no walls," Ben said, remembering Nanema.

"There is no need," Rema said. "If the port is

attacked, they will set fire to it and retreat to the city."

"That isn't the city?"

"No. Bakar is beneath us."

Ben looked over the edge. He could see a wide road which came from the port toward the cliff they were descending. Close beneath the cliff the road divided. One part seemed to dead end into the cliff and the other swung toward a saddle shaped notch in a cliff north of them. "I don't see anything down there but a road."

"Be patient. You will soon see." She smiled a taunt into her answer and continued down the trail.

The sun reddened and slipped toward the western sea making the thin path carved into the cliff face even more difficult. Ben shivered to think how bad this path would be in the dark.

It was dark when they reached the valley floor and Ben had still not seen Bakar. "Well, where is it?" he asked a little peevishly, following Rema around a curve in the cliff face. then he saw it. Like something from a surrealists paint brush, a wall and a ghostly group of buildings seemed to be birthing from the cliff a little above them. It shimmered with the light of oil lamps, flickering torches, and watch fires. The wavering eerie light of it sent a chill up Ben's back. Rema watched and was gratified to see his reaction.

"Beautiful isn't it?" she asked.

Ben nodded. "And spooky looking."

"It looks a fit place for ghosts," Othway agreed, his voice mixed of jest and fear.

"No ghosts," Rema assured them, "and no Servants of the Dark."

"Yet," Ben said.

Rema glanced at Ben. The worry she found there caught at her throat. She swallowed and said, "Come. Leear will be waiting for us."

"Who is Leear?" Ben asked.

"Keeper of the Flame," she said and started off, not giving Ben a chance to ask more questions.

Inside the walls of Bakar there was a palpable sense of excitement and anticipation. As the travelers made their way through the jammed, lamp-lit streets they could feel the electricity of it, but there was no tingle of fear. Everyone seemed to be moving toward the wall of the city which closed off the front of the cliff hollow and protected the city. Most carried something as they went; jars of oil and water, baskets of fruit and bread, and, more worrisome to Ben, clutches of spears and bags of arrows.

Rema had seen this before--too many times. "They prepare for a siege," she said.

Ben raked his lower lip with his teeth and thought about being caught between two armies. The thought did nothing for his disposition. "Maybe we shouldn't wait around to find out," he said.

"Well spoken, my Lord," Othway agreed

"Perhaps," Rema said and kept walking. Ben followed her, but his mind kept turning up mental pictures of them as three moldering corpses.

Lord Aris' shrine was not as impressive as Tarsa's Temple. In fact it was almost a disappointment in its simplicity. It was a large white domed roof supported on twenty-four slender columns made of white marble covering an area about half the size of a football field. The floor was raised twenty steps above the surrounding streets. It was not enclosed but gave the impression of being walled about with light--more light than the lamps and the altar flame could account for.

The three of them started up the steps but had not gained many when a short, round, bald-headed fellow wearing a bright yellow robe came from the shrine. His eyes fell on the little group and a smile lit his face. “Rema!” he cried and threw his arms wide as he hurried down to them.

“Leear,” Rema said going to the offered embrace. “I am glad to see you.”

“No more than I to see you. It looks as though the skills of a healer will be useful soon.”

Rema turned to the others. “Leear, this is Ben Fordham, the Voyager, and this is Othway.”

“Leear frowned. “I was told to expect you Rema and you Voyager, but who is this one?”

Othway shrank back a little, as though to shield himself behind Ben.

“It is a long and complicated story, Leear,” Rema said. “And we will be happy to tell it over wine and food. We have been traveling hard for days with Lady Tarsa’s minions at our heels.”

“Of course! Of course! How foolish of me. All three of you are welcome in Lord Aris’ Light. Come along.” He continued down the steps and the travelers followed him. He crossed the small plaza and went through the door of a building painted the same yellow as the robe he wore.

The room was low ceilinged and Ben had to stoop

not to bump his head against the roof beams. Light from several oil lamps placed in wall niches gave the room a warm friendly glow. "Please," Leear said, "rest yourselves. I will have food and wine brought. I must return to the Shrine. The people must see the Flame is attended." He bowed and left them still standing.

The room had several large divan-type cushions, four of which were placed beside a low oriental table. Rema went to the table and sat. Ben followed Rema's lead, but Othway went to a bare stretch of floor beside the door and sat. He looked uncomfortable and not because he was sitting on the cold stone floor.

"Come and sit with us, Othway," Rema said.

The little highwayman shook his head. "I am not welcome here. The Keeper said they did not expect me. I am unworthy to be here."

Rema frowned and said, "They just didn't know, Othway. It doesn't mean you are unworthy. Didn't you hear Leear say you were welcome?"

"He did not mean me--"he was cut short when a slender, graceful young girl dressed in a robe the same color as Leear's came in. She carried a basket of fruit which she placed on the table before them.

"This is Meya," Rema said. "She is Leear's youngest daughter." The girl smiled shyly and bent her head. Her face was almost heart-shaped with huge dark eyes, full red lips, and glowing skin. She promised to be a great beauty in the near future. "Meya will be a healer like her mother."

"I study with my mother now and help her, but soon I will go to the Valley."

"What valley?" Ben asked, but the answer was cut off by the voice of a woman from outside. Meya turned and went out. Ben looked after her. "What a beautiful child," he said.

"Her mother is beautiful too and skilled," Rema said.

Meya came back laden with a platter of meats and two long crusty loaves of bread. Her mother followed carrying a bowl of raw vegetables and a pitcher of wine. Rema had not exaggerated her beauty.

"This is Ginya," Rema said.

"You are welcome in this house, Voyager," Ginya said, smiling. Ben could feel the warmth of it in his heart. "Where is the other?" she asked then turned to look at Othway. "Please, come and eat. Those who travel with Rema and the Voyager are welcome too." She gave Othway another of those ice melting smiles and he could not refuse such an invitation.

When they were settled around the table Ginya said, "I am sorry to simply throw food on the table and run, but I am very busy with preparations."

"Preparations," Ben asked, afraid of what the preparations were for.

"For tomorrow," she answered. "It is good you are here Rema. Soon we will need all the healers that can be found."

The knot which had been in Ben's stomach since he had first seen the dust-stained sky behind them tightened. "Why, Ginya?" he asked.

"Tomorrow Lady Tarsa's armies will arrive."

Ben looked from Ginya's face to Rema's. "Then we should go now," he said.

The smile disappeared from Ginya's face. "We need Rema and all the other Servants of Light. The Balance is in question. Tomorrow many will fight and many will be wounded. A skilled healer is more use than ten swordsmen."

"Oh, God," Ben groaned.

Rema was torn. She had spent her life practicing the healers' arts and she knew what the fighting would be like. She had always hated it, but since Ben Fordham had commanded Othway and his partner and Rothean to peace, she felt an even deeper loathing for battle than her healer's loathing for it had ever been--yet there would be great need for her skill tomorrow. "Perhaps he is right," she said. The words came out with more accusation than she had intended; as though she were accusing Ben of cowardice.

Ginya turned to Rema, disbelief on her face. "But Rema…"she began.

Leear stepped through the door; the look of him mixed of dread and elation. All eyes turned to him. "It has begun," he said. "Ships have begun trying to unload troops at the port and an army has moved to seal off the pass."

"How do you know?" Ben demanded.

Leear frowned. "Lord Aris and word from the lookouts."

"Then there is no way out?"

"Why would you wish to leave now?" Leear asked in confusion.

"Oh, God." Ben breathed.

~ * ~

From the walls Ben, Rema, and Othway watched the battle for the port by the flickering light of ships set ablaze by catapults on the shore which threw flaming barrels of oil. The catapult shots were not accurate enough to actually hit a moving target except by purest chance, but they did not need pinpoint accuracy. When the flaming barrels hit the water, they burst and threw flaming oil over the water like napalm. The spattering, flaming oil ignited everything it touched--transport ships, landing boats, and the soldiers in them. The rolling flames lit everything bright as day.

The three travelers could not watch for long. The thought of the lives being spent made them sick and when the night wind from the sea brought the screams of burning soldiers and the smell of cooking meat, all three began gagging and vomiting. They had to be helped down from the walls and back to Leear's house.

"What are we going to do?" Ben asked hopelessly. The three had stopped vomiting, but not because the battle had stopped. They were all so empty there was nothing left to bring up. Dry heaves still racked them periodically, but they were trying hard to ignore them.

"There is nothing to be done except what I am trained for," Rema said, her jaws clenched against her own nausea. "I am going to prepare myself to help those who need help."

"I too can help, mistress," Othway said and was instantly taken with another bout of gagging.

Ben looked from one of them to the other. Both were gray and sweat drenched, but there was determination in their eyes and it would not be denied. His stomach suddenly rolled and clenched, but nothing came up.

"I am sorry, my Lord," Rema said, watching Ben's distress. "If I had known, we would not have come here, but…"

Ben shook his head. "I know. I know. And you are right. Since we don't have any choice we must try to help however we can."

She smiled feebly, gratified that Ben would agree. "We probably will not be needed until morning. I doubt any wounded will come back before then. Come. Ginya will have a hospital set up somewhere. We will go there."

Despite the shore batteries of catapults, Lady Tarsa's troops managed to affect a landing in the port. They did it with sheer determination and a willingness to throw wave after wave of hapless soldiers into the flames. The cost in blood and ships was appalling.

Bakar's army fought valiantly for the port, but when Tarsa's army had established a firm beachhead and would not be moved, they began to fall back toward the city, torching everything between themselves and their enemies, including not only the port, but also all the farmsteads and fields between city and port. They left nothing behind the advancing army could use.

Meanwhile another contingent of Bakar's force fought a holding action against Tarsa's cavalry which tried to break through the inland pass. The defenders were outnumbered three to one, but they never intended to hold by main strength. When it became apparent they could not hold any longer, they retreated and released the controlled avalanches that had been set up against just such a day. The rockslides careened down from each side of the pass crushing a hundred of Tarsa's cavalrymen and their horses and plugging the pass tight with a wall of dirt and rock three hundred feet high.

The infantry force which had come up the trail behind the travelers, swallowed the tiny lookout post on the cliff above Bakar's valley in one small gulp, but it did them no good. They tried to advance down the narrow path carved into the cliff face, but archers picked them off as though they were shooting targets until the bodies stacked at the bottom were a wall of bleeding flesh as tall as a man on horseback. On the third day, as the troops from the sea consolidated their beachhead, rested, and treated their wounded, the infantry above the city tried dropping men down ropes, but Bakar's wall was built under the overhanging lip of the hollow in the cliff. The ropes hung more than ten feet in front of the wall so the young boys of the city stood on the wall and knocked the soldiers off the ropes with rocks thrown from their slings. The soldiers fell like apples knocked from the high branches of a tree.

And so the siege of Bakar was set. Lady Tarsa's infantry held the cliff above the city but could not get down. Her cavalry held the inland exit from the valley but was stopped from entering the valley by thousands of cubic yards of dirt and rocks. The sea born troops held the port but were too weakened by the cost of the landing to storm the city.

Bakar stood firm, yet it was cut off from the rest of the world and everyone knew Lady Tarsa's army would not simply sit. Even now the infantry was moving back to another trail which gave access to the inland highway near the pass. Cavalrymen were already at work cutting their own pass over and through the avalanche. When the infantry joined them, a path would soon be opened, but more worrisome was what was happening in the ashes of the port. The remaining transport ships which had brought in the troops departed only to return a few days later and off load timber and rope from which the army holding the port began building siege engines: catapults, bridging towers, battering rams, and ladders.

Bakar attempted two sallies against the port but was driven back because the forces sent were not strong enough. A third sally was planned, but Leear and other city elders resisted, pleading that Lord Aris was mounting an army to relieve the city. "Why should we sacrifice more men in useless combat? If we wait, Lord Aris will save us."

The defense force argued against this, but at last the city elders won. No more sallies were made; only some scouting parties went out to keep tabs on the progress of the siege engines.

It was a stalemate, but it was not a stalemate which would last. When cavalry, infantry, and landing force joined and were supplemented by fresh troops brought in by ship, the siege engines would begin pounding the walls of Bakar. Stalemate would end and the bloodletting would begin again.

Ben, Rema, and Othway were in frustrated agony as the days of the siege passed. The nausea did not stop when the actual fighting stopped, though the gagging and retching eased. All three became thin to the point of emaciation. They could hardly keep food down so their bodies consumed themselves to compensate for the nourishment they were not getting.

What seemed to ease the sickness most was assisting the wounded. The man beneath your hands might scream and curse you as you cauterized the stump of his arm with a red hot iron, but provided he did not go too deeply into shock, with the bleeding stopped he would probably live and that helped the three to forget their own pain. But assisting the wounded only helped them when there were wounded. After the first few days of the siege, there were almost no wounded. Everything had just stopped where it was and the loss of that relief became a large part of the agony. Ben found that bitterly funny. "The fighting shreds my insides, but I find myself wishing for more so there will be more wounded to tend to take my mind off it."

The three sat in a large whitewashed room of a house which had been turned into a hospital. It was near the city gate for the sake of easy access and, at present, it was empty.

Rema nodded her agreement. "I am ashamed to say I was thinking the same thing."

"Can you not do something about this, my Lord?" Othway begged.

Ben glared at the little highwayman but softened at the pleading he saw in Othway's eyes. He understood what Othway was talking about. If he could command peace between the two robbers and Rothean as they were about to kill one another, why could he not do the same thing right now? He felt an almost overwhelming urge to run up to the walls of the city and begin screaming, "Stop, Stop, Stop!" but he fought the urge because he knew it would do no good. Besides, no matter what Othway and Rema thought, Ben was not sure he had actually commanded peace--and, even if he had, it had been on a much smaller scale. Here the scale was so large the combatants would not even be able to hear him.

"Surely you could do something…" Rema began then cut herself off. She knew there was nothing to be gained by it.

"My Lord," Othway began then stopped. He drew a deep shaky breath and began speaking with such intensity the words were like blows to Ben. "In my life I have killed many people. They meant nothing to me. They were only things to be killed and stripped so I might live. I have seen friends killed in battle. They meant little more than those I robbed. A few days of sadness at their loss. Nothing more…but now each death, whether friend or enemy, is like a sword through my middle. On the road to Rayhan you told me to put up my sword, and I have well and truly done so. But not only that, I have put away the heart which helped me to draw sword. I am changed!"

"And I am sorry!" Ben shouted at him. "I am sorry. I didn't mean too. I didn't set out to change you. Hell, I didn't even know there was such a person as you or such a place as this a few weeks ago! A few weeks ago I was sitting in a bar in LA trying to figure out where my next drink was coming from!" He rubbed his fingers across his forehead trying to ease the pain of what Othway was saying.

"No, my Lord! No!" Rema said, coming to put her arms around Ben. "Do not be sorry! It is better. Now is better."

"Yes," Othway agreed, reaching out toward Ben, but not bold enough to touch him. "Now is better. To have put up my sword is better!"

"Better?" Ben said bitterly, looking from one to the other. "How can it be better? We are going to end up corpses in this stinking city, and you can't even defend yourselves anymore because of me. How can it be better?" He stood suddenly and stalked out. Othway started to follow him, but Rema grabbed his wrist. "Let him go," she said.

Othway looked after Ben, seeming to want to ease the pain he had caused, wanting to protect him somehow, but the little highwayman probably knew there was nothing he could do.

The morning was already hot when Ben left the hospital and soon the heat baked away his bitterness, replacing it with thirst. He had been wandering with no particular destination, but when he looked around he found himself near the Shrine of Lord Aris, standing almost in front of the door to Leear's house and the Keeper of the Flame had just stepped out.

"Good Morning, Voyager," the bald priest said with a smile.

"Not *that* good I'm afraid, Leear."

"Still sick, eh?"

Ben did not want to hash over the whole thing again so he just nodded.

"Thirsty too, I'll warrant."

"As a matter of fact, yes I am."

"I thought so. Come," Leear motioned toward the door.

Inside Leear poured half a cup of wine from an earthenware pitcher then cut it with water. "For your tender stomach's sake," he said.

Ben accepted the cup gratefully and drank it down. It tasted wonderful, and because he had hardly eaten anything in days, he could feel the soft thrumming of the wine in his veins almost before the wine had reached his stomach. "Could I have some more please?" he asked. "A little less water this time."

Leear smiled and poured a cupful from the wine pitcher. "I was just on my way out to make my daily round of the wall, Voyager. Would you like to come along? After you finish your wine of course."

This was not the first time Leear had asked Ben if he wanted to tour the wall. Ben had always turned him down before, but now he decided to go along. Just being with the smiling priest in his bright yellow robes seemed to pick up his spirits. *Then again it could be the wine,* he thought, but shoved the thought away.

"All right Leear," he said. "If the wine doesn't sit well, I can always go back to the hospital, I suppose."

"Quite so," Leear said, patting Ben's shoulder sympathetically. "Quite so."

The soldiers greeted the Priest's round of the wall with joy. Men who were weary, or afraid, or bored would see the flash of his yellow robe, his broad smile and his sweat shiny baldhead and they would feel better. He brought encouragement and hope. He reminded the men they were servants of the Light, and they were helping to preserve the Balance--to preserve the world. Over and over he repeated the litany, "We live by the Balance. Lord Aris must triumph, for Lady Tarsa would bring ending," and the men would buck up and feel more determined to triumph.

A guard captain who had been looking out toward the port turned, smiling when Leear approached, but his smile became brittle when his eyes fell on Ben.

"How goes the watch, Captain," Leear asked, pounding the man on the shoulder like a comrade at arms.

"About as usual, Leear. We stand here and watch them, and they stand there and watch us."

"No movement at all?"

The captain shook his head. "Not yet, but I fear the stillness will not last. Scouts say the work of clearing a way through the pass is almost finished. A few more days at best. With those reinforcements they will bring their siege engines up and begin trying to batter down our wall."

"Can we hold against them?" Leear asked.

The captain shrugged then grinned like a skull. "The walls are strong and they…" he spit in the direction of the port "…may not find it so easy to bring up their catapults and towers as they think," he said, relishing the thought of battle to come.

A gust of wind brought the mixed stench of burning and rot up from the port. The smell made Ben's stomach roll and his face go gray. "I must go down, Leear" he said, barely holding his nausea in check.

The captain smirked, disdain radiating from him.

Leear touched Ben's arm sympathetically and said, "Go back to the Shrine, Voyager. Lord Aris comes soon to tell us of the progress of the relief army."

Ben nodded and turned away.

The captain looked after him for a moment. "Better

we should throw him down to Lady Tarsa," he said. "His long face and weak stomach steals the heart from my men."

Leear looked from the captain to Ben's retreating back but said nothing.

Lord Aris came at midday. His brightness made the noon sun seem like a weak candle. The plaza around the Shrine was jammed with people, all wanting to draw power and courage from their god and to hear the news of the army which was coming to their relief.

Ben, Rema, and Othway had not planned to meet, but they found themselves standing together near the top of the steps to the Shrine in a little knot.

Leear talked briefly with the God of Light first then came and directed the travelers to Lord Aris who darkened their eyes and looked over them for a long time before he spoke. "The power in you has grown, Voyager," he said at last. "And now there is power in these as well. What has happened?"

Ben did not understand but Rema did. "We were changed on the road to Rayhan, my Lord. Ben Fordham spoke to us and we were changed."

"Changed how?"

Othway, astounded at his own boldness, said, "He told us to put up our swords and we did. Not just for a time but forever."

The god's head turned as he examined each of them. Then he nodded and said, "So this is what has affected the Balance in such an odd way."

A stone of dread materialized in Ben's chest. "What do you mean?" he asked.

"The Balance has been fairly stable for a long while," the god explained. "Tarsa was contained and seemed content to amuse herself with such creatures as you, Voyager. But some weeks ago she suddenly woke from her quiet. She began to assault my strong holds with a determination not seen for a long time, and the Balance began to tip far toward the dark."

"You mean what happened on the road to Rayhan started all this?" Ben groaned.

"It would seem so, Voyager," Lord Aris answered.

The words turned Ben's legs to water and he sat down on the floor at the God of Light's feet.

"How?" Rema demanded. "My Lord Ben Fordham's command…"

Lord Aris' attention snapped to Rema at hearing her call the Voyager *my Lord,* but he did not interrupt her.

"…to put up swords saved at least two lives and maybe more," she continued. "To save life is to serve the Light, is it not?"

Aris looked thoughtfully at her for a long time before saying, "yes it is. Yet it seems to have had exactly the opposite effect, probably because Tarsa felt the Balance tip toward the light and reacted. Like poking a sleeping lion with a sharp stick. The question is what can be done about it?"

"Lord Aris," Othway began, "would the Balance not be restored if this siege was lifted?"

"Probably, but Tarsa will not listen to any such talk. You know how she is. She will not be happy until this battle is fought. She will not be happy until the end of the world."

"If my Lord Ben Fordham commanded peace…,"

Othway began.

Ben had slumped at the feet of the God of Light, but hearing this he looked up and said, “No! No, no, no! This is already enough of a mess with what I have already done, assuming I really did anything. Rema and Othway say I somehow commanded peace, but I am not so sure. And anyway, even if I did, it was a small area where they could all hear. With a battle going on it would be hard for even one or two to hear me, much less a whole army.”

“That can be handled,” Lord Aris said, considering what had been said. “The question is, do you truly have such power?”

“He does, Lord Aris,” Rema said definitely.

“You are not convinced, eh Voyager?”

“No, I am not”

“Nor am I,” the god added. “We must test it.”

“How?” Ben asked.

Aris thought a moment then said, “Leave it to me. I will set up a test. Now, be gone. Send Leear to me.”

## Chapter Nine

Early next morning Leear came to the hospital and called for the three. “Lord Aris waits with your test,” he said.

Ben had a feeling he was not going to like what was about to happen, but when he questioned Leear, the priest would tell him nothing.

Waiting at the Shrine were Lord Aris, the guard captain from the wall, several armed guards, and two bound prisoners. The prisoners looked to be in good condition. They had no visible wounds, but they were forced to kneel and kept their heads bowed.

“I felt in my bones you were in this,” the captain growled as Ben passed. “Beware how you stroll the walls hence forward. You may make a misstep.”

“Enough,” the God of Light commanded.

“What is going on here?” Ben asked with a steadily growing dread.

“Last night I sent the captain and some of his men out to bring in some prisoners,” Aris said. “These,” he inclined his head toward the kneeling men. “This is the test of the power Rema says you have.”

“Now wait a minute...” Ben protested but was

ignored.

"Captain, loose the prisoners and bring them here," the god commanded.

The captain shot a look of pure hatred at Ben but bobbed his head to acknowledge the order then stepped to carry it out.

When the prisoners stood before him, Aris said to them, "If you fight well and kill your opponent you will be returned to your troop unharmed and richer by the weight of one talent of gold."

The men glanced at one another then back at Lord Aris, unsure whether they should believe him, but the god did not expand on what he had said. "Arm them, captain," he commanded.

"What!" Ben, Rema, and Othway shouted with one voice.

Aris leaned back in his chair. "The only way to make a true test of this power to stop a battle is to create a battle for you to stop," he said. "Therefore we have the makings of a battle," he gestured toward the two prisoners who now held swords.

This was the true heart of the god Ben had sensed beneath the patient, caring being too whom he had told his plight the day after his rescue from the Valley of Voices, but he could feel no sense of satisfaction at having discovered the truth. "If there is no power," he said, "someone will die."

The God of Light shrugged. "Many die. These might have fallen yesterday, and if they fight well here and are returned to their comrades, they might fall tomorrow. We need a test, therefore..." he let the words hang.

After a moment he continued. “Captain, pick the two best swordsmen from among these.”

The captain did as he was told.

The captives, their swords hanging loose in their hands, watched and wondered if they could trust the God of Light, but when the picked men lifted their swords it was clear there was no choice but to fight.

“Very well,” Aris said. “Begin.”

The double-edged bronze swords clinked together as the opponents came to the ready.

“No,” Ben protested, his voice a croak of disbelief.

The fight began in earnest. Swords clanged and the combatants grunted with the effort. One of the captain’s men turned the sword of his opponent with a back step followed by a lunge and slash, finishing with his sword point low in perfect position to spill his foe’s guts with an upward slice. Othway seemed to fly toward the battling men. He threw himself over the arms of the man, stopping the upward slash, and as he stopped the blow he shouted, “STOP!”

The columns of the Shrine trembled with the thunder of the command. Othway was no longer the cringing highwayman, but a being of power and fearful command, a channel through which peace flowed to crash over the four swordsmen. “Bring no more death to your brothers!” Othway commanded, now ablaze with a crackling aura of power which reached to engulf the fighters.

The battling men stopped as though they had been pounded with mighty blows. They stared at one another for a moment then, as one man, fell to their knees weeping. Their swords clanged to the floor as they brought their hands up to cover their grief-stricken faces.

Everyone in the Shrine including Lord Aris stared first at the figure of the ragged little robber then at the weeping men who only a moment before had been battling to the death.

The guard captain looked upon them and shook his head in disbelief. “No,” he said. “I will not have it!” His sword hissed from its scabbard and, quicker than thought, slashed down on the nearest kneeling man. Blood and brain matter gushed from the cloven skull onto the marble floor.

Rema leapt at the captain. She said nothing, gave no command, made no sound save the rush of air when she moved. She seized the wrist of his sword arm and with strength far greater than her slender frame should have possessed, she spun the man to face her.

The captain was off balance and almost fell. His face was twisted with horror at what he had done and when he looked into Rema’s eyes his lips worked up and down but no sound came out. He looked down at his blood-spattered arm and the gore drenched sword blade and groaned, “No....” Then, “NO!” It was a scream which trailed off into a wail. His thick muscled shoulders began to shudder with sobs and he threw his sword to the floor with such force it chipped the marble then brought his arms up across his face an collapsed into writhing agony on the floor.

The other troopers who had been guards had drawn their swords, but they had not moved. Now they looked at one another and at the tableau before them and did not know what to do.

“Put up your swords,” Ben said. It was no command

full of thunder and fire, only a quiet request full of loathing. "Too many have died already," he said. "Put them away."

Othway and the three former combatants who remained alive continued to glow with blue fire which was not at all dimmed by Aris' sun like presence. The same glow was around Rema and the captain who continued to writhe at her feet.

The troopers sheathed their swords, dropped to their knees, and bowed to the floor before Ben. "Don't bow to me," he said, a despairing edge to his voice. "I'm no god." He put all the contempt he could into the *god.* "Stand up. Stand up and be at peace."

"Yes, my Lord," they all answered.

Ben turned to the God of Light, hating him--hating his arrogance and cruelty at spending lives as though they had no meaning. "You have your test," he said.

"Yes, Voyager. I have my test," he said and was gone.

News of the test spread and everyone was sure the siege would soon be lifted but then nothing happened. Days passed. Bakar held its breath, but Lord Aris did not return. Those standing watches on the wall reported that preparations among Tarsa's troops did not stop or even slow. They continued building and training with the siege engines and the work clearing the pass continued day and night. It was as though there had been no test. Ben might have believed it was an illusion except for the crashing weariness which speaking the peace had brought to Rema and Othway, and the continuing misery brought on by the siege which now effected the soldiers who had been involved in the test.

Two weeks after the test Tarsa's infantry and cavalry

cleared a path through the pass. Bakar's walls and the roof tops near the walls were jammed with people who watched as the army integrated itself with the landing force to form a battle hungry hoard the like of which none of them had ever seen before.

Leear had his hands full keeping the populous calm. Panic was just below the surface and each day Lord Aris failed to return brought it closer to the top. "Lord Aris has not deserted us," the priest said over and over, smiling and exuding faith and trust in the God of Light. "It is only that he is busy with the relief force coming to save us. He will return as surely as the sun returns after a rainstorm."

Ben was not so sure. On earth his parents had tried to teach him faith in God, but it had always seemed an iffy proposition at best. Now, on this world where he had actually met two gods, he was convinced that gods were no more worthy of trust than most humans. It was just possible Aris was going to allow the siege to continue, perhaps even let Bakar fall for reasons known only to him.

Tarsa's hoard began moving up from the port the morning after the pass was cleared. It was a slow process. The catapults and siege towers were unwieldy, but strength of numbers and cavalry horses hooked up as draft animals drew them half way across the valley before dark. Watch fires, numerous as stars on a summer night, let the city know the hoard had stopped for the night.

The situation seemed hopeless. Bakar seemed doomed to fall until brilliant light spread over the city like sunrise. Shouts of joy and relief went up. Lord Aris had returned to save them!

Ben was still not convinced and when Leear brought word the God of Light wished to see him and the others, he laughed cynically. "Why? More tests?"

"I do not know, Voyager, but please, all of you go at once. Time is short." Leear did not wait for any more questions. He turned and left, his usually comic figure radiating worry.

Aris sat before the flaming altar, his eye-scalding brightness swallowing the light of the fire as if it were nothing. "Are you prepared to stop this siege now?" he asked.

"How?" Ben asked in his turn. "Are we just going to go out there and tell a few thousand armed men, *Now make nice! Let's all play together like good little boys.*"

Aris laughed. "I only wish it were so easy. No, it will have to happen the same way as when these were empowered," he said, flicking his shining hand at the soldiers from the test. "We will precipitate a battle."

A chorus of protests rose from Ben and the others. "It will be a slaughter," Ben said through clenched teeth.

Aris shrugged. "I hardly think it will be a slaughter. You and these will see to that. Some will die and some will be wounded, but it is a sad fact of your power."

"My power! I'm not the one cooking up a battle!"

The God of Light shook his head. "You do not understand. I would rather none of this had happened. I would rather not be locked into a battle to tip the Balance back, but there is no avoiding it. Your power worked only in the presence of battle; otherwise you would have command the soldiers to throw down their swords before ever a blow was struck, but you did not. You could not. Even in the second before the first blow was struck you could not. You, Voyager, looked at me and said '*No*' but it had no power in it. It was only a word of protest. Not until the battle was well and truly joined did the bandit command peace. Therefore, though I despise the shedding of blood, we will precipitate a battle and you all will stop it."

"But..." Ben began, but Lord Aris waved him to silence. "It is better a few die so that many may be saved."

Ben stood with his mouth open, trying to think of some way to stop this, but there was none. At last he said, "Very Machiavellian of you," with acid sarcasm in the words. "Or maybe I should say *very godlike.* How can you be so willing to spend lives? Aren't you supposed to be the God of Light? Don't you have any concept of what it is to die? Is it because you are eternal?"

"I am eternal only so long as the world continues," Aris said, not defensive, only matter of fact. "I know what it is to end. I hold my life at the whim of the Over-God, and I am trying to preserve my life and this world. I have no desire to see those who serve me die, but I see no other way."

"How about we just surrender?" Ben asked.

"That would truly be a slaughter. Tarsa would have every man, woman, and child in Bakar butchered which would tip the Balance so far toward the dark it could not be brought back. It would be the end. The judging would come and all would be lost. Tarsa would have the Chaos which is her deepest wish, and the Over-God would sweep away this world. So, it is much preferable for a few lives to be spent here and now in order that all lives may not be lost in the future."

There was no arguing with the logic. Though the thought of the bloodletting made Ben and the others ill, they knew they had to carry out Lord Aris' plan. Ben drew in a deep shaky breath and let it out. "All right," he said. Bring on your battle. Let's get it over with.

~ * ~

Bakar's defense force spent the rest of the night preparing to march out to battle. Lord Aris did not remain in the city. Shortly after his conference with Ben and the others, his light, which had eased the fears of the city, disappeared. As always the disappearance of his light left a gray gloom in its wake, and the gloom let the mood of dread return to the people despite all Leear could do.

Dawn brought the city from dread to despair. Through the morning fog a hundred ghostly ships could be seen, many already off loading troops. The muted clank of armor and the eerie scrap of booted feet drifted up the valley to chill the hearts of Bakar's defenders. A murmur of "We are lost," went through the city.

Lookouts who had been straining eyes toward the port turned toward the camp of the besiegers. Something seemed odd there. Usually the first thing to be seen was smoke from fires rekindled to heat tea and breakfast gruel, but there were no fires this morning, yet there seemed to be a great deal of scurrying about. Something seemed wrong, but the lookouts could not see well enough to understand what it was.

In half an hour the sun peeked over the mountains

and burned off some of the fog making it easier to see the ships in the harbor. The lookouts began shouting with joy. "The ships are flying sunburst pennants! It is the relief force Lord Aris promised!"

A roaring wave of jubilation rolled down from the walls like an incoming tide. All Bakar began shouting and cheering and some citizens even broke out wine jars to celebrate victory. Leear and the defense force commanders had a hard time regaining control enough to tell the revelers the battle was not even joined yet much less won.

The defense force marched out as soon as the officers damped down the soaring spirits with a little reality. They formed into a wide wing sweep, extending two arms across a front which would move forward to push the encamped army back into the force, which was now advancing from the harbor. The maneuvers were guided by drumbeats and bugles to tell each flank when to hurry or when to ease its pace.

Tarsa's army was caught between the two advancing forces, but it was an army made up of battle hardened veterans who would not panic in the face of a difficult situation. The infantry formed a defensive line against the force coming from the city while the cavalry formed up in attack wave lines and trotted toward the port to harry the troops already on the shore and slow the debarkation of the rest.

The infantry engagement was long in coming, and when it finally did come, Tarsa's troops were puzzled by the manner of the engagement. Sections of Bakar's line would charge forward, their flanks protected by their fellows, strike a few blows then retreat as though trying to draw Tarsa's troops piecemeal into some trap, but there could be no trap on a plain where no other armies could be hidden to suddenly spring forth.

The cavalry was as perplexed as the infantry. They charged any place troops seemed to be massing, but the enemy lines faded and broke before each charge. The troops would drop beneath their large heavy shields and let the horses run directly over them, and when the charge had passed they would rise and strike the horsemen from behind with light javelins. It was like trying to fight smoke! And as the already landed soldiers kept the cavalry busy, ship after ship off loaded its cargo of fighting men.

Lord Aris came directly to the hospital, appearing like something out of a fairy tale from Ben's world. "Prepare yourselves," the God of Light said.

"We are as prepared as we are going to be," Ben said. "When do we go?"

"When the armies are fully engaged."

"How will we know, my Lord," Rema asked.

"I will know," Aris answered.

Ben thought, *I will know too,* for already he could feel a sort of rage building atop his sickness. That rage increased and increased and increased with each escalation in the number of soldiers engaged in battle.

The clash and retreat went on for hours. Tarsa's generals saw what was happening, but they were powerless to stop it. If they pulled their infantry back toward the port to help the cavalry, the Bakar infantry advanced, closing the battle into an even tighter circle. If the cavalry withdrew from the port to help the infantry, the speed of unloading from the ships tripled and the situation got worse. No matter what they did they were forced to fight a defensive fight with the troop strength against them increasing moment by moment and their own strength decreasing with each fallen man.

The afternoon wore on toward evening and the last of the ship-born troops landed and formed to finish enclosing Tarsa's stranded army.

The same rage Ben felt showed in the faces of all the humans waiting in the hospital for Lord Aris' command. Even when the wounded men began to trickle in, it was not assuaged. Rema tended the wounded and the others helped her, but their rage against the battle grew. It could not be distracted now.

Toward sundown something occurred to Ben which made a shiver of fear run down his back. "Will Tarsa come when it gets dark?" He asked the God of Light.

"Yes."

"Is this going to be like the siege of Troy with gods walking around the battlefield assisting their troops and maybe fighting side by side with them?"

"I do not know this Troy, or these gods of which you speak, but we gods do not war one with another. We can help in some things, but not in the actual fighting. For that we can only watch and weep for the battle lost." Aris fell silent and turned his face toward the sky. "They are joined," he said. "To the wall all of you! Go up and wait at the center. We will stop this now."

Without word or thought the seven ran from the hospital toward the wall.

Lord Aris was waiting when they arrived. "I must

darken your eyes more," he said and without waiting permission touched the temples of each of them. Blackness like the very bowels of the earth engulfed them. It was a crashing blindness which came near to panicking Ben.

"I can't see anything!" He wailed and others added their voices to his.

"You will see by my light when I remove my veil," the god said. "The night will become like day."

"All right, all right then! Let's get on with this!" Ben shouted, his rage squeezing his fear into a tight little ball inside his mind.

"Prepare to feel the wall slip away from beneath your feet," Aris said, as he dropped his veil.

It was as the God of Light had promised. Night suddenly became day and the light illuminated the valley as though it were desert noon. The humans all felt the first stomach turning second of drifting free in the air and all fought it like fish on lines, but the clash of arms soon stilled the panic and concentrated the anti-battle rage in all of them.

Much blood had already been spilled during the day, but now with the appearance of Lord Aris, the fighting intensified. The dead lay in heaps and those so wounded they could no longer fight writhed and screamed in agony. Dead and wounded were ignored by those engaged in battle. Swords, maces, shields, hands, feet, and minds all were turned to one purpose: kill the man before you then be on to killing the man who took his place.

The stench of blood and spilled bowels rose in a miasma so thick it was almost visible. It turned the stomachs of the seven who were now spread equidistantly along the battlefront, forcing all of them to gag and causing their rage to build. At first they saw only the sweep of the battle, over-awed by the huge despair of it, but soon the whole resolved into individuals slashing, sweating. and bleeding.

--Here a skull crushed by a mace, spattering red and gray ooze over the arm of the mace wielder.

--There a soldier drove his blade into the midsection of his enemy who collapsed in screaming agony as his intestines spilled onto the ground.

--A soldier lost his footing in the slimy mud created by the blood of a dead man. The slip was his death. A sword bit through the side of his neck nearly severing his head.

--And over it all was the deafening clash of weapons and the screams of men caught up in battle frenzy.

Shrieking, gibbering horror rose up in Ben and the others who had been commanded to peace. It clawed at their minds and twisted their stomachs. Their hearts pounded inside their chests and the rage grew until they could not hold back the words "Stop! STOP! STOP! NO MORE!"

Thousands of eyes snapped away from enemies at the thunderous command and up to those floating above the battle. The very air shattered with the command and the ground shuddered with the crash of it. The blue glow of the Speakers combined with Aris' nova brightness and froze the warriors with upturned faces and still raised weapons.

"Peace be with you all, forever," the Speakers commanded in voices amplified by the power of the God of Light. "Throw down your weapons!"

In the blink of an eye the battle was finished. All over Bakar's valley men who had been intent on slaughter threw down their weapons and fell to their knees. Many wept. Some went into the shivering writhing convulsions the guard captain had fallen into after the test, but all combat ceased.

"Down," Rema cried. "I must get down, Lord Aris. There are wounded who need help."

"I have called others," the god said. "They will be here soon."

The other Peace Speakers also demanded to be let down. The cries of the wounded no longer covered by the cacophony of battle rose to a piteous crescendo.

Ben touched earth beside a man whose hands were pressed tight over a sword cut in his side just below his rib cage. Bloody bubbles rose and burst between the man's fingers with each breath. *He is going to die soon. And I can do nothing to help him.* He might have wept for the loss of the one life, but there was no time to waste on tears. There were wounded soldiers all around that he might help. A few steps away a soldier was bent over a wounded man.

"What can I do to help?" Ben asked the soldier's bent back. Something seemed familiar about the man.

"Water," the other said, his voice splintery with emotion. "Bring water."

"From where?"

"Back there," he hooked a thumb toward where the army camp had been. "There are water barrels. Take a helmet to carry it in. There are many loose ones around…" the last words broke off.

Memory suddenly came clear in Ben's mind. This soldier had once given Ben a drink of water from his own helmet. It was Borj.

The wounded man Borj was trying to help drew a gasping breath which gurgled out as he died. Borj hung his head then massaged his temples for a moment before looking up. "I killed that man, my Lord," he said. "I killed him. If only the command had come a moment sooner..."

Ben knelt beside Borj and put his arm around the bear-like shoulders. "I'm sorry Borj. I wish I had, but..." he stopped and drew a breath. "I wish I had. Come help me get some water. Maybe we can keep some of these others alive."

Borj nodded and they stood.

Thunder grumbled. Real natural thunder. A few drops of rain spattered down, blown on a wind, which was not natural. Ben felt the chill and heard the roaring before he saw the cloud of darkness and it made his whole body shake. Primal terror made him want to flee, but the sight of the boiling black cloud paralyzed him. It rolled up the valley from the sea without touching the ground. Aris rose to meet the cloud. His light beat against it but did not penetrate.

The wall of blackness opened and Lady Tarsa, looking just like the statue in the Temple at Nanema, was revealed amid a boiling mist. She was naked, as was Lord Aris. They were beautiful and terrifying beyond anything Ben had ever imagined. The gods faced one another and appeared to converse. There was no gesticulation or other sign of argument.

Minutes passed then Tarsa retreated a little and the cloud once more enfolded her. Suddenly they were gone, both cloud and light, and the darkness crashed down. Storm clouds made the night darker and the flashes of lightning seemed to make the darkness thicker. The rain increased from a drizzle to a torrent, pounding down on the dead and dying of the now finished battle.

# PART TWO

# THE SPEAKER

*"Think not that I am come to send peace upon the earth: I came not to send peace, but a sword."*
Matthew 10:34

*"The peace of God, it is no peace,*
*but strife closed in the sod.*
*Yet, brothers pray for but one thing--*
*The marvelous Peace of God."*
"They Cast their Nets in Galilee"
Hymn
American Episcopal Hymnal of 1928
Music by D. McK. Williams
Verse by W. A. Percy

## Chapter Ten

The weariness of speaking the peace, while overwhelming to the former soldiers, was much less so to Rema and Othway and less yet to Ben. Tolerance or strength appeared to build with each use as a muscle will grow stronger with use. It was a good thing too, for after the lifting of the siege, the three needed all their strength to cope with what came next. There were hundreds of wounded to be healed and hundreds of dead to be buried, and those problems were huge. But they diminished with time and another, more overwhelming problem arose. The assault by adulation.

Mobs formed anywhere the seven who had broken the siege were thought to be. They could not walk in the street without people accosting them with worship. Everywhere they went crowds fell to their knees and bowed their foreheads to the earth. People spoke in whispers about the power of "The Speakers," but for Ben it was worse. He was the first to have spoken the peace; therefore he was singled out for special adulation. Not only did the crowds bow in worshipful adoration, they reached out to touch him. If the crowd was so thick those at the outside edges could not possibly reach him, they would lift their children high so they might see "The Speaker." Mothers practically threw their babies at him! And all begged to be blessed by "The Speaker."

"This must cease," Rema said, red faced and annoyed after pushing her way through the mobs between Leear's house and the hospital. "I told all of them to stop treating me as though I was a god, but they don't listen.

The seven speakers were gathered in the hospital to drink tea and to hide out from the adoring mob. "I too have told them I am only Othway, a former bandit and not one to be worshipped, but still they bow and call me *my Lord Speaker.*

Ben would have laughed except he knew how serious the problem was becoming. "I know what you mean. Remember how many times I told you not to call me my Lord, Othway?"

The little bandit looked sheepish and nodded. "Granted," Ben continued, "the problem has gotten somewhat larger, but it is still the same problem. And it is twice as bad for me."

"What can we do about it?" one of the others asked.

"That is a really fine question," Ben answered. "I wish I had a really fine answer for it."

"And something else, Ben Fordham," Rema said, more serious worry displacing the annoyance in her voice, "Bakar cannot continue to support so many for much longer. Yet no one wants to leave! They all want to be near the speakers, and especially near "*The Speaker.*"

Ben wiped his hand down his face and sighed. "I know, I know. I've thought about just leaving. Sneaking away in the night."

"It would do no good," Rema said. "They will seek until they find where you have gone then they will follow. They are devoted."

"Could you not simply command them to stay while we leave?" One of the new speakers asked.

Ben shrugged. "It didn't work with Othway. Besides, it isn't just us. What about all the new speakers."

The former soldiers looked confused, but Rema understood and groaned. "I had not considered that," she said.

"Neither has anyone else."

The others still looked confused, "What?" They all babbled at once.

"When we spoke the peace to stop the battle, we created a few thousand new speakers," Ben explained.

All fell silent beneath the weight of that bit of news.

"Perhaps that is the answer," the former guard captain said after a time.

All turned uncomprehending eyes to him.

"They are all speakers now," he said. "Can we not tell them to go forth and speak peace to all the world? By making them share in our predicament perhaps we can ease our predicament."

Ben stroked his beard, which was now longer and streaked with silver, as he thought about it. "It is worth a try. Maybe I can get on to this Valley of Seers and maybe home."

Rema brightened. "Better yet, we can tell them all to go home and speak the peace to all they meet!"

Heads bobbed all around the room, but Ben wasn't

so sure. Unforeseen consequences seemed to be the rule here just like they had been back on earth. Still, he didn't have any better idea so he said, "Very well. Tomorrow we send everyone home."

That evening, after supper with Leear's family, Ben explained the plan, but rather than exciting Leear, that one's face grew longer with each word.

"What's wrong, Leear?" Rema asked.

"Nothing. Nothing is wrong."

"I have known you since I was a child, Leear, and you are a very bad liar. Something is bothering you. What is it?"

Leear blushed then knitted his fingers together and held them folded over his mouth as if to hold the words back, but at last he said, "The world is back in Balance because of you, Voyager--or perhaps I should call you Speaker?" There was a bitterness in the words which did not fit with the man Ben had come to know and like. "You have snatched many from the service of the dark."

"That's good, isn't it? Lord Aris said the balance was tipped far toward the dark. Now it is tipped back the other way, right?"

"Yes, but…" Leear stopped and looked from face to face, seeking understanding for what he was about to say.

"But…" Ben prompted.

"These new speakers will tip the balance too."

"Toward Lord Aris," Ben said. "That's a good thing isn't it?"

"Lord Aris is the God of Light and the God of Reason. He wants only to maintain the Balance. Now the Balance is right, but...but what of all these new Speakers?

They too will snatch servants from Lady Tarsa, and it will tip the Balance too far toward the light. If that happens, everything Lord Aris has tried to preserve--everything I have worked to preserve--will end. Lady Tarsa, the Goddess of Endings, The Goddess of Chaos and Darkness will triumph, for the Over-God will wipe out his creation."

Ben understood what the Keeper of Aris' flame was saying, but he also understood there was nothing to be done about it. "You're right," Ben agreed, "but it can't be helped. I wish I could, but I can't undo what is done. These new speakers may affect the Balance if they go, but they will certainly affect it if they stay here much longer. They have to leave or Bakar will be destroyed as sure as if Tarsa's army had over run the place, and it will unbalance the world too, won't it?"

Leear folded his hands against his lips again. His knuckles were white with displeasure at the conclusions, but he couldn't argue with them. "Yes, you are right."

"The best solution is to send them all home, and let me get on toward the Valley of Seer's so I can maybe do the same thing."

There was nothing comic about Leear now. His mouth was a grim line and his gaze darted back and forth, not focusing anywhere. "Yes," he said at last, "the sooner you are gone from this world the better." He stood and stalked out of the room without another word.

~ * ~

A nightmare brought Ben out of sleep; it was a

childhood nightmare come back to haunt him. A feeling of menace, danger, and dread jolted him awake like being grabbed with a clammy hand.

The room was black, with only the slight twinkle of the stars coming through the window. He listened for some sound, but there was nothing. He tried to put the nightmare fright out of his mind, but it wouldn't go. There was still a feeling of menace gripping his stomach. The quiet scuff of a foot sharpened his ears and another sound which might have been a sob of labored breath made him call out, "Rema?"

The assassin sprang, but some warning from the dream caused Ben to roll a little so the leap was not perfect. Still, the killer had the advantage. He was determined, he was on top, and he was not tangled in bedclothes like Ben was.

The knife blade burned as it slid between Ben's ribs just below his heart. He grunted with the pain of it and tried to roll free. The weight shift surprised the killer, and it pulled the haft of the knife out of his grip.

The door burst open and the feeble yellow-white light of an oil lamp spilled into the room. Othway and Rema stood frozen with shock by what they saw. Leear, a look of insane determination on his face, was struggling to get his hand back on the dirk sticking out of Ben's left side. He succeeded in less than the length of a breath. Ben cried out as Leear twisted the dirk, trying to lift the point into Ben's heart.

"STOP!" The command rang out and auras crackled about both Rema and Othway as they commanded the peace. Their lightning reached out for Leear and stuck him down as though he had been clubbed across the back of the head. He collapsed like a bag of wet sand across Ben.

After a moment Ben, with Rema's help, managed to struggle out from beneath the weight of Leear's unconscious body. "I'm all right," he said. "I'm all right," but the look on Rema and Othway's faces told him he wasn't all right. He followed their eyes down to see the handle of the dirk protruding from his ribs and suddenly he felt faint. He looked into Rema's eyes and said, "I'll never see Maggie again, will I?" then crumpled into the healer's arms.

~ * ~

"Leear missed killing you by less than the width of a finger," Rema said.

Ben had come to looking into the healer's golden eyes and feeling her strong but gentle hand holding his. He vaguely remembered her and others talking to him in the past few days, but the memories were distorted. They were wrapped up with dreams of Maggie, his parents, and Aris, and he could hardly distinguish between fever delusion and reality.

Now he sat up in bed and Rema fed him some of the same bitter, meaty, wonderful broth he had eaten the night after Rothean and the others had saved him in the Valley of Voices. Rema fed him because between the pain of the wound, the pad of the bandage covering it, and having his left arm strapped tight against his side, he could hardly move.

"The blade did not touch anything vital. It was a miracle, and surprise at having it sticking out of you kept you from trying to pull it out which might have killed you. You might have nicked a lung or turned the blade enough to nick your heart, not to mention the bleeding. Fainting was the best thing you could have done."

"The best thing I could have done was to not have tried to cadge a drink from that toad-mouthed little bastard, Mardian," Ben's grimaced was only partly feigned bitterness. At least he could not see the tattoo on his left forearm. Having to look at it as he lay wounded in the world it represented would have been more than he could take. *It would probably send me into a permanent case of the screaming meemies.*

Rema smiled. "Perhaps so, but you didn't, and you did faint--which probably kept you alive. Even so, it was a near thing. Leear's knife was not clean. What its blade failed to do its dirt almost succeeded in doing. You were fevered for three days."

"Umm. Accounts for the dreams. I even dreamed Leear came in here."

"That was not a dream. After he recovered from being struck with the peace he came. He sat with you during the time I slept. He waits outside right now."

Ben tried to draw a deep breath, but it pulled the wound wrong and he winced. "You might as well send him in," he said grimly. "Just make sure he isn't armed."

A smile flickered over her face, but disappeared when she realized he was only half joking. "Do you really feel up to it? He has waited all this time. It will not hurt him to wait a little more if you are too tired."

"Just send him in."

She looked a little longer at her patient but finally stood and left the room.

Leear looked different from the wild-eyed madman

who had driven a knife blade into Ben. He looked exhausted and full of regret. He knelt beside the bed. Without saying a word he lowered his head and began to cry with deep racking sobs.

The sound embarrassed Ben. He did not know what to do and ended by reaching across with his free hand and patting the back of Leear's bald head as though he were a dog. The movement hurt and Ben sucked in breath through clenched teeth.

Leear lifted his eyes. "I am sorry, my Lord. I will go now. I did not mean to hurt you further." He made a move to rise.

"No, it's all right. Stay. Rema said you had been waiting a long time."

"My waiting is nothing, my Lord. I only waited and prayed you would live. I prayed you would not die before I could ask your forgiveness."

*But then go ahead and die quick,* Ben thought, and felt bad for having thought it. "It's all right, Leear. It appears as though I'll live."

"I am glad. I do not think I could have lived if I had killed you, Speaker."

Ben found himself feeling sorry for the man who had tried to kill him. "I understand, Leear. I have turned your whole world upside down. For all I know, I have destroyed you all."

Perhaps, my Lord, but knowing peace is better even if the Over-God ends us."

"I'd like to believe that but I don't know..."

"It is better, my Lord. Believe me."

They looked at one another for a long time, and Ben looked away first.

"I will let you rest now, my Lord," Leear said, standing up.

"Please, don't call me 'my Lord.' I am not a god. I'm nothing but a man, the same as you."

Leear shook his head. "Speaker, you may not be like Lord Aris, but you are not like me," he said and went out.

Later Rema returned, bringing more broth. She changed the dressing on the wound as he sipped from the bowl. After a little he asked, "What is the situation outside?"

Her hands hesitated a moment in wrapping the bandage around Ben's chest, but it was the only indication of her lie. "All is well."

"That's good. Now tell me the truth," he said through teeth clenched against the pain.

She smiled a little ruefully. "Food is low. No one has eaten a full meal since day before yesterday. And the wells are muddy with overuse. Cistern and barrel water from the night of the battle has helped, but it is almost gone now."

"You should have gone ahead and sent them all home," Ben said with a worried twist of his mouth.

Rema stopped wrapping bandage around his chest. "We tried, but they would not go. They refused to leave until they could see you we're all right."

"Oh, Lord," he said.

Rema continued wrapping.

"I have to get up," he said, and tried to do it.

Rema pushed him back. "I will bring the toilet jar. Lie still."

"Not that!" he snapped. "The mess outside! I have to get up!" He started to raise himself.

"No," Rema said and pushed him back again without much effort.

"I will not be responsible for people starving or dying of thirst," he said and tried again to get up.

"No," she said again, pushing him back hard enough this time to make him grimace with pain. "You are too weak! You might tear the wound open again or something worse."

"If I do not go out, the people will suffer. I've got to go so they will go home."

Rema recognized the determination in his eyes, but would not let him win. Instead she offered a compromise. "Tomorrow," she said. "Everyone will be fine until tomorrow. I will arrange it so it won't be so taxing."

"I am fine…" he started to argue.

"No," she said, firmly. "Tomorrow."

Ben felt light headed from his attempts to rise and there was a dull ache in his side which did more to convince him than Rema's fierce look. "All Right! All right! Tomorrow!"

Next morning Rema brought four burly ex-soldiers, Borj among them, to the room and told them to pick up the bed with Ben in it.

"Hey, wait a minute," Ben protested. "I can walk."

"I doubt it," Rema answered and nodded at the four to continue.

"I'm not a baby or a king! Put me down," he demanded, but they ignored him and went out with Rema close behind them clucking like a mother hen.

The bed and the bearers marched through the city and a crowd jammed the crooked streets behind them, barely keeping a respectful distance.

On the plain outside the city, a few hundred yards from the wall, a platform taller than a man had been built. The procession worked its way down the broad road from the gate. The road was made into a narrow trail by the mob lining its sides. At the platform the four lifted the bed up, shoved it onto the platform, and climbed up themselves. They took positions at each corner of the bed and stood quietly. Rema knelt beside the bed and did not take her eyes off Ben. For more than a half hour people continued to flow out of the city like water from a spilled bucket. They surrounded the platform and waited.

When the mob stopped expanding and fell quiet, Ben said, "Help me up."

Borj and the former guard captain did so. His balance was not good. His head spun like a carousel and his knees felt wobbly, but he was standing. The bearers held him until it appeared he would be able to remain upright alone then they stepped back.

Somewhere at the back of the crowd a ripple of cheering began and grew to a roar. Ben looked over the thousands of up-turned, expectant faces and felt his throat close with emotion. The adoration and faith he saw there made his insides go watery with dread. *They expect me to have some kind of answers,* he thought. *They expect some kind of Salvation from me,* but there was no way out now. He was here and they were there, and there was nothing to be done, but what he had planned so he cleared his throat and began speaking as loud as he could manage.

"People of Bakar, and all former warriors," he stopped, thinking he sounded like a politician addressing a convention, but there was no going back now so he cleared his throat again and continued. "As you can see I am alive and mending. This city--this valley, cannot support so many people. If you all stay here much longer, there will be much suffering, and there has been more than enough of that already. So I beg of you all…I command you, if you wish me to put it that way--I command you to go home. Return to your families and continue your lives. Let this time of siege and blood go to the past. Leave it all behind and go home.

"You are all speakers now."

There was a ripple of denial, but Ben lifted his right hand as high as he could, wincing with the effort, and the crowd fell silent again.

"It is true," he continued. "All those commanded to peace become speakers, so you who were warriors become speakers now. As you go home tell everyone of the Peace of Bakar. If you meet those who still slay their brothers, speak the words of Peace to them then tell them to go home.

"I do not know what will come of all this. This Peace may unbalance the world and destroy us all. For that I am sorry."

Again there was a ripple of denial which Ben silenced with an upraised hand. "I am sorry if my Peace has destroyed the world, but I could not help it. I came from another place by will of Lady Tarsa, and her will had a part of this destruction, but I spoke the Peace, and now you will discover you have no choice but to do the same. Leear and the others all say no matter what happens, Peace is better. I hope it is true for I--and now you--can do nothing save help the Peace to grow. Therefore, go your way toward home speaking the Peace to all, until the end of the world."

Ben suddenly felt weak and weary. Rema saw the grayness of him and the sway of his stance. "Help him," she said, and Borj stepped forward to support him. The crowd stood, as though waiting for something more, but there was nothing. After a moment Borj shouted, "Well, what are you waiting for? You heard the Speaker. Go home!"

A laugh spattered through the crowd like summer rain then grew to the pounding splash of a downpour as it mixed with clapping and cheers. It ended slowly, drop by drop as people broke away from the crowd and turned toward home as the Speaker had told them.

## Chapter Eleven

Not everyone went home because not everyone had a home to go to. Several hundred of those who had been Tarsa's warriors had been with the army since they were children. It was the only home they had ever known, but clearly they could not return to that so they were left with no place to go.

Ben talked with Rema and Leear and both said the displaced soldiers should stay in Bakar. The city's population had taken a beating in the battle. There were many widows and orphans who had no one to care for them. "It will be difficult," Leear said, "but in the end it will help Bakar to recover." Rema agreed, and when the idea was presented to the city fathers of Bakar, they agreed too. So it was done and life in Bakar began to return to normalcy.

One of those who had no home was Borj, but he was determined not to stay in Bakar and become a farmer or seaman. "I will stay with you, my Lord." He told Ben, sounding disturbingly like Othway had sounded when he refused to stay at Rayhan with his injured partner.

"First off, Borj, I am not *your Lord,* or anyone else's. I am plain Ben, or Ben Fordham if you must."

"Yes, my Lord," Borj answered and grinned.

"Not *Yes my Lord!* Yes, Ben," he repeated, trying to sound stern.

"As you wish, my Lord Ben."

Ben sighed and gave up trying to stop him. No doubt it would change in time as it had with Othway. "You should be finding a wife and getting ready to carry on with your life, Borj," he said, coming at the real subject from a different angle.

"I am prepared to carry on my life, my Lord Ben. I will stay with you."

This sounded so much like Othway it made Ben flinch. "Look, Borj, I'm leaving here as soon as I am well enough. I am going on to the Valley of Seers--"

"Yes, my Lord Ben, and I am going with you."

"No you're not! You are going to stay here and make a life for yourself, or whatever else you want to do, but you are not going to come with me. Bad enough I have Rema and Othway to worry about."

Borj shrugged. "I do not want anything, but to go with you, my Lord Ben. And you will not need to worry about me. I can take care of myself."

"No you can't! Not anymore you can't! All that changed the instant you were commanded to Peace!"

Borj thought about that for a moment but shook his head. "My Lord Ben, I have been a warrior since the time I could lift a dagger. I have never known anything but weapons and war. I have been commanded to Peace, but I still have the skills of war, so I will use my skills to protect you."

"Protect me how?" Ben asked, his voice rising in

exasperation. "You can't so much as throw a stone at anyone."

"It is true, my Lord Ben. All my old weapons are gone, but I have a new weapon now--stronger than any weapon I have ever had before. I have the Peace."

"Wha…what…" Ben stuttered to a stop. "That's ridiculous!" he said at last.

"No, my Lord Ben, it isn't. Never have I held a weapon which could disarm not only the foe before me, but all the warriors within the sound of my voice."

"It doesn't work that way!"

Borj shrugged again. "Not quite, but close. It is still a powerful weapon.

"All right, all right, but I have the same weapon, and I had it before you did. I am more than able to use it to defend myself. I don't need you, so stay here!"

Borj grinned and shook his head, seeming to enjoy Ben's frustration. "No matter how skillful one is with his weapons he cannot watch his own back. You must sleep sometime. You learned that the hard way when Leear tried to murder you. I will watch your back. It is what I am trained for."

Ben stared at this bear of a warrior who grinned apologetically at having to disagree with his Lord. This man's upper arm was as big around as a tree, and his neck was so thick it was as though his rather pointed head sat directly on his bull wide shoulders. He looked to be the perfect strong, stupid soldier who always did what he was told and never questioned his superiors, yet he had reasoned Ben to a standstill, not only with stubbornness like Othway had done, but with real reasoning. And there was no arguing with him which left the same option as with the *my Lord*-ing--stall long enough and perhaps Borj's stubbornness would wear off. "Fine," Ben said. "We leave for the Valley of Seers as soon as I can travel. Mean time, go see Leear. He'll put you to work."

Borj shook his head. "My work is to guard your back. It started some days ago."

Ben's defeat was complete. He lowered his head and chuckled. "All right, all right! You win. You are now my official first bodyguard and hand-holder."

Borj bobbed his head in a mocking bow of acceptance. "As you wish, my Lord Ben."

The next day Othway came to see Ben. He nodded his shaggy head in greeting at Borj who was sitting not far away. The ex-soldier nodded in answer and continued the business of protecting the Speaker, meaning he sat, quiet and alert, within arms reach of Ben.

"I am glad Borj is going to be your bodyguard, Ben Fordham. I failed miserably at it," Othway said.

"Don't feel guilty about it, Othway. Who could have guessed Leear of all people would turn into a danger."

"Still, Borj will do better."

"Maybe so."

Othway nodded and continued to sit but didn't say anything more. Ben let the silence stretch on for a time, but he could tell Othway hadn't said all he had to say so he prodded the bandit. "Is there something else?"

"Yes. I am glad Borj is going to be your bodyguard...," he began again and stopped.

"You said that."

"Yes, I am glad because it makes what I must do easier."

"And what is it you are going to do?"

The bandit hesitated another moment then said, "I am going to leave you."

"What?" Ben said, taken completely by surprise.

"You told us all to go home," Othway began. "Well, I have no home except the roads where I used to rob travelers. So I am returning to it."

"What? That's crazy! Better you should stay here! There's nothing on the road for you. I mean, you can't even go back to robbing people to stay alive. Just stay here, or come with us to the Valley of Seers if you must," Ben said, hardly believing he had just said it. He had once worked so hard to be rid of the little bandit and now was asking him to stay.

The moment was not lost on Othway. He laughed and his eyes twinkled. "No, Ben Fordham, I cannot stay with you," he said, still chuckling. Then he turned serious. "You said, *Go home and if you meet those who still slay their brothers, speak the words of peace to them* which is what I am going to do."

"Come on, Othway! That is like being some kind of wandering preacher. Besides, it is like Leear said, the more peace gets spoken the farther the world tips out of Balance. You and the others might bring on the end of the world!"

"Yes," Othway agreed. "And it will be better to have the world end in peace than continue in blood as it was before."

The words stole the breath from Ben's chest. This

shaggy little man, ex-bandit, ex-murderer, speaker of Peace, had changed. He was no longer the annoyance who had tagged along from Rayhan. Now there was a conviction, a power, a saintliness in him...

Ben let go of that thought like it was hot iron! "You can't, Othway! You can't! I didn't mean it like that. I didn't mean to start some kind of religious movement. I mean, if you're going to be a wandering preacher. that makes me--Oh Lord! No!" He waved his hands to fend off what was happening. "You can't do this!"

Othway smiled, and it was the same smile Ben had seen in Renaissance paintings of saints. "Oh God, what have I done?" he breathed but no answer came.

Hours of talking did not change Othway's mind. The former highwayman just smiled and continued to assert he was "*going home to the road to speak the peace.*"

At last Othway stood and said, "You are the Speaker, Ben Fordham, but you have always said you are just the same as all other men. If it is true and I am like you then I have the power to choose what I will do. So, what I choose is to speak the peace upon the road. I had hoped you would wish me well, but one way or another I am going."

Ben was exhausted. His head ached and his wounded side throbbed, but worse was the feeling he had created some kind of monster. And, to his surprise, it was all mixed up with a feeling of love and concern for the little robber. "Very well, Othway," he sighed. "If I can't talk you out of this, at least be careful. I have a feeling what you are going to do is dangerous, and I don't want your life on my conscience."

Othway smiled his saintly smile and said, "How could

it be dangerous, Ben Fordham. The Peace will protect me."

"Like it protected me from Leear?" Ben said with a cynical lift of an eyebrow.

Othway shrugged. "You are still alive."

Ben shook his aching head. "Just be careful. Please."

"Yes, my Lord," Othway answered then bowed in a manner which set Ben sputtering with protest and went out.

Othway left the next morning. Rema, Leear, Ben, and the now ever present Borj stood on the wall and watched as the little robber marched down the highway from the city gate passed the platform where Ben had sent the new speakers home. He turned toward the pass cleared by Tarsa's troops.

"I want to leave as soon as possible," Ben said when Othway was only a dot crossing the saddle of the pass. "Tomorrow if we can."

"You are not healed yet," Rema said, concern in her voice. "You are still weak."

Ben raked her with a withering glare. "I don't give a damn. I want out of this valley as fast as I can move. The sooner I get to this Valley of Seers the sooner I get home, and that can't be anything but good for all concerned. We go tomorrow, understand?"

Rema looked as though she had been slapped and started to protest but held her tongue for a moment before saying, "Yes, my Lord Speaker." She kept her eyes down in surrender.

Her bowed head and "Yes, my Lord." made Ben fee like a brute, but he didn't correct her. When he felt Borj and Leear's eyes on him, he glared at them until they bowed too.

Borj had everything ready and waiting at Aris' Shrine the next morning. He had procured two packhorses and three saddle horses. The packhorses had been loaded with supplies. Leear provided all three with new clothes including cloaks and boots with soft uppers and hard leather soles. The cloaks and boots seemed much more than the weather called for and Ben asked about it.

"Soon the rain and cold will begin," Rema said, "and we will be going north toward the autumn. Also, the only way into the Valley is high in the mountains where it is always cold."

Even with everything in readiness they almost did not depart, The Speaker's command notwithstanding. Ben was still weak and sore. He was no horseman at the best of times, which this was not, and the stirrup-less saddle was almost his undoing. He grabbed a handful of coarse mane and tried to vault into the saddle the same way he had tried on the day of his arrival in the world of the gods with the same result. Only this time those watching cared if he hurt himself. When he fell on his rear and grabbed his side, Rema, Leear, and Borj were on him like parents of a not too bright child.

"Get away from me!" He snapped and they backed away. He got to his feet slowly, still holding his side, and dusted his behind.

"My Lord," Rema began, but cut off when Ben glared at her. She blinked at his anger and started again. "Ben Fordham, perhaps we should wait another day at least."

"We go now!" he said, his teeth clenched against the pain. "Borj, gimme a hand!"

Borj stepped forward then interlaced his fingers to

make a step, but when Ben placed his foot ready for the boost Borj began shaking with barely controlled laughter.

"What's so damn funny?" Ben growled and took his foot down.

"I am sorry, Ben Fordham," Borj said. "It is just--this is so much like the first time I set eyes on you."

"Umh," Ben growled and unconsciously ran his tongue over the sharp point of the tooth Borj had chipped when he had rapped Ben across the mouth that first day.

Rema looked worried and grim and angry at Borj for laughing at Ben's pain, and her concern twisted the blade of guilt which had been in Ben's heart since the day before.

"Just so you don't hang me belly down on this one like you did last time," he said with a crooked smile, trying to ease his guilt.

Borj almost collapsed with manic laughter and even Rema could not help smiling a little. "I am sorry, Ben Fordham," Borj said after he gained some control of himself. "Please forgive me. It was nothing personal then and my laughter is not personal now."

"No, not much it's not," Ben said sarcastically as his tongue touched the broken tooth again, but he found himself on the edge of laughter too. "Just boost me up, will ya?"

Borj did.

When they were mounted, Leear and his family stood on the steps of the Shrine of the Flame to say good bye. "The Valley of Seers is far and the way is dangerous, Speaker. Travel carefully."

"Thanks for everything, Leear," Ben said, not thinking of the dirk with which the man had tried to kill him, but Leear thought of it.

"I am sorry for trying to…" his voice trailed off.

"It's all right. I'm sorry my coming has made such a mess of your world."

Leear shook his head. "Othway said to me a few days ago, *'Better the world should end in peace than continue in blood.'* We are in the hands of the Over-God now and whether we see another tomorrow or not, it is better to live in Peace."

"I hope you don't regret those words someday, Leear," Ben said then stuck out his hand to shake Leear's. Leear took it and as he did Ginya also reached up and took hold of it. Before Ben could snatch it back they had both kissed it.

"Travel safely, Speaker," Meya said with tears in her eyes.

A shiver went up Ben's back. Leear, Ginya, and their daughter Meya all wore the same beatific smile Othway had worn.

They traveled slowly for days, stopping often during the day and early at evening. Ben was really in no shape to travel, but he didn't open the wound again. Eventually his body, still strong despite the abuse, healed itself.

They took no particular precautions save trying to avoid people as much as possible. That was Ben's doing. "If we avoid people, we avoid the chance of having to speak the Peace," he said.

"Perhaps we should leave the road," Rema said,

thinking out loud.

"Will it get us there faster?"

"No. The fastest way north from here is the highway. It will take us through some villages and near the city of Teca, but if we go carefully, we should have no trouble."

"I worry about Lady Tarsa's patrols," Borj said. "We will have to deal with the problem if it arises. With the defeat of so great an army as the one which set upon Bakar there may not be many soldiers left to patrol the roads."

"I hope you're right. No soldiers means no fighting, which means no speaking the peace. Let's go."

After a month the weather began to change from hot to cool and then on toward rainy and cold. The trek became uncomfortable, especially sleeping wet. They slept in inns where they could and it was not so bad but things soon began to change. In the beginning the hamlets and inns were welcoming places. The people knew who the Speakers were and were happy to have them. Often the innkeepers would not even accept money for food and lodging, but with each step farther along the road the welcoming spirit shrank. After the first couple of weeks hostility began to show in the hamlets they passed, and it seemed to grow with each mile. They began avoiding inns.

"I do not understand," Borj said, as they sat around a small fire waiting for tea water to boil and gnawing on strips of smoked dried meat which Ben thought of as jerky, but which the others two called trail meat. They were camped in a glade a few hundred yards off the road. The country was deep conifer forest which reminded Ben of California coastal pinewoods. It had been raining most of the day, but now the moon and stars were breaking through the clouds.

"With every mile the hostility seems to grow," Borj continued.

"Are you sure it isn't just your nerves, Borj?" Ben asked, but he knew it wasn't. He could feel it too.

"Teca is not far ahead," Rema said. "What will it be like in a city with thousands of people?"

"Can we go around?"

"I had thought to stop for a day or two and renew our supplies, but now…" Rema shrugged, worry clouding her golden eyes.

"I think perhaps Ben Fordham is right," Borj said. "Better to go around. To be amid a few thousand hostile strangers is not a choice I would willingly make."

"We still need supplies. Our hard bread is gone, the wine is gone, and the tea is almost gone. Soon we will be down to trail meat and water."

"Can we live off the land?" Ben asked.

Both of the others shook their heads at once. Rema explained. "It would take too long for too little. We could waste hours hunting and gathering. Besides, the road is too well traveled for the pickings to be rich. Everyone hunts and gathers to add fresh food to their trail rations. At best we might get some skinny rabbits and wild greens, and there won't be much of that now either because the weather is changing too fast."

"One of us could go into Teca and bring back what we need," Borj said, poking the fire with a stick.

"And which one of us might that be?" Rema asked, knowing Borj meant she should go.

"I do not know Teca much...," xhe began.

"All the better. You will not be known."

"I do not like leaving Ben Fordham," he said as though Ben was not right across the fire from him.

"Hey!" Ben said. "What am I, a sack of rocks sitting over here?"

Borj glanced up and smiled an apology. "I'm sorry. It is just --I have not left your side for weeks.

"Then it is time you had a night out, Mother," Ben said. "I'm a big boy now. I can take care of myself and Rema can hold my hand for a little while without your help. And she is a lot easier to look at than you are."

Rema smiled and blushed, though the dark and the red of the fire hid it. "We will be fine Borj," she said. "As long as you don't stay gone too long."

The ex-soldier's sharp eyes cut from one to the other as he considered. "Can I trust you two here alone in this pretty place?" he said at last, grinning from ear to ear.

Rema snorted derisively but blushed enough for it to show despite the darkness.

Ben pretended offense. "A month ago I was '*my Lord*' now you're accusing me having designs on Rema. What happened to all the awe you used to hold me in?"

"It has been beaten out of me by weeks of hearing you whine about your sore back side," Borj said, laughing.

"Ah." Ben said.

Borj left before first light the next morning leading the unladen pack horses. "I will try to return no later than tomorrow evening, but do not worry if it takes a little longer.

I intend to poke around for some news."

"Be careful, Borj." Rema said.

"I will be invisible," he said with a wave as he left the glade.

"What do you think he is going to find out, Rema?" Ben asked as they watched Borj fade into the misty dawn.

"I don't know, but I fear it will not be good for us."

When the sun was fully risen, Rema said, "I am going to put together a wild stew."

"I thought you said the pickings would be slim and it would take too long?"

"And that is true, but what else have we to do while we wait for Borj?"

"True enough, I suppose. I wish there was a place to take a bath. It has been days. I itch."

Rema's eyes became misty as the morning and her lips curled in a wistful smile. "The hot pools in the cavern near Nanema," she said, remembering.

"Too close to the Valley of Voices to suit me, but if we could find something like that around here, I would be in so fast I wouldn't even make a splash."

"Ah well," she said, shaking off the thought. "There is nothing like it near here, and it is too cold to go into the water of the stream down there," she flicked a hand toward the other side of the glade.

"Nice idea though."

"Yes it was. Come, let us get supper." She walked in the direction of the stream and Ben watched her for a moment, thinking how graceful she looked. Her long strong legs stretched out in sure steps and her hips swayed ever so slightly. He suddenly realized this was the first time he had been alone with Rema when he was not hurt, sick, or afraid to the point of paralysis and even those times had been short. Memories of her washing him and doctoring him in the cavern of the hot springs flickered through his mind, and the accidental glimpse up her long thighs to her womanhood featured prominently in them.

He caught his wandering fancy and dragged it back to reality. *Maybe Borj was right. I can't be trusted alone with Rema!* He got up and trotted after her.

It took most of the day to gather what went into the stew. There were roots dug from a boggy place beside the stream and leaves of plants which looked like weeds. Then there were grasses and tubers and seeds. The only thing he recognized was wild onion, but when the fruit of their day's work was dumped into Rema's cooking pot with trail meat, the aroma was mouth watering. The stew tasted better than it smelled.

After they had eaten they sat wrapped in their cloaks against the growing chill of the evening. They sipped tea made from the last of their supply.

"I wonder how Borj is doing," Ben said.

Rema's face had been calm and smiling all day, but now Ben's words caused lines to score her forehead. She pulled her cloak tighter around herself and shivered. "It will be cold tonight," she said, changing the subject.

"I'm sorry. I didn't mean to make you worry."

She shrugged. "I have a feeling in the pit of my stomach what Borj finds out will not be good news."

"Or maybe it will be," he said, trying to erase her

worry lines. “Maybe everything is in fine shape now. We haven’t even heard of one of Tarsa’s patrols in days and days, and no one has tried to harm us.”

“That is one of the reasons I am worried. It is not natural for the world to be so quiet and safe. Before the Peace, raids, strikes, and battles large and small were daily happenings. Now...”

“Maybe the Balance is so perfect it has stopped all that.”

Rema shook her head. “Lady Tarsa is not concerned about the Balance except to destroy it. Nothing could stop her mischief before and nothing can stop it now.” She swirled her tea around her leathern cup and studied it as though she might find some answer there.”

“None of our worries will make anything better,” she said after a while. “So let us not think about tomorrow,” and began clearing up the dishes.

The night was cold and clear and no cloak or sleeping robe could keep the cold out. The ache in Ben’s side where Leear had stabbed him made him wish they were sleeping in a nice warm inn. He flopped and turned and drew his knees up then straightened them out again, but there was no way to get comfortable.

“It still pains you?” Rema asked from her side of the low burning fire.

“I didn’t mean to wake you,” he said.

“I wasn’t asleep. Does it pain you?”

“Only when I am cold or wet or tired,” he laughed.

She appeared as though by magic and knelt beside him. “Let me see,” she commanded and turned to the fire to get a light. She whirled the stick in the air to get it blazing again.

"It's too cold," Ben complained. "And there is nothing you can do about it anyway."

"You might be surprised. Sit up and let me see." Her command brooked no more resistance so he unrolled from his bedding and sat up. He lifted up his jerkin on the left side and Rema held the flickering torch close. She ran her finger down the welt.

"It appears healed, but if it still pains you it must not be completely healed inside," she said. "There is no fever in it so I think it will be all right. It would be better if we could stop somewhere warm for a few weeks. It could heal properly then. It is a miracle Leear did not kill you." She stroked her hand up to his arm pit then back down to his hipbone. The touch felt proprietary, not clinical like the moment before.

"Yeah, yeah. You said that before. Can I put my shirt down now? It's cold," he said, not meaning to sound as cranky as he did, but the stroke--the caress, had caught him by surprise. It had set off some mental pictures and some physical reactions he was not prepared for.

Rema snatched her hand back as though she had touched something hot and looked at the hand as though she did not recognize it as hers. Ben let go of his jerkin and it dropped back into place.

"I will make a poultice to draw out the pain and brew a potion to help you sleep," she said looking anywhere but at Ben. She was usually bold with her glance. She got up and added wood to the fire.

Ben wrapped up in his cloak and sleeping robe but

did not lie down again. He watched as she made her preparations, unable to take his eyes from her. She heated water then poured a little of it into a conglomeration of herbs taken from her medicine box. She wrapped the poultice in a piece of soft leather which had been pounded thin and turned back to Ben. "Show me the wound again," she said, still not looking into his eyes.

He opened his bedding again and lifted the jerkin.

She put the warm, wet bundle of herbs against the wound, flattening it so it covered completely. "Hold this in place," she commanded.

The poultice wrap had tails on each end, and when the mat of herbs was over the wound she put her arms around Ben to tie it in place. Ben's chest was wide enough to make Rema have to pull close in to reach around him, and her head was directly under his chin. The smell of her hair, sweet and warm and heady as spring engulfed him and he thought, *how could she smell so wonderful?* Then he felt her lips brush his chest in a kiss so soft he thought he had imagined it at first, but then he felt it again.

Ben lifted her chin with his fingers and looked into her eyes. "Are you sure, Rema?" he whispered.

She tightened her embrace and turned her cheek against his chest. "I was sure from the first day," she said. "But Maggie from your world held your heart. Does she still?"

Ben thought about that for a moment. When Leear stabbed him the last thought he remembered was of Maggie, but now Maggie was so far away both in time and distance and experience. There was very little chance he would see her again, but more, he truly realized for the first time that Maggie had left him and would not be his again even if he got back to his world.

"No, Rema," he said. "You hold my heart now."

She looked up into his eyes and saw it was true.

## Chapter Twelve

Before dawn the pounding hooves of a horse coming fast awakened Rema and Ben. They unrolled from their sleeping robes just as Borj drew his blowing, lathered mount to so hard a halt the horse sat down upon its haunches.

"Borj, we didn't expect you until this afternoon--where are the packhorses?" Rema and Ben began, but Borj cut off their questions.

"Lord Aris and Lady Tarsa have leagued themselves against all Speakers," he said, bending down, hands upon knees, panting from his miles long gallop.

Ben and Rema stared at him with their mouths open, uncomprehending. Rema came to her senses first and denials began falling from her lips. "No, that cannot be. Lord Aris is Light, Lady Tarsa is Dark. They cannot be in league, and even if they could Lord Aris--"

"The Balance," Borj said straightening up. "It has swung too far toward the Light because of us. Lady Tarsa would be happy to let the Balance tip so long as it brings chaos and ending, ,but Lord Aris must preserve the Balance therefore he has leagued himself with the old dark to restore it. All Speakers are subject to arrest. That did not go well at first," he snorted ironically. "Soldiers tried to take the Speakers by force and gained the command to Peace for their efforts. Now Speakers are taken by stealth or by simply walking up to them with no weapon drawn and laying hands upon them. Their mouths are bound then they are clubbed insensible. If they are not dead by the blow, their tongues are cut out while they are unconscious."

"Oh, God," Ben breathed. It was worse than anything he had imagined--but Borj was still talking.

"That is not the worst," he said, losing even the gallows humor from his voice and unable to look into their faces. "They have set up poles along the road."

Rema had taken Ben's hand when Borj began; now her grip increased until her knuckles were white and the circulation was diminished in his fingers.

"What are poles, Borj?" Ben asked, dreading the answer.

Borj swallowed, still unable to look into their faces. "Sapling trees about as big around as your wrist are stripped of their limbs and sharpened at the top. The victim is bound and placed so the point begins up the--" he stopped, swallowed, and drew the stony mantle of a veteran soldier about himself. "The victim is jammed down upon the point so it is driven up through the bowels. To be jammed down hard is a kindness for then the point reaches the heart and lungs quickly, but if the executioners are cruel--I have seen poles cut short enough so the victim's toes touch the ground with the point only a little into the bowels. It is a long, slow death. I saw a man stand three days once--" He stopped, drew a deep shuddering breath and continued. "For mercy sake I beheaded him at the end."

Rema let go of Ben's hand and threw her arms around Borj.

Ben stared in open-mouthed shock for a moment then his knees would no longer support him and he sat down hard. "Oh, God. Oh, God," he said as though he had only enough breath for the plea.

Rema released Borj from her embrace and looked into his face. "How many?" she asked.

The former soldier of Darkness shook his head. "I do not know. At least a hundred in Teca and I heard some say a thousand in Cynar. The one who helped me heard a hundred a day were poled beside the north gate of Cynar. He said they keep the Speakers gagged or cut out their tongues then keep them in the court of Lady Tarsa's temple. She stretches out her pleasure by poling only the hundred at a time."

"And Lord Aris allows this?" Rema asked still unable to believe and yet believing.

"It is the Balance," Borj said. "He will do anything to maintain the Balance, even allow Lady Tarsa to exercise her pleasures."

Disbelieving shock at the barbarity of it all had been Ben's first reaction, but as Borj ceased to talk and they sat in silence, an acid ball of loathing began swelling in his chest. Not loathing for Tarsa or Aris, but for himself. The gods were committing horrors but it was because of him. If he had not spoken the Peace, these would not have died. "I killed them," he whispered, not knowing he had spoken aloud. "My Peace killed them all and it will kill more."

Borj and Rema both heard his whisper in the quiet dawn and they turned on him with denials. "No, my Lord," Borj cried.

Rema pulled Ben into her arms as though he were a sick child. "You have killed no one," she said.

"You are the speaker of Peace, my Lord," Borj insisted.

"Without me they would all be alive."

"No!" they both denied. "It is the gods! It is the Balance!"

"This must be stopped," he said, not hearing their denials. "I cannot have any more blood on my hands. This must stop."

"How?" Rema asked. "We can only speak the Peace to those who do battle."

"I must go to Teca and stop this."

"It is too late, my Lord," Borj said. "All those to be poled have been. There is nothing to stop now, unless more Speakers are captured."

"And Cynar?"

Borj shook his head. "If the rumors are true, there are many more yet to die there," he said.

"How far is Cynar?" Ben demanded. Borj and Rema both began protesting, but Ben ignored them. "How far to Cynar?" he asked again.

"Three days hard travel east through the mountains," Borj said.

"Is it a city or a town?"

"A city. Bigger than Bakar."

"It is a strong hold of Dark," Rema added.

"I don't care," Ben said. "I don't care what god rules there. There is no difference between them now anyway. They are both dark and they must be stopped. I must stop them."

Ben wanted to start for Cynar that instant, but it was impossible. Borj was sick with exhaustion, and he had ridden his horse almost to death. He had left the packhorses in Teca because they would have slowed him down too much. The man who had helped him had given him all the cured meat, hard bread, tea, and wine he had in the house, but it wasn't much.

Rema stirred up the fire and re-heated what was left of the wild stew for Borj. She tried to get Ben to eat some too, but it was as though he could not hear her. He squatted, wrapped in his cloak and stared into the fire with an intensity such as she had never seen. It was as though he had become stone and it made a sliver of ice sharp as a needle jab at the base of her heart.

The morning passed. Borj ate, drank some tea, and fell into exhausted sleep. Rema tended his horse as best she could, watering and feeding him carefully then rubbing him down with hanks of grass, but what the nearly blown animal really needed was a week of rest.

Noon passed and still Ben did not move. Rema glanced furtively at him and the needle of ice pricked her heart more viciously. He did not even seem to blink his eyes.

Ben's thoughts were focused only on Cynar and the poles set up beside the gate. There was a molten rage building in his belly--a power induced rage, which petrified his limbs but electrified his mind. For the first time in his life he knew the hunger for revenge. He wished a troop of soldiers would suddenly come marching down the road. He would destroy them with the sword of the Peace. He knew now what Borj had meant when he called the Peace the most powerful weapon he had ever possessed. He did not think of the need to precipitate a battle in order to create an overwhelming need to speak, but only the crashing, crushing command to Peace--Peace which struck every warrior who heard the command to his knees and tore away the very ability to violence. More, he wished to have the very gods before him. He would command them to Peace and be obeyed though it cracked the very foundation of the world!

"Ben Fordham..."

The voice was so small it barely penetrated his rage.

"Please, Ben Fordham..."

He knew the voice, and remembered he loved the person, but he was absorbed in rage and could not be called forth from it.

"Please, my Lord, please! Come back to me. I am afraid. I love you. Please come back to me."

Her touch was so light he hardly felt it, but the warmth of her hands, one on each side of his face, penetrated his concentration and he turned his eyes. Rema's beautiful face was only inches from his own, her eyes bright with unshed tears and her cheeks stained with those already shed.

"Don't cry, Rema," he said and found his voice rusty. He touched her cheek and the gesture seemed to release her. She threw her arms around him and squeezed as if to press herself into him.

The day was gone. The black of night was upon them,

broken only by a soft glimmering of stars. Ben had sat from dawn to dark without moving, but to him it was as though only a moment had passed. "Don't be afraid," he said. "I'm here now."

They held each other in the stars' glimmering and kept silent for a long time. Rema's body continued to shudder as though she were freezing. "They will kill us at Cynar, my Lord," she said. "They will bind our mouths and we will die on the poles."

"No, they won't. It's all right. We won't die. There is power in me, in all of us, and it is growing. Aris saw it and he knows it is growing, and he is afraid. We won't die."

"They are gods," she said, gazing up into his darkness obscured face.

"It doesn't matter."

She searched his eyes in the reflected starlight. "Is it true, my Lord, or are you just saying these words because I am afraid?"

He lowered his mouth to hers in a gentle kiss. "It is true, Rema. I swear it is true."

~ * ~

Cynar was different from both Bakar and Nanema. It was placed upon an island which had been created by diverting and dividing the flow of the river Mychos. The city was built of dark stone hewn from the mountains and looked like a sinister black ship sitting in the midst of the river. The west wall, shaped like the prow, divided the current and created a swift flowing moat around the city. Two bridges crossed the moat, one on the north side and one on the south. The broad avenues which crossed the bridges and entered the gates led arrow straight to the swelling dome of Tarsa's temple which dominated the city's center.

The three Speakers made no attempt to hide as they came down from the mountains. They joined the heavy traffic of horses, carts, and people on foot which flowed toward the city. Many noticed them, but any who recognized them turned their eyes away quickly as though they were afraid or ashamed.

As they neared the north side bridge, the traffic slowed to a crawl. It was the poles. They were set at about ten-yard intervals, fifty on each side of the highway, the last pair at the beginning of the bridge. When the throng moved between the first pair, it slowed and eddied as people looked at the naked, impaled bodies. There was no atmosphere of carnival or amusement. These people had been brought up in blood, death, and war, and the power of Lady Tarsa who's city Cynar was, but even that had not hardened them enough to find pleasure in the agonizing death of those on the poles.

The afternoon sun was hot here. No cool taste of autumn had come to the eastern side of the Sabard Mountains and the heat added its torture to the agony of the poles. The three Speakers stopped as they passed between the first two poles. These two, a man and a woman, were already dead and Ben found himself being thankful for it. He remembered Borj's mercy to the man who had been three days alive on a pole. Fat blue-green flies swarmed over these bodies and smaller carrion birds pecked and tore at the dead flesh. The eyes had already been eaten away and the flesh was beginning to bloat in the heat. Dry blood streaked the short expanse of the poles which were exposed and around the base of each was a crusted puddle covered with ants and flies.

Ben did not recognize either of these. Probably their own loved ones could no longer have recognized them. Their tongues had not been cut out; instead they had leather gags tied over their mouths with thongs. The thongs were pulled so tight they cut into the cheeks of the dead Speakers. Ben wondered if they had been man and wife, or if they had once been servants of opposite gods. It did not matter. Now they were united in death before the gate of Cynar, and the horror, the barbarity of it, caused the wrath in Ben to glow and rise like lava from the depths of the earth.

A crackling aura of power grew around him as he looked at the poled Speakers. The crowd which eddied and flowed between the poles saw it and flinched. Many fell to their knees and threw their arms over their faces. A low wail of fear and mourning which seemed to rise from the very earth began. Ben neither saw nor heard any of it. The bodies impaled beside the highway were the only things which filled his eyes and his mind. He was again fixated like the day Borj had brought the news, but now there was no rigidity in him. After a few moments he swung his horse toward the gate of the city and kicked it into a run. The crowd parted like sod before a plow blade, but Ben did not notice. He did not know if Rema and Borj had followed him and he did not care. Only the bodies on the poles flicking past his charging horse mattered. He saw each tormented face like a snapshot before his eyes. Dead strangers, some with tongues cut out, others gagged--faces, which would be forever tattooed upon his mind as surely as Mardian's tattoo was upon his arm--as surely as their blood was on his hands.

A face flickered past and suddenly Ben reined in so hard his horse skidded to a stop and reared in protest. Ben slid down and ran to the Speaker poled on the right side of the avenue. That one's face was twisted and swollen with agony, but he was still alive.

It was Othway.

Like the first two Speakers along the gauntlet of horror Othway had only been gagged. Ben stared a moment then drew his knife and cut the cruel thongs which had bitten deep into Othway's cheeks. "Oh God, Oh God! What have I done?" Ben begged the skies.

Othway croaked, "Water," his voice like ancient, crumbling parchment.

Ben unhooked his water bag from his saddle, unstoppered it and lifted it to the little bandit's mouth, unmindful the water would probably give him more agony than relief.

Othway drank then turned his head away and he coughed out a mist of bloody droplets. "I knew," he breathed.

Ben leaned close to hear the whispered words. "Knew what, Othway?"

"You would come." He coughed again and the pole drove deeper into his vitals wrenching a scream from him.

"Oh God, Othway! I'm sorry, I'm sorry!"

"No," Othway gasped. "No! Speak! Speak the Peace to them, my Lord."

The little bandit's command was like a slap to bring

Ben out of hysteria. "Yes, Othway. I will. I promise," he said and kissed the other's sun blistered forehead.

Othway smiled and died.

Every movement on the avenue had stopped. Even the soldiers walking their posts upon the walls had ceased their march. Every eye was turned toward Ben Fordham as he stepped back from Othway's body, turned toward the city, and lifted his arms above his head. "You gods are gods no more!" he cried. "There is no mercy in you! These people were innocent. They did nothing, but bring an end to some of the murder and death of this wretched world and you have murdered them for it. You are not fit to be gods! You are less than human!"

The keening moan from people and earth rose like the winds in the Valley of Voices.

"The Balance is not worth this," he continued. "The Balance is void! Cynar no longer serves Dark or Light for now there is Peace! PEACE!" He turned, swung up into his saddle, and drove his heels into the horses' sweating sides. The steed shot forward through the gate and plowed through the mob toward the city's center--toward Tarsa's Temple.

Ben did not stop at the wide stairs which lead up into the temple but pounded up between the demon carved pillars into the gloom of the sanctuary and across to the Holy of Holy's. He slid down from his horse and onto the shining expanse of floor before the towering statue of the horned Goddess of Dark. The horse, eyes rolling with terror and barely under control when Ben was astride, bolted and disappeared deeper into the Temple as soon as it was free.

Power--shining, crackling, intense power--radiated

from the Speaker. He despised these gods, and the strength, the bitterness of his despise shook the foundation of the temple and engulfed the statue of Tarsa with such heat the alabaster began to smoke and melt.

Suddenly fists were beating against his chest and a voice was screaming "no, no, no!" Lau, the priestess from Nanema who had brought him to the Valley of Voices for Lady Tarsa's pleasure was pounding at him. The cold disdain she had once shown him was no longer. The contempt was ripped away by awe and fear which changed her into a clawing, spitting, pounding animal screaming for him to cease; screaming for guards to come and stop him from destroying her very life.

Ben laughed. Such a puny hateful thing she was. He swept her aside with his arm then lifted his hands above his head and cried, "The gods no longer rule in this place. Tarsa, you are finished!"

The statue trembled as under a powerful blow and crashed down onto the altar in a cloud of shards and dust. The Speaker lowered his arms and surveyed his work. Lau cowered at his feet. He glanced down at her then stooped to help her to her feet. "Call your guards now," he said.

Astonishment came over Lau's face then she backed away a few steps, turned, and ran.

Ben watched her go then strode back across the sanctuary toward the crowd jamming the door. They began to retreat down the steps as the Speaker neared. He stopped at the top of the stairs and looked over the mass of people below. Rema and Borj elbowed their way out of the mob and ran up the steps to him. When they came close enough he reached out and caressed Rema's cheek. "You see," he said. "I told you we wouldn't die."

Her smile was like sunrise after a night of storm.

A clatter of armor and measured tread of soldiers drew every eye in the precincts of the temple. Ten armored guards marched toward the three Speakers, but they did not come with assurance. They stopped a pace away and the detachment's leader apologetically cleared his throat. "High Priestess Lau commands us to bind your mouths and take you into our custody," he said, eyes cast down.

Ben smiled in answer and said, "Peace be with you and with all your soldiers. High priestess Lau does not command here anymore. The gods no longer rule in Cynar. Put up your swords forever." It was not the *Command of Peace*. There was no thunder, no shaking of the earth, no lightning; only quiet words of peace.

The leader of the detachment ran his eyes over Ben's face and the faces of Rema and Borj then he looked toward the interior of the temple. Lau stood inside the shadows of the demon pillars, wreathed about with smoke and dust. Her hands were at her side, the false horns skewed on her head.

The soldier turned back to the Speakers, drew his sword, and dropped it with a clang at the Speakers' feet. "Peace be with you also, Speaker," he said then turned and walked away. His detachment watched him melt into the crowd. When they could no longer pick him out from any other, they drew their swords, dropped them on the marble floor, and mumbled, "Peace be with you, Speaker," before filtering into the crowd themselves.

A murmur rose from the mob. Ben turned to them

and lifted his hands. "Peace be with you all. The power of the gods is broken in Cynar. Go and take the dead from the poles and bury them. Give them honor and remember they came only to speak the Peace."

A thousand faces stared up at them and, as at Bakar, Borj said, "Don't just stand there! Go and do as the Speaker has told you." Then he turned to Ben who had suddenly found it necessary to lean heavily on Rema. "Come, my Lord," he said. "There is an inn where you can rest."

"I don't think I can walk, Borj," he answered just as his knees buckled.

Borj and Rema caught Ben as he collapsed. Borj scooped him up as though he were a child and carried him down the steps and through the dispersing mob, and as he went many turned to touch the unconscious man in those iron arms before going to bury the dead.

## Chapter Thirteen

A dark, swirling vortex of dread sucked at Ben Fordham, threatening to swallow him up without a trace. He fought the twisting current with every fiber of muscle and will in him, and he seemed to be winning until a gigantic hand rose from beneath the surface and pushed him under. The dark, viscous liquid which he had thought was water became blood and it flowed into his mouth and nostrils with a personal, vengeance-embittered will--a hunger to mix his blood with itself. He gagged and choked and tried to fight his way to the surface again, but the blood was like thick jelly and the hand of the Over-God kept pushing him deeper and deeper and deeper into the vortex...

Ben jolted upright in bed, gasping for breath, with the terror of the dream still clutching at his heart. He struggled to make his diaphragm pull down and his lungs to fill. After a moment of suffocation, he managed to draw in a breath, then another, and a third. His heart still felt as though the Over-God squeezed it, but the feeling began to ease. He brought his hand up to wipe his sweat slick face.

Rema, sleeping beside him as she had since the first day in Cynar, had heard the beginning of the dream and had reached out to touch him, but her touch no longer stilled the nightmares as it had at first. Now she sat up beside Ben and put her arms around him. He was clammy and trembling. "All is well," she whispered soothingly. "There is peace in Cynar and all is well. Sleep."

Ben shook his head, trying to shake the nightmare from his mind. After a moment he got up and went out to relieve himself. When he came back he was no longer shaking and his breathing had returned to normal but sleep was long gone. He sat on the edge of the bed.

"Shall I brew a sleeping draught?" Rema asked, putting her hand tenderly upon his back.

"No. The dream isn't gone. If I go back to sleep now, it will come back."

Three weeks had passed since Ben had spoken the Peace and cast the gods out of

Cynar. The power to do it had come from his rage at what Aris was allowing, and on the morning after speaking the Peace, he had felt like mighty Zeus standing on the pinnacle of Olympus casting thunderbolts down at the wicked, blood-thirsty godlings. On the third morning recognition of his own arrogance had battered its way through the triumph. He had indeed ejected the gods from Cynar and thereby unbalanced the world even more than breaking the siege at Bakar had. That unbalance had pushed Aris to allow yet more poles to be raised beside more cities in a futile attempt to re-establish the Balance, but the Peace had pushed the world and all the people in it toward destruction. Since that realization Ben had been under an assault of dreadful guilt and horrifying dreams.

Ben had been subject to nightmares since he was a child, but they were nothing like these. Now there was no escaping them. They came every night--the blood vortex; the new poles being raised beside the gates of other cities; the Valley of Voices; Tarsa and Aris pulling him to pieces like a well cooked pheasant. Rema brewed sleeping draughts, but they did not help. In fact they made the dreams worse in some ways because they held him in sleep when he wanted desperately to wake.

"Do the dreams grow worse, my Lord?" Rema began, and seemed to regret the words even as they left her mouth.

"Don't call me lord!" Ben shouted and shot to his feet away from her touch. "I am nobody's lord!"

"I am sorry Ben Fordham," she said, on the verge of tears. "Please--I am sorry. Come back to bed."

After a time he relented, sorry he had shouted, but meaning what he said. He sat down on the bedside, caressed her cheek, and felt the tears there. "I'm sorry, Rema. It's just..."

"I know," she said. "You feel guilt for those who died, but their deaths are not on your hands."

"The Peace..."

"The Peace has freed Cynar."

"And destroyed the world," he said bitterly, putting his head in his hands.

Rema wiped eyes and nose on the sleeve of her nightgown like a little girl. "Then so be it," she said. "Othway believed it better for the world to end in peace than to continue in blood and death."

"And look what it got him! Him and a few thousand

others with him! And others even now!"

This was generally where these midnight discussions ended, with Rema on the edge of worship for the Speaker and Ben on the edge of despair.

After a time Rema coaxed Ben into lying down again and she held him to her as though he were a frightened child.

"What am I going to do, Rema?" he whispered. "Everything is wrong. Everything I touch is destroyed one way or another. Even back home. I thought I wanted to go back, but there is nothing there for me even if I could get back. What am I going to do?"

"Ben Fordham, please do not be angry for what I am going to say, but I think you have no choice in what you will do. I think you will go on speaking the Peace and changing the hearts of the people."

"I can't! Isn't it bad enough..."

She put her hand over his lips to stop the words. "I think you will go on. I think you have no choice. Whether you will accdept it or not, you have become a third god upon the world..."

"I don't want to hear this!" he said and tried to get loose from her arms, but she held him tight.

"I do not care!" she shouted. "I do not care what you want! You will hear it, and you will believe it!" She rolled over and sat astride his chest, holding him in bed with all her strength. "You are the god of Peace on this world," she cried. "It doesn't matter what you want or what you believe. Everyone in Bakar and Teca and Cynar and Nanema and in the whole world believes it except you! Even the gods believe it now. Before Cynar I did not quite believe it, but now--how could I not? You have commanded the very gods to depart! You have broken their power here, and you have no choice but to continue. You cry about destroying the world, but you have not! The world still stands..."

"And the Over-God..."

"The Over-God will do what he will do. He will judge, and he will decide when it is the time for judging. Until then you have no choice but to continue speaking the Peace."

Ben was stunned by the vehemence of her. Her eyes burned with the fire of worship and fear and pity and love, and that fire scorched his soul. He struggled to get out of bed and away from those scorching eyes and could not. "And what about you?" he said, thinking to strike back, to get free. "You have the same power I have. Does it make you a goddess?"

Rema shifted her weight, but still held him. "I have a small power which you gave me, but it is not like yours. You command all to Peace though they have not even drawn sword. A word from you and the hearts of the soldiers Lau sent to seize you were changed! They had not even begun to draw weapons, and yet they were changed."

"I don't know that they were changed," he said petulantly, relaxing beneath her.

"They drew their swords and dropped them at you feet. A word from you and their hearts were changed."

The pearl glow of dawn seeped in the window. "Maybe they just saw the situation was impossible," he said at last. "Maybe they just decided they couldn't win anyway so Peace was better."

"And is that not a change of heart?"

"The Balance..."

"Damn the Balance!" Rema screamed and pushed herself off his chest to stalk across the room.

Ben's mouth fell open in surprise, but after a moment anger replaced surprise. "Damn the Balance?" he cried. "Peace is better? That's easy for you to say. It isn't on your head. There are no poles going up and speakers being killed on them because of you! You aren't the one they are looking to as some kind of replacement god! When the Balance was right they killed each other, but everybody knew where they stood. Then I come along and destroy the Balance. All of a sudden there are no rules anymore. Now blood and death aren't a few here and a few there. Now there are thousands dead in a battle stirred up so I could speak the Peace, and more thousands dead on poles beside the highway. And when this Over-God comes back, if he comes, he's going to take one look at the mess I have made out of his nice orderly world, and it is going to be the end. Everything is going to wink out, goodnight, dead, the end. And it is all going to be on me! I snatched power out of the hands of the gods, so the fault is mine. I will have destroyed the whole world! What are a few thousand dead in battle compared to that?"

Tears poured down Rema's face and great shuddering sobs of frustration and anger wracked her. "Peace is better! If the world ends now, no matter what, Peace is better!" She said through teeth clenched in determination. Then she whirled and stamped out of the room.

~ * ~

Cynar began to fill with pilgrims. Day by day more came, all with the same desire: to see the Speaker.

At first Ben saw a few of them, but soon there were so many and he was so deep in despair he could not continue, but his refusal to see them did not make them go away. Borj and Rema pleaded with him to see them, but he sent word out they should all go home. They sent word back that they would go home if it were his command, but only if it was his command.

"Then I'll command it!" he said. "I don't want to see any of them!"

"Ben Fordham," Borj said, "some of these have traveled weeks just to catch a glimpse of you. Has your heart grown so bitter--have you grown so god-like--you can refuse them?

Ben went scarlet at the jab, but said nothing.

Borj waited for an answer but when none came, he said, "There is one here you must see if there is any mercy in you. An old woman. She has traveled from Yanek which is across the great sea to the west. She says she has known you would come since she was a child and when you first spoke the Peace to Othway, her fire leapt up and told her to come to Cynar. She knew you had come. The journey has taken months, and she is weary almost to death, but still very insistent that she must see you. Please, if you will not see any other, please see her."

Ben looked into the earnestly pleading eyes of him who had been both captor and friend and remembered Othway. *I knew you would come,* the little bandit had said. "All right, all right," he said with less than good graces. "I'll see the old woman but only her!"

Borj's hard, craggy face glowed with satisfaction. "Thank you," he said. "I will bring her." In a moment Borj returned with a bent, decrepit old woman. She looked tiny and fragile beside his bulk, but she would not allow him to help her. She hobbled along leaning upon a tall stick, and everything about her was gray--tattered clothes, strands of hair, which had escaped around the edge of her cowl, the skin of her hands and face, her eyes. She was like a wisp of gray cobweb moving toward Ben, and the sight of her sent a shiver up his back.

"Speaker," Borj began. "This is Arna of Yanek. She is a Seer."

The icy prickles along Ben's spine increased. "Speaker," she said with a bow, polite, but not deferential. Her voice was as dry and soft as a thousand years of dust. She still leaned upon her stick, the very picture of patience.

"Borj, bring a chair," Ben said, unable to pull his eyes away from her.

Borj hesitated. The old woman looked harmless, but he remembered harmless looking Leear's wild eyes as he had tried to turn the point of the dirk up into the Speaker's heart.

Seeing his hesitation she snapped, "I am no danger to the Speaker," the iron in her words belied the softness of her voice. It surprised Borj and the Speaker, and seemed to strike a cord of command from Borj's past. His eyes cut from the old woman to Ben and back then he nodded and left to bring back a chair.

When Arna was seated Borj said, "I will bring tea."

"No," she commanded. "Brandy. My bones ache

with travel and waiting."

"Yes, Ma'am," Borj said, not quite coming to attention before he went out.

"You are a Seer?" Ben asked. "As in 'The Valley of Seers'?"

"Yes."

"I was going there..."

"And you will continue there, Speaker, but first you will take what I am sent here to give you."

A trickle of fear ran through Ben's veins. "And what is that? A dagger through the heart?" he asked, not sure such a thing would be bad.

Arna snorted. "Do not be a fool. There is too much for you to do yet. No, I am come to strike you with the Peace."

Ben looked into the gray eyes for a long moment, feeling a calming power come from them. "I do not understand," he said.

Borj came in with a stone bottle and two leathern cups. The old woman watched in silence as he poured, set the bottle down, and left.

Arna sipped from her cup and smacked her lips. Ben touched his cup to his lips but did not taste the brandy. The old woman's presence so concentrated his mind everything else was excluded.

"You have brought Peace to the world," she said. "And because of it you have no peace. You fear you have destroyed more than you have preserved and you are weary. You cannot rest, though you are the weariest mortal ever to have lived. Therefore you need Peace."

Ben laughed with cutting bitterness. "Peace! It has probably killed the whole world. If that is the kind of peace you are bringing me..."

"The Peace has not done that," she said. "Nor have you. The gods have done that."

"But until I came--"

The old woman cracked her walking stick hard against the stone floor. The sound was like a shot. "It serves no purpose for you to blame yourself. It is easy to let the gods be guiltless if you find yourself guilty."

"The gods are guiltless in this!" he said. "They have only done what they have always done. They have followed their natures."

"That is only partly true. They have choices within their natures, but it doesn't matter. What does matter is you are here, and you have need of the Peace. Blaming yourself does not help the world, the people, or you. Instead, think what can be done."

"There is nothing to be done!" Ben said, shaking his head.

"Then that is what must be done--nothing, but I do not think it is so. I think what must be done is to speak the Peace."

Ben stared at the old woman with disbelief. "Speaking the Peace has brought the end of the world!" he said.

"Very odd," she said, calmly sipping her brandy again. "I do not feel ended."

"Don't mock me old woman! You know what I mean. The Balance is broken and it means the Over-God will call the judgment."

"No doubt. But as yet, he has not. So speak the Peace until the judgment."

"If I go tramping around the country speaking the Peace, even more poles will go up outside even more cities, and I cannot live with any more blood on my hands."

"Ah," Arna said. "And has your hiding here in Cynar stopped the poles?" She waited until he had shaken his head. "Is that blood not on your hands as much as the other?" she asked, her tone softening a little.

Ben looked at her and thoughtfully bit his lip. The poles outside other city gates weighed heavily on him.

"I have spoken the truth and you know it, therefore you have but one choice," she said and reached for the stone bottle.

"And what is that?" he asked with acid sarcasm. "To have another drink to numb the pain? I tried that on another world. It didn't work. It's one of the things that got this thing on my arm," he nodded at his left forearm.

The corners of the old woman's mouth turned up a little. "The tongue of the Speaker should be sharp," she said. "Sharp enough to speak the Peace to the gods."

Ben's mouth dropped open in disbelief. "Speak the Peace to the gods?" he said with a hollow laugh. "You must be truly tired of living to want the world completely destroyed."

The old woman shrugged off the jab and sipped her brandy. "You say the world is already ended, but it is not. You say the Peace brings death; it does not. The gods bring death. So speak the Peace to them and end death."

"And end the world for true!"

She shrugged again. "The world is already ended. Judgment comes. It is inevitable. There is nothing left now but to continue to the end. So continue, Speaker. There is no going back, so continue."

Ben lifted his hand to his mouth as he turned what she had said over and over in his mind. At last his eyes re-focused upon hers and he said, "I don't know if my tongue is so sharp old woman. Can I speak the Peace to the gods? Do I have power over the gods?"

"I do not know, but if you have, the Peace--the final Peace--will come." The ancient seer smiled with chilly irony for a moment then added, "If you do not, your death will come, which will bring you peace." She drank down the last of her brandy and pushed herself to her feet with her stick. "I must rest now, Speaker," she said and turned toward the door; after a few steps she turned back and pierced him with her eyes. "Peace be with you, Speaker."

Ben swallowed hard and tried to look away from her, but couldn't. "And with you, old woman," he answered her.

She favored him with another of her devastatingly icy smiles, turned, and hobbled out.

After some days of thought Ben had Rema and Borj bring Arna to him. When the three arrived and the old woman was seated with a cup of brandy in her hand, Ben asked Borj, and Rema to sit too. Ben took a deep breath and said, "I will speak the Peace to the gods."

Rema and Borj just stared at him. Arna cackled with satisfied delight.

"Then..." Rema stammered, "are you a god?"

"No. Just a man."

"But..." Rema began.

Ben held up his hand to stop her. "I do not know if it is the right thing to do. The Seer," he nodded at Arna, "believes it is the only thing I can do…"

Arna answered with a nod of her own.

"And who am I to contradict a Seer?" he continued, his words tinted with resignation. "So, I will speak the Peace to the gods if I can figure out how. First I must find a way to stop the poles from being raised. How can I do that?" He looked from face to face--Arna to Borj to Rema.

"Can you not stop them as you did here in Cynar?" Rema asked.

"It took three days to come to Cynar. How long would it take to go back to Nanema? How long to Yanek? We would all die of old age before I reached even a small fraction."

Borj who still possessed of a soldier's mind said, "You could send armies."

"Except I don't have armies."

"Yes you do, Ben Fordham!" Borj insisted. "The pilgrims. There are thousands of them. Send them home as you did at Bakar, but tell them to assault their home cities with the Peace. They will become armies as they march, speaking the Peace along their way."

"These armies won't have the power of the Speaker," Rema objected.

"It isn't needed," Arna said, tapping her stick with excitement. "The cleansing of Cynar was done by the rage of the Speaker at what the gods had done. If other Speakers feel that rage, they can cleanse other cities. As with speaking the Peace, people needed only to be granted the power to do it by the Speaker and it could be done. It is the same with this. Now the Speakers know it can be done, so they can do it."

After some thought Fordham nodded his agreement. "Then I will send out my armies tomorrow," he said thinking, *I am dispatching armies to do my bidding just like the gods before I came.* The thought chilled him to the very marrow of his bones.

~ * ~

Ben, Rema, and Borj stood just inside the pillars of Tarsa's temple and looked out. Rain made everything reflect with wet gray light and made the mob, which eddied and flowed through the square below the temple steps, look like a turbid river.

Despite the chilly rain, thousands had begun gathering in the square before dawn. Word had filtered through the streets that the Speaker was going to appear and give them a message. The relief which greeted this news was so great even the miserable weather could not dampen it.

Ben did not feel the relief. He was weary and his nerves were raw. The nightmares had come again, worse for all of Arna's promise of peace and rest. The gray weather chilled him and he shivered as he looked out at the rain and the waiting people. He was not convinced what he was about to do was the right thing, but he could not think of anything else. He could not just sit in Cynar and let the servants of the gods continue to raise poles and kill Speakers. The very thought made his stomach turn. The thought of sending these people who waited so patiently in the rain out like armies to attack those cities still loyal to the gods made his stomach turn too, but it seemed to be the only choice.

When the morning was as light as it was going to get, Ben stepped from between the pillars. Borj was on his right, slightly behind him, and Rema was on his left. They stood quietly until the crowd noticed them and ceased its murmuring. "Speakers," he began, too softly. He realized it, cleared his throat and started again. "Speakers, there is Peace in Cynar..."

The cheer seemed to start everywhere at once and it built until the pillars of the temple behind him resonated to the sound.

Ben looked and listened and thought, *My God, what have I done?* At last he held up his hands and the crowd began to quiet again.

"There is Peace in Cynar," he began again. "but in other cities there is no peace. In other cities the servants of the gods still pole Speakers. In other villages Speakers still have their tongues cut out so they may not speak the Peace. I am sickened by the pain and death and horror of it, and, since I have cursed you with my Peace, I am sure you are sickened too. Lord Aris will say this torture is for the sake of the Balance. He will say the Peace has all but destroyed the world--has brought the judgment of the Over-God to no more than a breath away, and perhaps it is so. If it is the fault is mine, but Borj," he turned and touched that one's shoulder. "Borj, who was a soldier of the Dark, says Peace is better. Rema," he took her hand. "Rema, who was a servant of the

Light and a healer, says Peace is better. Othway, who died upon a pole outside the gates of this city said, 'though the world end tomorrow because of it, Peace is better.'"

A low growl of agreement rumbled through the crowd like far off thunder.

I do not know if it is true," Ben continued. "But true or not I know the pain and the dying must stop. I know we have the power to stop the pain and the dying. We can command it to stop." He cast his eyes over the crowd. There was no movement, no shuffling of feet, no whispering. Even the children, some babes in arms, were silent in anticipation. The only sound was the oppressive hiss of the drizzling rain. Every face was turned toward him and every eye was focused upon him, and the burden of those faces, of those eyes, weighed so heavily upon him he almost collapsed beneath it.

Rema and Borj, attuned to everything about Ben Fordham, knew his weariness and stepped closer to his side to support him. Then, from the crowd, the bent, fragile figure of Arna hobbled up the steps and took her place with the others, lending him her strength as well.

After a moment Ben said, "You are an army. An army of Peace. You can command Peace now; therefore you must do so. All you pilgrims return to your cities and towns and gather Speakers as you go. Make yourselves into hoards which flow like a tide over the earth, washing away all the spilled blood with your command to Peace. Take the Balance into your hands. Take your fate from the hands of the gods and into your own hands, and as you go, I will go and attempt to speak the Peace to the gods themselves."

A gasp of in-drawn breath greeted this.

"I do not know if I will succeed. I do not know if what I have told you to do is right, and I will not blame you if you decided the Balance of the world is more important than death and pain. I do not know what will happen if we succeed. The Over-God may well decide it is time for the judgment and the end, but this is what I will do. Now you must choose what you will do." He cast his eyes over the crowd once more then turned back into the temple. Rema, Arna, and Borj followed him a moment later.

## Chapter Fourteen

Cynar became a ghost town almost overnight. Though the rain increased from a drizzle to a cold steady down pour, and the river Mychos swelled and beat against the city walls; though the roads became rivers of mud, and the lanes became miry sink-holes, the weather did not dampen the spirits of the army of Peace Speakers. Thousands who had come to the city as pilgrims departed as soldiers, marching out to assault the world with the Peace. Even citizens of Cynar, men, women, and children, abandoned their previous lives and joined the army of Peace.

Ben Fordham and the ever-present Borj stood atop the gate tower from which soldiers of the dark had watched "The Speaker," give water to the dying Othway. They watched the stream of humanity plow through the mud away from the city. Ben prayed to whatever merciful divinity was listening that he had done right.

A figure, bundled against the cold rain, stepped from the narrow door behind the two and shouted, "Speaker!"

Ben turned, prepared to be attacked as after the battle at Bakar. Borj sprang forward to place himself between the attacker and the Speaker.

"Rema told me I could find you here," said the man, throwing back the hood of his cloak to expose blazing red hair and beard to the miserable weather. A long, puckered scar ran from hairline to jawline down the left side of the man's face dividing the eyebrow and the beard. He was showing a mouthful of strong white teeth in a grin which could melt stone.

The man seemed familiar, but Ben could not quite place him. Then it came to him like a flash of lightning. "Rothean!" he shouted and pushed past Borj to throw his arms around the man who had rescued him from the Valley of Voices. The two pounded each other on the back with joy while Borj looked on, not quite knowing how to react.

"I didn't recognize you with that scar," Ben said, leaning back to look into the others face.

"Speaking the Peace can be dangerous to a warrior's health," Rothean said with a laugh.

Ben's smile turned rueful. "I'm sorry,"he began.

"No, no! Do not be sorry. He who gave me this and those with him, saved my life the next day by speaking the Peace to a troop of Tarsa's cavalry while I was still insensible."

"What are you doing here? Is your family with you?"

The grin flew from the big red head's face. "No, my Lord."

Ben winced at the appellation but said nothing.

"I buried my wife at Achema," Rothean went on. "I do not know where my children are. I hope they are mercifully dead. I would not have them in Lady Tarsa's hands, either as playthings or servants."

Ben felt as though he had been kicked in the belly. "What happened, Rothean? Was it because of the Peace?"

"No. It was because of the Balance."

"Oh, God! Your wife wasn't..."

"No," Rothean hurried to say. "She was not poled. There was a time before the Peace, my Lord Speaker, when servants of Light and Dark contended solely for the sake of the Balance. A raiding party of Tarsa's servants swept through Achema. They carried off children and killed any who resisted. I found the village looted and burned when I returned after you spoke the Peace to me."

"I'm sorry, Rothean."

"When I buried Leah, I wanted revenge..."

"And I stole it from you with the Peace..."

Rothean took hold of Ben's wrist with a grip which crushed for the first instant then released to gentle pressure as he shook his head in denial. "You stole nothing, my Lord. I left the ruins of Achema seeking revenge. I was not even armed! After Rayhan I had thrown away my sword, but armed or not I wanted revenge, or so I thought. That is really how I got this," he hooked a thumb up at his scar. "I found a double handful of Tarsa's raiders camped beside the road and charged among them. It was madness! I had no weapon, and I did not know I had the power of the Peace! I think I simply wanted to die, but when one drew his sword and started his cut, my soul cried out. The words flew out of my mouth. It was just like when you spoke on the trail to Rayhan. Thunder, lightning, shaking earth, and the Peace, but even the Peace cannot stop the already committed sword's cut. I had my revenge but it almost killed me."

"Ben Fordham," Borj said, reaching out to touch the Speaker's shoulder.

"Oh Borj!" Ben said with a laugh of delight. "Rothean, this is Borj, former soldier of the Dark. Borj, this is Rothean former soldier of the light. Borj is sort of my self-appointed body guard, Rothean."

Borj offered his hand to Rothean and they shook, but Borj added, "Can we take this discussion indoors? It is cold and wet out here."

Ben looked startled and Rothean laughed. "A true soldier," he said with a nod toward Borj. "Practicalities first."

Borj answered with a crooked smile and a shrug then lifted his hand toward the door.

They stepped into the first wine shop they found which looked as though it still boasted a proprietor. The publican, a tall skinny fellow with a long blond beard, was awe struck that "*The Speaker,*" would stop into his wine shop and was more than willing to bring them wine. He set a pitcher on the trestle table with a smile and a bow. "My Lord Speaker, drink all you want, but after this pitcher you will have to help yourself. The wife and I go to join the army of Peace."

Ben looked at the man and the happiness of meeting an old friend once more disappeared. "You don't have to go, my friend," he said.

"Oh, but we do, my Lord Speaker. You go to speak the Peace to the gods. How can we do less than to speak it to our brother men?" he said.

Ben racked his fingers through his wet hair and nodded. "Then travel carefully, my friend," he said.

The publican smiled and bowed. "With your permission, my Lord," he said, and walked though the door at the back of his shop.

Ben watched his back disappear through the beaded curtain which served as a door between the living quarters and the wine shop. "I hope I haven't sent him and his wife and all those others to their deaths," he said.

Borj shook his head. "Perhaps some will die, but less than are dying on the poles now. The sooner we speak the Peace to the gods the sooner these will be out of danger."

The publican and his wife, a short dark woman with a round figure and a merry face, returned. They were dressed in cloaks against the rain and each carried a travel pack slung over their shoulders.

"My Lord Speaker," the woman said, "we are nothing special I know, but would you allow us..."

Ben knew what was coming and it made his insides churn. He had fought hard against the people's desire to bow down to him and refused many such requests, but how could he refuse after such hospitality. "I am no god," he began, "but if you really want…"

The two fell to their knees and seized each one of his hands and kissed them. "Peace be with you," he said.

"And with you, Speaker," they answered in the way which was becoming ritual among the Speakers. Then they rose and left the shop.

The three sat quietly for a long time until Ben shook off the silence and asked, "So, why are you here, Rothean?"

"Apparently for no reason at all," he answered. "I had a feeling you might have need of a former soldier, but I see you have all the bodyguards you need." He nodded at Borj. Before Ben could say anything Borj said, "You thought wrong, Flame. Your help will be more than welcomed, if not by the Speaker then by me. Even I must sleep."

Rothean's grin flashed like sun from behind clouds. "It is only proper that "The Speaker" have his own personal guard since he has dispatched an army."

"Wait a minute," Ben protested. "Don't I get a say in this?"

As one Borj and Rothean said, "No."

~ * ~

Ben gathered his *Personal Guard* in the common room of the inn where Borj had carried him after the destruction of Tarsa's temple. A former soldier of the Dark, a former soldier of the Light, a Healer, and an old woman Seer--they seemed a pitiful force to be setting out to assault the very gods, and the assault was looking more and more problematic.

"Well, how do we go about this if we can't call them to us somehow?" Ben asked, exasperated. "What, am I just going to march into heaven or wherever they are? Is it even a physical place or is it 'somewhere else' like heaven is supposed to be back on my earth?"

There was no tangle of voices trying to answer him.

At last Rema said, "Lord Aris and all his Flame Keepers always spoke of 'The Home' as if it were a place somewhere here in the world, but I don't know if any mortal has ever been there. I wish we had Leear here to explain the secrets of the Priesthood of the Light. I always had a feeling he and the rest of Aris' priests had some kind of secret. And, like Seers, they do go away somewhere for a time before they actually begin serving as priests."

Ben said, "Aris talked about Tarsa taking me to 'The Home' from the Valley of Voices if Rothean and the raiders hadn't freed me. That makes me think it is a place in this world, but we still don't really know. I mean, maybe Tarsa would have translated me to 'The Home' the same way Mardian translated me here," he shook his tattooed forearm at them. The movement made some stray beam of light glint off something in the Voyager's Mark as though it were metal and Ben looked closely at it for the first time in many days.

The Voyager's Mark was a beautiful piece of work and no doubt about it. It stretched from the bend of his elbow down to his wrist and most of the way around his forearm. Ben remembered the tattoos on Mardian's body. They had impressed him, but those were crude scratches compared to the one on his arm. Now he looked at the Voyager's Mark and tried to decipher the symbols of which it was made. Some of them he understood from asking Rema, and some he understood from knowledge which came from within him. Many of the symbols he 'remembered' from childhood dreams just as he 'remembered' certain places in this world, though he knew he had never seen them before. He had chalked it up to some sort of déjà vu.

Centered on his forearm was a craggy, cloud-wreathed mountain peak. Atop the peak was an open column construction like one of Aris' shrines. Carved into the stone of the mountain directly beneath the shrine was a colonnade of the demon carved pillars Ben had seen in Tarsa's Temples. Golden sun glinted from the blindingly white clouds around the peak. *Olympus,* Ben thought. *Definitely a place where gods would dwell.*

"The Home is a place in this world," he said. "See?" He pointed at the glowing center of the Voyager's Mark. "Do any of you recognize the place?"

All heads moved back and forth in denial.

"Speaker, have you forgotten our first conversation?" Arna asked.

All eyes turned to her. "The Valley of Seers. The rest of the knowledge you need will be there," she said. "Now you know The Home is a place in this world. In the valley they can tell you how to reach it."

Ben knew she was right just as he knew the symbol in the Voyager's Mark was The Home. "All right," he said. "How soon can I go?"

"We can be packed and ready tomorrow morning," Borj said.

"Not we, Borj. Me."

"No!" All of them said at once.

"My Lord Speaker," Arna began in the cold commanding voice of their first meeting. "Do not be a fool. You are The Speaker, but, as you continue to point out, it does not make you a god. You are so burdened with dreams you can barely stand without help. You know almost nothing of the ways of this world. Only the help of Borj and Rema and Rothean has kept you alive thus far. If you leave Cynar alone, you will be dead within a few days and probably not even from the wrath of the gods or for the sake of the

Balance. There are dangers here which can kill you just as dead as sword or pole. These three must go with you. The world hinges upon them as much as it does upon you.

"And what about you, Arna?" Ben asked, the question tinted with bitter sarcasm. "Do you not wish to come along too?"

The old woman's gray eyes became like blades and the laugh which cackled out of her had nothing humorous in it. "I would go with you if I could, Speaker, but the length of my life is used up. I will stay here in the city made derelict by the Peace and wait for the end, either of my life or of the world. Therefore get you on with your doom, so I may get on with mine."

~ * ~

At first they traveled boldly, mingled with those marching out to assault the world, but as they drew farther away from the city of Cynar, the crowds thinned, first to a trickle, then to an occasional traveler, then to almost empty roads--at least empty of friends. Twice they found evidence of ambushes. Groups of travelers they assumed were Speakers had been set upon with arrows and slings. The attackers had given no chance for the travelers to speak the Peace. They had killed from hiding and left the bodies for the scavengers, not taking the chance that one of them might be left alive to snatch them from the service of the gods. But finding those scenes of slaughter was nothing compared to what they found two weeks along the road. As they neared a village called Nohar, the breeze brought a stomach turning stench of death to them. Many poles had been raised along the road some time before the Army of Peace was sent out. Skeletons with a few rags of putrid flesh were all that was left. A flock of vultures squawked and fought of the scant remains and were forced to share what little was left of their horrific food with the ants, flies, and smaller carrion birds.

"Why were they left like this?" Ben asked. "How can the people of the village stand the smell?"

None could answer him until they moved on into the village. In the square at the center of Nohar was the rest of the village population. Another flock of carrion birds, large and small, squabbled over the corpses which had been dumped there. Some of the corpses' mouths were bound but some were not. Some of the dead were not Speakers at all.

"Why?" Ben cried, trying hard not to gag.

Borj shook his head. "The blood thirst," he said. "I have seen it happen in battle, but never like this."

"Is this happening all over the world?" Ben whispered, only a breath from screaming despair.

"This happened before. These have been dead for a long time," Borj said.

"We must go," Rothean said. "They may have left watchers."

"We should bury them," Ben said.

"Yes," Rema agreed.

"We do not have time, Speaker." Borj said. "These dead are long dead. They do not know or care. You must speak the Peace to the gods as soon as you can to help the living remain alive."

Ben swept his eyes over the heap of corpses and the

squawking flock of scavengers, and wiped the cold sweat of barely controlled nausea from his face with his forearm. "You're right. I don't like it but you're right," he said.

They rode on, trying not to hear the flapping wings and raucous cries behind them.

~ * ~

The dreams had never ceased to plague Ben, but after Nohar they became worse. He never slept more than a few minutes at a time and most of the time he was in a sort of pseudo-sleep--not in the dream state but not awake either. He was more like a barely sentient stone balanced upon the horse. The others came to think of him more as some precious cargo rather than a living being. Each of the three took turns riding beside him to keep him from falling out of the saddle but of necessity, most of the chore of tending to him fell to Rema.

"How much farther, Rema?" Borj asked some days after Nohar. It was mid-afternoon and they had stopped to water and rest the horses.

"A week until we begin the trail to the valley. About three days after that if the trail is clear."

"I do not like the way the Speaker looks," Rothean said.

Ben sat leaning against a boulder wrapped tight in his cloak against the cold. His eyes were closed and his breathing was shallow.

"He has no color," Rothean continued. "He eats almost nothing, and he has not said a handful of words for days."

"Between dreams and despair, what would you have him do?" Rema snapped. "Perhaps he should dance about like a puppet for your amusement." She was more tired than she had ever in her life been, sleeping almost as little as the Speaker.

Glancing over at the huddled figure of the Speaker Borj said, "He is one, you know?"

Rema turned on him like a cat protecting her single kitten. "Is what?" she spat.

"A puppet. A puppet of the gods--or of the Over-God."

The other two were taken aback. "He is the Speaker!" Rothean said. "He commands--"

"He has no choice!" Borj said, not taking his eyes off Ben. "Just as he had no choice when Sko and I took him from the tower and threw him over a saddle. Arna of Yanek said he had to work out his doom as she had to work out hers."

Rothean and Rema stared at the former soldier of the Dark and realized he was right; they knew they had no choice either.

Two days later they turned off the main north-south road onto a track which led east and deeper into the mountains. Within hours they had left all signs of human habitation save the track itself which was hardly more than a wide path chiseled into the face of the gray stone cliff. After a time even signs of life became scarce. There was some green, but even it had a look of desperation about it. Every bush seemed to cling to life by only the thinnest of threads.

Ben, in one of his lucid times, looked at the harsh

gray stone and asked, "Why would anyone ever come here? Who built this road?"

"Probably the Seers of old," Rema said. "They are almost the only ones who ever come this way."

Ben shivered because of the cold wind whipping down the canyon and because of the desolation. "The road to exile," he said.

"Only for some," Rema said. "Some Seers pass this way and never return from the valley, but some--healers like me and others like Arna--pass this way in both directions. Few pass it a third time," she said.

"Those who stay in the valley," Ben began and stopped, not sure he really wanted an answer to what he was about to ask. He was afraid he would discover the valley was really a sort of colony for lunatics as such places had been on ancient earth.

"The Seers who stay are of different mind than most."

"You mean they are insane?" he asked and felt despair bubbling up in his chest.

"No--well, perhaps some are for they see and hear things which others do not, but most are of the same mind as everyone else. However, for reasons known only to them and the Over-God, they find it necessary to leave their places and come to the Valley of Seers to live."

"The Over-God?" Ben asked.

"Yes. The Seers of the valley are children of the Over-God."

"What does that mean?"

Rema thought about her answer for a time. "They are

not subject to Lord Aris and Lady Tarsa in the way of other humans."

"Aren't you a servant of Aris."

She nodded and shrugged. "I chose to serve the Light."

"Did that make you subject to the gods more?"

Again Rema thought before she answered. "Perhaps, I have never thought of it before."

"Why are you a Speaker, Rema?" Ben asked.

She looked sharply at him. "You commanded me to Peace, Ben Fordham. Along Rayhan's stream when you commanded Rothean and Othway."

"Still--you were not a warrior. You never lifted a weapon in your life. How could I command you to Peace?"

Rema could not answer him.

The travelers were camped beside a crossroad called 'The Pillars.' The weather had turned bone aching cold though the sky remained clear. The trail they had been traveling continued north. The other trail, so thin it was more like a crack in the canyon wall, climbed through a narrow defile marked off by two towering natural obelisks of granite.

"We will have to leave the horses here," Rema said, her words wrapped in clouds of steam. "Above The Pillars there are places barely wide enough for a person to walk. A horse could never make it."

"If we abandon them here, they will be wolf bait," Rothean protested.

"There is no choice," Rema said. "The Speaker must go on and the horses can't."

They all looked at Ben, wrapped tight in his cloak

against the cold, slumped beside the fire. He was once again in the twilight of not quite sleep yet not quite wakefulness.

"Can the Speaker walk on into the valley?" Borj voiced the concern they all felt.

"He must go to the valley one way or another. Remember what Arna said."

"Then, like it or not, we must abandon the horses and go on," Rothean said. "Borj and I can carry him if need be."

Rema nodded. "I will try to help the Speaker sleep tonight," she said. "Perhaps he will be fit to travel tomorrow."

The other two looked at her skeptically but said nothing.

Rema put a mixture of herbs into a pot of boiling water and removed the pot from the fire the moment after. While the potion steeped she went to Ben. "My Lord," she said softly. He did not react so she spoke louder.

Ben's head came up and he looked around with uncomprehending eyes. After a moment some light of understanding came to him and he said, "Is it time to go on?"

"It is time to sleep, my Lord."

Even the dark and the flickering light of the fire could not disguise the fear which jolted him at her words. "No," he said. "The dreams--leave me alone."

"I have made a potion…" she began.

"They don't work, Rema! They make the dreams worse because I can't wake up from them!"

"This one is different. It will not force you to sleep, only make your body relax so you may slip into sleep. You will be able to wake."

"No, Rema. Please," he begged like a frightened child.

She put her hands one on each side of his drawn, bearded face. "My Lord, you must sleep! If you do not, you will die. I will watch as you sleep and wake you at the first sign of a nightmare."

He gazed into her eyes for a long time then dropped his forehead against her breast. "All right, all right," he said.

Rema held the cup to help Ben drink the steaming, bitter stuff then wrapped herself together with him in their sleeping robes and cloaks. She put her arms around him like a mother holding a frightened child and felt his trembling subside as the relaxant began to work.

The whirlpool dream began the instant Ben slept, but he did not feel the usual choking paralysis of fear this time. Exhaustion and familiarity were like a thick pane of glass between him and the viscous blood, and there was something else too. He felt protected against the hand which reached up to drag him under. Before, he had always swum as hard as he could, trying to get away, but when the hand clutched him this time, he felt no urge to escape. He let himself be dragged under. Usually when the blood whirled over his head he began to feel choked which woke him. This time the blood closed over him and he woke, but there was no horror to it. His eyes opened and he found Rema's arms wrapped tight around him. Her deep slow breaths told him she was asleep, but her hands were locked together in a grip so strong he could hardly move his arms.

Ben breathed in. The chill air was touched with smoke and the scent of horses, slightly musty sleeping robe and the brassy aroma of Rema's breath. There was only the sound of the wind and the crackle of the low burning fire. So peaceful. He did not even realize he was asleep again until the unearthly roaring wind of the approach of Tarsa's cloud brought awareness. He was again in the Valley of Voices chained to the altar. The stomach turning roil of greasy cloud was upon him, but like the whirlpool, this dream was something he watched, not something in which he was trapped.

The cloud engulfed him and he should have been swallowed by fear, but he was not. Something was between the horror of the cloud and himself. He usually woke when the cloud covered him, but this time he did not and after a few seconds the darkness of the cloud opened to a new dream--Lady Tarsa, horned and draped as he had seen her in temple statues stood before him. She was not the huge being of the statues or of the conference with Aris after the battle of Bakar. Here she was of a more human size--a little shorter than Ben's six feet plus--and she was beautiful beyond words--beyond thought. Ben felt his maleness come alive with desire just to be in her presence. To have her kiss, to have her touch, to have her embrace him with arms and legs as her femininity swallowed him! Any man could die from the joy of such ecstasy. Would happily die!

She reached out and stroked her fingers down his cheek and neck then down his naked chest. Her touch was like the smooth heat of warmed oil and when she drew her finger tips around his nipples, the sensual agony of it made him cry out with pleasure and pain. The goddess smiled as his muscles clenched and relaxed against her touch. Her lips were shining wet and slightly parted.

"You could be mine," she breathed as she trailed kisses down his chest and brought her caressing hands lower to his loins. "All you must needs do is leave off thought. Feel only. You may have all." She stepped back and her drape disappeared. Her skin was like the alabaster of her statues, but her flesh was not cold stone. She opened her arms to him and smiled the ancient promise of fulfillment as she showed herself to him. Her breasts were heavy, but firm. Crowned with virginal pink nipples, yet there was nothing else of the virgin about her for the nipples strained up with desire. There was an air of ripe womanhood about them. These breasts were filled with nourishing milk, and more than anything, Ben wanted to suckle them. His eyes traveled down the goddess' perfectly rounded belly to the welcoming golden curls of her pubic triangle. The sight of it was a torture more painful than the chains which bit into his wrists.

"I am yours," Tarsa whispered as she stepped close to him and rubbed herself ever so lightly against him.

There was no resisting. No stopping her. She ripped off Ben's silken breechcloth and pulled her body tight against him. The heat of her was consuming! Irresistible! And Ben's body reacted.

Tarsa laughed deep in her throat with a sound that might have been the feral growl of a she panther in heat, and pulled Ben's maleness into her. Carnal ecstasy began to radiate through him. He was being consumed by an irresistibly beautiful, infinitely fertile woman who was...

A ghastly, vomit breathed, ravenous crone who devoured him both above and below. A vortex of dark which sucked the marrow out of his bones.

Ben struggled to pull away, but he was chained and could not. He could not resist! He was chained...

"Shhh," Rema's soft breath whispered in his ear. Her arms were tight around him, protecting him. "It is only a dream," she whispered. "Only a dream. I am here with you. Sleep, my love."

Ben's eyes opened to the flickering light of the low burning fire and the fog of his breathing on the night chill. Rema's arms were still locked around him, but her breathing told him she was awake. Her soft lips were close to his ear as she whispered and her warm body molded itself against him. He turned himself within her embrace so they were face to face and, without a thought, she brought her leg across his hip to pull him into a protective full body embrace. After a moment she kissed him then cradled his head against her shoulder. He was asleep in moments.

Twice more during the night dreams attacked Ben, but in them he felt himself protected; and each time they reached some climax of terror within the soft steel grip of Rema's embrace. Her warm whisper of assurance insulated him, and each time he woke he found himself still wrapped in her protecting arms.

## Chapter Fifteen

"*All hope abandon ye who enter here,"* Ben thought as he looked at the Pillars looming through the morning fog. Rema said the trail was dangerous enough without fog so they sat around the fire sipping hot tea and waiting for it to clear. Rema and Ben sat side by side, the same cloak wrapped around them both. It was as though Rema was unwilling to release the Speaker from her protection.

"You look more rested this morning, Speaker," Rothean said. "Rema's potion must have worked."

"Her potion and her presence," Ben answered.

Rema blushed.

"I don't know what I would do without her. Without all three of you," Ben said. "I cannot believe I ever considered trying to do this alone. Thank you all."

"Speaker, it is we who thank you," Borj said. "You have brought us the Peace and are tortured in dreams for it."

Ben looked long at each of them and found Borj had spoken what they all believed. He almost said again that this Peace was a dubious blessing at best, but he did not, knowing they would only tell him Peace was better even if it destroyed them all.

Sunlight finally burned through the fog, distilling the air to a bright clarity. The sky ached an icy blue, and the wind whaling down the canyon was sharp enough to freeze blood in the veins.

They traveled with Rema in the lead and Ben between Borj and Rothean. The trail up the cliff face beside the canyon became narrow an hour after they passed between The Pillars. An hour later narrow was far too generous a term for it. The cold wind growling down the canyon made their hands and feet numb and threatened to blow them off the thread of a trail. They had to concentrate on each step lest they find themselves hurtling toward the canyon bottom. Borj and Rothean were silently glad the Speaker was able to walk, for they could not have carried him. There were places where they had to inch along with backs against the canyon wall holding their packs in front of them.

Rema tried to keep an eye on the Speaker, but in truth there was nothing much she could do but worry.

At mid-morning they came to a hollowed out place in the canyon wall where they could rest out of the wind. Rema took the opportunity to examine Ben, feeling for fever and looking into his eyes. Nothing seemed amiss and it worried her more than if he had shown some sign of illness. “How do you feel?” she asked.

Ben smiled. “I’m fine. I’m still tired, but at least I know what is going on around me. There are some days back there I don’t even remember.”

Rema nodded her understanding. “We will repeat the treatment this night,” she said.

Ben lifted his hand to her wind chapped cheek. “I

think you can save your potion. Having you hold me did more good than all the potions in the world."

She took his hand in hers and kissed his palm. "I would that we might sleep together in peace forever, Ben Fordham," she said, blushing. "And I will hold you again this night, but I will also brew the potion and you will drink it."

Ben smiled and shrugged. "All right, if you say so, and if we can find a place big enough to lie down." He looked over the edge of the chasm. "If you sleep a little restless here, it could be fatal."

"There is a traveler's shelter ahead if it has not been swept away by an avalanche. We should be able to reach it before night."

They did not. A little farther along from where they had rested a rock fall had covered the trail, and they were forced to pick their way carefully through the debris. Danger of twisted ankles and broken bones was in every step and it slowed them to a crawl. They reached the shelter only because of desperation. The last hour of travel was lit only by what little moonlight reflected from the canyon walls. They would have stopped on the trail, but there was not enough room to sit down safely much less lay out sleeping robes.

The shelter was where it belonged and the four, exhausted and near frozen by the icy wind, were giddy with relief to find it. The place was made of stone stacked like a half dolman covering a hollow gouged out of the canyon wall. The refuge was well stacked with firewood so they lit a fire and prepared trail meat stew and hard bread. When they had eaten, Rema prepared the sleeping potion.

"I hope this works again," Ben said his earlier

bravado lost to reality and weariness.

"I will hold you tight, Ben Fordham, and wake you at the first sign of a nightmare."

He gave her a half smile and drank the bitter stuff down.

"Good," she said. "Sleep well and tomorrow we will reach the valley."

"I'm not sure if I'm glad or not," he said, feeling the potion radiate from his middle. "I keep thinking this valley is nothing but a place of madmen and maybe I'm on my way there so I can't hurt myself or anyone else. I mean, for all I know I am really still in my world, only I'm in an asylum wrapped in a wet sheet because I am in the middle of a paranoid delusion."

Rema gazed deep into his eyes, wishing she could help him with more than potions and embraces, but there was nothing more she could do so she said, "Sleep now and do not dream, Speaker."

Ben nodded and they lay down.

The usual dreams began almost immediately when Ben slept, but they seemed to have lost their power. His sleeping mind recognized them and disregarded them. When the new dream of captive sexuality presented itself, the goddess became Rema at the moment of change and the conclusion was joyous release, both from the imprisoning altar and the sexual tension. Ben sensed a feeling of frustration coming from outside him. Things had not gone the way they were supposed to have gone. Ben was supposed to have been possessed by terror not joy. The malevolent power was confused and it retreated.

Ben woke to find himself still safe in Rema's arms. Her sleeping breath whispered in his ear and the tiny sounds of Borj and Rothean's sleep added depth to the quiet darkness. The fire had burned low, but the hut was still warm. He could hear the wind howling up the canyon outside, and the sound of it made him shiver, but at least it was a real thing not a thing of dreams. Ben tried to turn carefully, but the movement woke Rema.

"My Lord?" she asked.

Her beautiful face was inches from his. Her body was molded protectively against him, her golden eyes reflected the warm flickering of the fire, and he sank into the depths of them. The vision of her from the dream was still in his mind, still in his body, and he could not stop himself from kissing her.

Rema responded. Her lips were soft and moist, sweet and warm as a spring morning. "I dreamed," he whispered, "and you came to save me. I love you Rema. I want you. I want to be with you forever."

"Oh my Lord, I have loved you from the first moment I saw you. I am yours until the end of the world." They made love, slow, gentle, and quiet then they slept.

Ben was upon the slope of a rounded hill, bare of trees and bushes--even of grass. A blade sharp wind brought the reek of spilled blood and bowels down on him. Bile rose in his throat as memory of the dead in Nohar came to his mind. On the crest of the hill four poled bodies were silhouetted against the brassy sky. Ben gagged at the sight and smell and tried to look away, but in every direction he looked he found the four poles. An invisible hand dragged him to the top of the hill and threw him to the ground beneath the poles. Ben tried to cover his head with his arms to shut out the sight and the stench, but the invisible hand would not allow it. His head was pulled up and his eyes met Othway's. The little thief stared down at him with accusing eyes.

The horror and guilt and helplessness which had engulfed Ben outside Cynar's walls came again to tear at his bowels. He turned his eyes away from Othway, but found himself looking into another accusing pair of eyes. Rothean's. The big red bearded warrior was in a paroxysm of agony, but despite the pain he whispered, "Your Peace is torture and death!"

Beside Othway and Rothean were Borj and Rema and all four of them cried out, "Your Peace has killed us all!"

Ben wept and tried to hide his face. "No!" he denied. "No, no, no! I did not do this!" but Othway was truly enough dead on a pole outside the gate of Cynar. He had died in agony telling Ben with his last breath to speak the Peace..."

Yes. Telling him to speak the Peace! Not condemning him for having done so. *The Peace preserves. It doesn't destroy and death cannot change that!*

A voice, or was it a thousand voices, whispered on the wind. "Peace," they breathed. "Peace be with you, Speaker."

A wash of anxiety, which was not his own, flowed over him.

An ember of the fire popped and Ben opened his eyes. The dream was gone and rays of gray daylight filtered through the crevices between the stacked stones of the shelter. Ben turned in Rema's sheltering arms, but this time she did not wake. It had not been her voice in the dream. *Then whose?* He wondered. *Whose?*

The Valley of Seers was bowl shaped--the remains of an ancient volcano, so huge the opposite side of the crater was blue with distance. A pall that reminded Ben of Los Angeles smog hung over it as though the volcano might still be active, but Rema said it was not. "Steam still spews out of the ground in some places to mix with the smoke, and the ground still shakes sometimes, but there has not been an eruption within memory."

They stood upon a platform carved out of the rim of the crater. To the left of the platform was a dolman-shaped traveler's rest like the one from which they had begun their climb that morning. It marked the ending place for the trail up from the travelers' shelter and the beginning place for a course of stairs which led down the inside of the almost vertical wall of the crater. The stairs disappeared into the haze far below them.

"Where does the smoke come from?" Borj asked.

"Manufactories and hearth fires," Rema said.

"There must be thousands of them."

"Yes."

"What do they do?" Rothean asked.

"They wait," a voice, deep and raspy, but feminine said from inside the travelers rest. In a heartbeat Borj and Rothean's warrior reflexes brought them to guard positions between the Speaker and the voice.

A woman, not old, but not young either, stooped and came out of the shelter. She was tall like Rema, with gray streaked black hair gathered in a knot at the back of her head.

She looked like a strict, but loving schoolteacher.

"Nora!" Rema cried, her voice full of joy.

"Peace be with you, Rema…"

Ben's glance sharpened at the greeting.

"…And with you, Speaker." Nora went on. "And also with Borj and Rothean who are warriors but not warriors." She smiled with a pointedness that told much about her sense of humor.

Borj and Rothean eased their readiness a little, but did not relax or move from between the Speaker and the woman.

"It was your voice in the dream last night wasn't it?" Ben said.

"Mine and thousands of others, Speaker. Thousands who know the Peace and return it to you."

"Another seer, Arna, wished me peace back in Cynar, but so far her wish hasn't helped much."

Nora's black eyes pierced him. "Arna promised you peace, but to have it in dreams as on earth, you must command it."

"Command it?"

"It is yours to command. Command it."

Ben thought on what she had said for a moment then asked, "What are they waiting for, Nora? The Seer's of the Valley."

"You, of course," she answered, still smiling and not at all confused by the change of direction.

"Me? Rema led me to believe there have been Seers in this valley for a long time--a lot longer than I have been in this world."

"That is true."

"Yet you are waiting for me? All of you?"

"Yes."

"Why?"

Nora took a step toward the Speaker. Borj and Rothean hesitated to let her pass them, but after a moment they separated and Nora walked between them. She gently took his left wrist and turned his arm so the Voyager's Mark showed. "This is you," she said, touching the picture of the broken wheat sheaf. "This is the Valley of Seers." She touched a part of the tattoo which looked like a field of ripe wheat. She looked up into Ben's eyes. "You are here to harvest the wheat of this valley," she said. "To bind it into sheaves."

"Why? Why me? And why is my sheaf broken?"

"Each straw is a life and many lives have been broken because of you," she answered, not accusingly only stating a fact, "and more, the broken sheaf means a breaking of the old ways. It is a sign of ending."

"Ending?" It was like a blow which drove the breath from his body. "I've brought the end of the world, haven't I? I have destroyed you all."

Nora shook her head. "You have brought the harvest. As for destruction...," she shrugged. "That is for the Over-God to say. We are, however, set toward a doom because of you.

"Come, I have hot porridge and tea inside. We must reach the valley floor before dark. The steps are treacherous enough in daylight."

"What of the Balance, Nora?" Rema asked as they ate. "Aris and Tarsa have joined. The Balance is destroyed, is it not?"

Nora shrugged. "The polings have stopped. There is an uneasy truce between Dark and Light. It is a Balance, but not as of old." She fell silent for a time. "Perhaps there is a new Balance. Perhaps the gods and their servants are on the one side and the Speaker is on the other."

"Then, if I stop now--if I leave this world--if someone in this valley can send me back to my world..."

Nora shook her head. "Only the Over-God can send you back." She hesitated a moment, looking from Ben to Rema and back. "I think you do not really wish to return to that other world now," she said. "It was not truly your world, was it? You did not fit there either, and there are those here who hope this world is a better fit than the other."

Ben could suddenly feel Rema sitting close beside him, and the thought of being parted from her almost pulled the heart out of his chest. Without her he would have died. Without her he would die. "No," he said at last. "I didn't fit there either, and I have nothing to go back there for, even if I could."

Nora nodded.

"But the Balance...if I stay here in the Valley, won't that preserve this new Balance?"

Nora's eyes bored into him. "You cannot stop, Speaker. No more now than when you first spoke the Peace beside Rayhan's stream. The doom is set. Now the only choices you or any of us have left are which roads to take to reach it. If you do not go on, if you stay in the valley, the doom will be reached by some other means. It will come, one way or another, so think of all that has passed, before you think of hiding here."

When she fell silent, it was like a clap of thunder and in the echoing silence Ben remembered how hiding in Cynar had not stopped the poles from being raised. "What is this doom?" he asked after a little. "What is the end?"

"I do not know. Seers know only what they can see. What the Over-God lets us see. I and many others have seen the doom, but we do not know what it is, only that it is."

"I can see a part of it," Borj said. All eyes turned to him

"Have you become a seer then?" Nora asked with a half smile and a lifted eyebrow.

"No. I am only a soldier. A warrior for the Peace, and a warrior knows battle is in his destiny. We set out to bring the Speaker to the gods so he might speak the Peace to them. That is a part of our doom I can see."

"And if I can't?" Ben asked.

"Then the Over-God will make another choice," Nora said.

"Then there is another doom?" Rema asked.

Nora smiled again. "If the Over-God wills it," she said. "Come now. We must go."

Not far down the stairs into the valley the wind which had scourged the travelers for days disappeared. A little farther down they passed through the layer of haze and the panorama of the valley spread out below them. The floor of the valley appeared nearly flat except in the center. There a rising like a navel, or perhaps more like the center of a splash when a stone is dropped into the water, rose. "That is Hollow Mountain," Rema told them. Surrounding the mountain was a tight packed group of thatch-roofed buildings and surround the town was a patchwork of farm fields.

Afternoon had advanced to dusk by the time they reached the valley floor. At the bottom of the stairs a path led toward the Hollow Mountain. It widened as they traveled down it and soon a few houses began to line it. When the five passed the houses, it was as though some alarm had rung for each door flew open and spilled forth everyone who had been inside. By the time they were halfway to the Hollow Mountain a crowd trailed them. Those who followed along kept a respectful distance at first, but there was an electricity about them Ben could feel. They wanted to swarm over him and touch him as the people of Bakar and Cynar had. They wanted to bow to him and the knowledge was like a stone in his stomach.

Soon the noise of the crowd was so loud it announced them like a fanfare. Houses they had not yet reached spilled forth their people and the road was jammed. This new mob had none of the restraint of the first people who had followed them. Hundreds of hands reached out toward Ben and if they could not touch "The Speaker," they settled for touching "A Speaker" and progress slowed to a crawl.

Whether Nora signaled for them or not Ben could not tell, but from somewhere a dozen husky young men formed themselves into a phalanx around the little group and began to wedge through the crowd a little more easily.

Darkness fell as they approached Hollow Mountain. By then they had all been touched so many times the slightest brush was painful, but all thought of pain disappeared when lights began to snake back and forth up the slopes of the mountain ahead of them.

Hollow Mountain was not really a mountain at all; it was a lava flow which had formed in the center of the ancient volcano. The dome had swelled to more than a thousand feet high and at least five miles in diameter. Tiered paths had been cut into it from bottom to top and now people with torches marched rank on rank up the tiers until the mountain looked like a massive Christmas tree alight with a thousand candles.

As the Speakers drew closer the need for the phalanx grew less. The crowd did not thin, but it seemed to give way before them until they stepped out of the mass onto a flat plaza at the foot of the mountain. Before them, across the plaza, was a huge double door like that used to close a city's gate. It was bound with bronze strips and looked sturdy enough to resist a battering ram. When they were clear of the crowd, they stopped to look back. Rema stood beside the Speaker holding his hand. Nora stood on his other side and Borj and Rothean, alert and protective, stood near by. The crowd was like a sea lit by flickering torches and lamps. It looked as though every person in the valley had jammed the area around the lava dome.

"Speaker," someone from the crowd called out. "Speak the Peace to us before you go into the mountain."

Ben swept his eyes over the crowd. "Peace is already in this valley. I can feel it. Why do I need to speak the Peace in a place where it already is? Here there will be peace forever."

Many voices cried out, "Not so, Speaker! Not so!"

Another anonymous voice came from the crowd.

"We will continue forever in peace only when you command the gods to peace, Speaker."

A chill of fear sliced through Ben Fordham--a chill of doubt. "I do not know if I can speak the Peace to the gods," he said.

A murmur of questioning and denial rose and after a moment Ben held up his hands for quiet. When it came he said, "I do not know, but as soon as I learn the way to the Home I will go there and try."

A collective sigh of satisfaction came from the crowd and Ben felt the crushing weight of their hope--the bone rattling fear of perhaps not being able to live up to it, and the twisted thought that even if he could speak the Peace to the gods it would accomplish nothing except destruction. Nevertheless, it seemed he had no choice but to continue. Nora had talked about doom, as had Arna the ancient Seer from across the sea. "Get you on with your doom so I may get on with mine," she had said. No matter his doubts or fears he was left with no choice but to get on with it.

"All of you go home and rest now," he said. "I only hope this doom I am told is mine will not prove to be the end of all here. Peace be with you." He did not wait for an answer from them or to see if they obeyed but turned toward the doors which led into Hollow Mountain.

The caverns inside the mountain were not like those Ben had seen before. Here there were no stalactites or other water sculpted formations. The honeycomb of tunnels was mostly ancient lava tubes, but there were also many passages which had been painstakingly chipped through the solidified lava. Nora led through the torch lit corridors, turning and turning at many intersections until none of them could have found their way out again.

At last they stepped from the maze into a gigantic, echoing chamber lit red-gold by a thousand oil lamps. It was many yards across and a hundred feet tall with a sand floor which sloped from the walls down to another swollen lava dome in the center of the chamber. It was about twice as tall as Ben was.

"There is your chart, Speaker," Nora said and pointed at the frozen lava bubble in the center of the chamber. The room was covered from top to bottom with pictographs, but it was a map--a map Ben had not the vaguest idea how to read.

"It shows the circle of the earth," Nora said and stretched up to touch a place almost too high for her to reach. "We are here. At the base is the ocean which surrounds the land. Here," she stooped to touch some pictures just above the blue section which represented the sea. "Here are the plains."

"I don't understand, Nora," Ben said. "Where is the Home?"

"There," she pointed at the top of the bubble, "The center of the earth's circle, amid the barren lands.

Ben shook his head. "I still don't understand."

"It is all right, Speaker," Rothean said. "I understand."

Borj, standing beside Rothean nodded his own understanding.

"I will trust you then. You haven't failed me yet."

The plaza outside the mountain was dark and empty

when they returned. There was an eerie silence where only a little while before there had been the murmur and shuffle of the crowd.

"Where did they all go?" Ben asked.

"Home, as you commanded, Speaker. They have gone to consult their visions and wait."

"It could still be a long time--maybe months. It is a long time to wait."

Nora shook her head. "You are wrong, Speaker. The time is short. We have waited long, but now...," she shrugged. "A few more weeks. A few more months. Soon." She turned and walked away saying, "Come. You must rest well tonight. Tomorrow is the beginning of the end."

Ben watched Nora's form fading into the dark and thought, *I hope that is only a manner of speaking,* before following the Seer.

The dreams appeared, and at first Ben was terrorized, but as Rema held him he realized the dreams were just dreams. He also remembered what Nora had said, "Peace in dreams, as on earth, is yours only if you command it." *Yes, they are my dreams and I can command them.* The thought caused anxiety to radiate like that which he had felt when the voices had spoken the Peace in the other dream. The gods...

Ben was again at the foot of the round hill, but now instead of four poles there were thousands, and each pole bore a dead Speaker. After a moment of dread, terror, and guilt, Ben shouted, "No! This is not true! This is a dream and if I can command Peace on earth, I can command it in my dreams."

The radiant anxiety became fear! The gods were

afraid--afraid of him! Afraid of the Peace! Ben laughed with relief then he ceased laughing and said, “Peace be with you!” He swept his eyes over the poles then lifted his hand and swept it from side to side. “Peace be with you all!” he said and the poles were gone. “You gods! You gods! Peace...”

And the dream was gone.

## Chapter Sixteen

The morning was clear and cold. Nora, carrying a bag of torches, led them around Hollow Mountain to another, smaller set of bronze bound doors than those by which they had entered the mountain the day before. "These have not been opened for many years," she said. "It will probably take the strength of all of you to open them now. Inside, you will find a cavern corridor which spirals downward. You cannot lose your way; there are no turnings. At the other end you will meet another door. It is barred on the inside. Open the door and leave it open. The time for protecting this valley is ended.

"Take these," she extended the bag of torches to Ben. "You can get horses in Doran at the bottom of the mountain," she said, looking over each of them as if to memorize their faces. "Go carefully. The doom is set, but the gods will not accept it until it is forced upon them."

"They are afraid," Ben said. "They came to me in dreams last night and I remembered what you said about commanding Peace in my dreams. I spoke the Peace and they were afraid. They fled."

Nora nodded. "And because they are afraid they are more dangerous than before. There may not be any more poles raised, but the gods still wish all of you dead, especially you, Speaker. Go carefully."

She waited for acknowledgement of the advice, and when all had nodded their understanding, she put her arms around Rema and whispered something to her. Rema's face took on a look of utter astonishment and she began to say something, but Nora stopped her. "It is so," Nora said. "And it is in the hands of the Over-God."

After a moment Rema nodded and Nora turned to the others. She embraced each of them, hugging Ben last. "Think of the harvest, Speaker," she said. "Do not be afraid of the doom. No matter what happens Peace is better."

"I hope you are right, Nora," he answered.

~ * ~

The Speakers reached Doran and found horses and supplies just as Nora had told them. They also found a population in turmoil. Speakers of the Army of Peace had come to the city so Peace reigned, but there were still those who served both the gods. These did not chance direct attacks on the Speakers for fear of being struck with the Peace. Instead they attacked subtly. They had begun whispering that Ben Fordham was dead--that he had been killed in an ambush. This was a lie not easily believed, but as time had passed with no word of the Speaker, the lie had taken on the patina of possibility. Speakers of the Peace said it was a lie and even went so far as to say, "It matters not at all whether Ben Fordham is living or dead. We speak the Peace! There is no longer need to die at the behest of the gods!"

Then The Speaker came to Doran. The lie collapsed and the city erupted with celebration which was enough to delay the departure of the Speaker, but, added to that, there were three assassination attempts which produced three new Speakers and a new scar on Borj's leather armor.

More than half the population of Doran tried to follow the travelers when they departed. Ben sent them home, but all of it took time, patience, and strength.

At mid-morning two days north of Doran the travelers rode though rolling hills splashed with the blazing color of late fall woods. The day was quiet and warm as autumn fought its final battle against the on coming winter. Time, tension, and miles of road had worn on them all and the day was like an elixir against weariness. "How long will the journey take us from here?" Ben asked.

"It depends, Speaker," Rothean answered. "This road is wide and well traveled. If we do not meet with any more celebrations as in Doran, we should reach Amlek within two weeks. The city is on the edge of the wasteland. Beyond that...," he shrugged. "The chart from Hollow Mountain shows the wasteland as about as wide as from here to Amlek, but I do not know how easy the travel will be."

"If the land is like the wasteland to the south," Borj said, "the way will be hard. There will be no water and little fire wood."

"We'll deal with the trials as we encounter them," Ben said. For the first time since coming to this world of the gods he felt he was doing the right thing and nothing could stop him. The beautiful day, the closeness of the three people with him, the comfortable rolling gate of the horses, all blended together to lift his spirits to a more positive plain than it had reached for a long time.

"Ben Fordham…" Borj began then stopped, not wanting to bring up anything to destroy the peace of the day.

"Go ahead, Borj."

He thought about it for a moment then shrugged. "My Lord Speaker," he said, ignoring the wince the title always produced in Ben. "Have you considered how we will reach the gods when we come to the Home?"

Ben blinked at the former soldier of the Dark. He had not thought of anything past getting to the Home.

"A fine question," Rothean agreed with a nod. "The gods fear you. I doubt they will throw open their gates at our knock."

Ben looked from one to the other, waiting for them to go on, but they didn't. "All right," he said after a little, "I understand the problem, but I don't have a solution. I am open to suggestions."

Borj scratched thoughtfully at the mat of beard upon his throat. "If we had an army..." he began.

"No!" Ben said

"Not that it matters," Rothean said. "We do not have an army."

"Crowds have tried to follow us from each village," Borj said.

"Those were mobs, not armies. Using them as armies could just get a lot of people hurt."

"No more than those in the Army of Peace," Borj said.

"That was different," Ben said. "They didn't set out to assault the Home of the gods."

"I agree with the Speaker," Rema said.

"No one need be hurt," Borj said.

"In the middle of a siege?" Ben snorted. "How could anybody get hurt in the middle of a siege?"

"Borj is right, Ben Fordham," Rothean said. "The gods will probably make no resistance to an army of Speakers set against them. They dare not. They know every sword set against us can suddenly be struck down with the Peace, so they will set no sword against us."

The rain of arrows was almost silent as it fell on them. The sound of the shafts piercing the air was more like bird song than the hiss of death. Arrows sprouted from each of the Speakers as if by magic, and those missing the Speakers struck the horses and set them bucking and kicking in pain.

Ben was unseated at the first jump, and he landed hard just as his pain-maddened horse wheeled and kicked. One of the hooves glanced off the side of his head knocking him unconscious and slamming him hard against the ground. The shafts of three arrows, one in his shoulder, one in his thigh, and one in his calf, snapped off under the impact, jamming the heads deeper into his body. The horse bounded a few steps farther and went down still kicking and screaming.

The surprise was so complete it gave the hidden bowmen time enough to draw and release a second flight before the Speakers, all wounded, reacted and spoke the sky shattering, earth shaking command to Peace.

Even as they spoke the Peace, Rema, Borj, and Rothean dove from their bucking, plunging horses to try to protect the Speaker. The silence of the Peace crashed down. Ben's horse thrashed and screamed in its death throes then fell silent, leaving only the gasp and wail of weeping which came from the ambushers struck down by the Peace. However, even the Peace could not stop the arrows already in flight. Some of them thudded with little harm against Borj's body armor, but Rothean and Rema had no armor.

After a moment Rema and Borj rose, still stunned by the suddenness of the ambush, and looked around. "You are bleeding, Rema," Borj said.

She examined herself quickly to find she had several bleeding nicks and one arrow lodged in her cloak. The worst wound was in her thigh. An arrowhead had sliced the muscle open, but not stuck. "Nothing too much. And you--are you hit?"

"Scratches. Rothean?"

They turned to find Rothean's body stretched beside the Speaker. An arrow stuck out of his back.

Rema reached out and held her fingers against Rothean's neck for a moment then shook her head at Borj's questioning look. She took her hand away and clenched it the same way she clenched her emotions closed so the tears stinging her eyes did not fall. She turned to the Speaker.

The side of Ben's head was already swelling and turning blue-black where the hoof had grazed him. Rema carefully checked the pulse in his neck.

"Is he…?" Borj began.

"Alive," she answered. "Come. Help me. Let us get off the road."

Borj glanced at Rothean's body then looked away

quickly, trying not to think of how many other dead friends he had seen. "Where?" he asked.

Rema's eyes landed on a huge cedar tree which stood out like a dark green blaze amid the red and gold of the woods. Its intertwined branches drooped into a natural shelter.

"There," she pointed. "Go gently and watch his head."

~ * ~

Ben opened his eyes and closed them again. His head hurt. Then he remembered--a guy with a hammer. *Yeah. Santa Monica Blvd. Right! Yeah, the fire. That's right. You didn't stay out of trouble again, did ya?* He could almost hear his father's voice saying, "…and it wasn't even your fight…"

*And Maggie! Oh my God! Maggie. She is gonna be so mad! She'll kill me!* He let the thought go. It made his head hurt worse. *So, this must be a hospital or something.*

He opened his eyes and pain lanced through his skull, but he managed to squint against it this time. After a moment his vision cleared, but he was puzzled by what he saw. There seemed to be a weaving of dusty sunbeams and dark green branches not far above his face. *What the hell? What kind of hospital is this?*

Then it all came back to him and he tried to sit up.

"Lie still, my Lord," Rema commanded holding her hand against his chest. "You will start bleeding again."

"Bleeding? Oh, yeah, the arrows. My head hurts."

"Your horse threw you and kicked you in the head.

Lucky it was only a graze."

"No wonder I have a headache. I thought I was back in the hospital on earth after the guy tried to brain me. Good thing I have a hard head." He fell silent for a moment then asked, "How's the horse?"

"Dead, my Lord."

"Oh. Poor thing. Everyone else?"

Rema looked away. "One of the bow-men broke a wrist when the Peace struck him down."

"That's not so bad. A broken wrist. Everybody else is all right then?"

Rema's face was stony and she did not answer.

Her face told Ben there was more. "Who else?" he demanded.

She drew a ragged breath and said, "Rothean."

"Oh." Dread crept into the center of Ben's chest. "Is he hurt bad?"

Rema bit down hard on her emotions. Tears stung the corners of her eyes, but she could not let them fall yet. "He is dead, my Lord," she said.

"Dead?" Ben knew the word, but somehow he couldn't make any since of it. "How?"

"An arrow pierced his heart, my Lord. He died quickly." Tears began to trickle down her cheeks no matter how hard she fought them.

What she said still did not make sense to Ben. Rothean could not be dead. He was a warrior for the Peace. He couldn't be dead. "No," Ben said softly. "No," he said again and tried to sit up against Rema's restraining hand. She pushed him back down.

"Please, Ben Fordham, your head. Lie still. You will hurt yourself worse. And there is still an arrowhead in your leg. Moving around could make it dig in deeper."

He stopped struggling for a moment and lay back, but after a moment he shook his head though the movement gave him pain. "It doesn't matter," he said and pushed himself up on his elbows. Rema tried to restrain him again, but he took her hand off his chest. "I must see Rothean," he said. "Where is he?"

"He is dead, my Lord."

Ben shook his finger back and forth in denial, as though fending off her words. "I must see Rothean," he said. There was a spark of madness in his eyes and it frightened her.

"You cannot, my Lord," she said, trying to stop him, but the strength of his madness was unstoppable. "Please," she begged him. "Your head. And you will open your other wounds again."

"Where is he?"

"Borj and some of the others have gone to bury him."

"No," Ben denied, wagging his finger again, his madness growing from spark to flame. He crawled out through the branches with Rema right behind him. He stood, tottering and swaying, his hands squeezing the sides of his head as though to keep it from bursting open.

Down the slope at the side of the road the bowmen who had ambushed the travelers sat. They turned at the sound of Ben's coming through the branches and stood when they recognized him. Ben glanced at them but did not take notice. He had only one thing in his mind. "Where is Borj?"

He demanded through teeth clenched against the pain in his head.

Rema, with an arm around him trying to steady him said, "I don't know." Already blots of fresh blood marked the dressings on his wounds.

He straightened and shouted, "Borj! Where are you?" His sight dimmed with pain reaction tears, and his knees buckled. Rema grabbed him around the waist and kept him from falling.

Borj stepped from among the trees on the other side of the road and said, "Here, my Lord."

Ben blinked his eyes clear and pulled away from Rema. He limped toward the former soldier of the Dark. The crowd of soldiers parted and Ben pushed through without noticing them. Rema followed and the soldiers closed in behind them. "Where is he?" The Speaker demanded his voice thin but not to be denied. "Where is Rothean?"

Borj looked from the Speaker to Rema and back. After a moment he turned and said, "Here," and walked back into the trees.

Ben and Rema followed him and the soldiers followed a little behind them. A few steps from the road through a screen of trees in a tiny clearing two soldiers stood in a knee-deep hole. One held a stick which had been sharpened for use as a digging tool; the other used a large flat piece of bark as a spade. A heap of dirt was on one side of the hole and Rothean's body, wrapped in a cloak, was on the other side.

The gravediggers recognized the Speaker and dropped to their knees, but Ben took no notice of them and went to the bundle. The other soldiers stopped at the edge of the clearing.

Ben stood over Rothean's body for a moment then dropped to his knees and lay forward with his hands and face on the bundle. His shoulders shook with sobs.

All the new made Speakers stood like statues, torn with guilt, knowing they were the cause of the Speaker's agony.

Rema knelt beside him. Her heart felt each of his sobs as though they were her own and wished with all her being she could take his pain away. She put her arm across his broad shoulders and felt the shaking of them. "Please, my Lord," she whispered. "He is dead. Please come away. You will hurt yourself more."

"No," he denied and sat back on his hams. "This cannot be!" He pulled the tight wrapped cloak open and pushed the hood away from Rothean's face.

"Please, Ben Fordham," Rema begged. "Stop. He is dead. Stop it!"

"He is not dead, Rema!" Ben shouted. "It is a dream! Just like before. It is a dream!"

Rema put her hands on his chest, trying to calm him. She could see the madness in his eyes--could see the madness would swallow him up so that his mind would never return.

"He is not dead, Rema! It is a dream!" he shouted again then through clenched teeth, "A dream."

With the suddenness of a candle being blown out, the hot madness was gone from his eyes. A semblance of calm, of chill control, which was really only a shield against reality, took its place. "He is only resting," Ben said with stern reasonableness. "He spoke the Peace and it always makes you tired. Now he needs to rest. We are in his dream as you were all in my dream"

"No, my Lord," Rema denied, her voice thick with fear, tears streaming down her cheeks.

"Yes! See? Watch, I'll wake him now." Ben turned back to the too still body on the ground and began to stroke the flaming red beard. "You have rested a little now, Rothean," he said. "...but you can't rest long. We have to go on. We have to, so maybe you had better wake up now. Come on. The Peace is with you so you can wake up now. Come on. Wake up. Live, Rothean…"

Rema tried to pull Ben away, but he threw her arms off and laid his hands upon Rothean's chest. "Live Rothean," he said softly. "The Peace preserves, it does not destroy, and I need you still, so you must live."

And Rothean took a breath.

Every sound in the world ceased. No noise of insect or rustle of wind or sigh of in-drawn breath or shuffle of feet broke the stillness until Rothean's chest expanded a second time. He breathed in another long, slow, deep breath of the crisp air and his eyelids flickered open to show eyes still vibrant with laughter and more deep blue than the sunny sky.

A gasp and murmurs of, "He was dead…," and, "The Peace preserves…," rose from the group of former soldiers.

Rothean lifted his hand and brushed a tear from Rema's cheek then looked at Ben. "You must rest now, my Lord," he said. "All is well."

The Speaker took a deep breath and pushed himself, swaying, to his feet. He put his hands to his head, trying to hold in the pain. "My head hurts, Maggie," he breathed and crumpled into Rema's arms.

~ * ~

When Ben came too this time he knew where he was, or at least what world he was in. He didn't recognize the stone hut he was in or the bed he lay on, but he knew it wasn't a hospital on earth--or at least he thought he knew. He had a memory of the ambush and or Rothean's death, but then again he seemed to remember Rothean, Borj, and a bunch of others picking him up.

The leather flap which served as a door to the hut opened and Rema came in carrying a large wooden bowl. She did not look toward Ben, but hurried to the side of the hut where she put the bowl on a rough table. She was closed into herself, her back hunched and her arms held tight against her sides.

*She looks so tired and thin,* Ben thought. "Rema--" His voice sounded creaky to him

Rema spun toward him so fast she stumbled against the table. "My Lord," she breathed.

"I wish you wouldn't call me my Lord," he answered, sounding more cross than he had intended.

"Oh, my Lord," she breathed again, and made the two steps between the table and the bed in one leap. She fell to her knees beside the bed and gathered him to her breast as though he weighed no more than a child.

Ben put his arms around her in return and felt the tremors of her happy tears.

"It's all right, Rema," he said, stroking her hair. "It's all right. Don't cry."

"Oh, my Lord, we thought you were lost. It has been so long. After you called Rothean back we feared…feared you would never awake!"

"Called Rothean?"

Rema leaned back and looked deeply into his eyes, seeking any hint he was still delirious. She found nothing except confusion. "You truly do not remember?"

"I remember the ambush, and I seem to remember you told me Rothean was dead then I seem to remember Rothean telling me to rest. I'm confused."

"Do you remember the horse kicked you?"

He lifted his hand to his head. "Yes. It was here, right? Must not have been much though. It isn't even sore."

"Because it has been two hands of days since it happened."

"Two...you mean I've been unconscious for ten days?" he asked, not disbelieving, but astonished.

"Not unconscious the whole time but not in your right mind either. You would wake enough for me to feed you broth or a little gruel, but you were never really aware."

Ben was stunned and his perception of the world suddenly dimmed and tilted a little disconcertingly.

Rema felt the change and laid him back down on the bed. With her hands free, she wiped at her tear stained face and blew her nose.

Ben tried to understand what she had just told him, but the information would not click into place so he left it alone and asked, "Where are we?"

"Manek. It was a road garrison for Lady Tarsa's troops."

"Was? What is it now?"

Rema shrugged. "A place of Peace."

"Peace?"

Rema shrugged again. "This was the closest place with shelter, so we brought you here."

"And they just opened the door and let us walk in?"

"Almost. The guard called down, 'Who are you?' when we stopped outside the wall, and Rothean answered, 'I am Rothean, who was dead and am now alive. Open in the name of him who called me from the dead.' That was all it took. The gate opened and we came in." She suddenly remembered the others and popped to her feet. "I must tell Rothean and Borj," she said, and without another word she was out of the hut, leaving Ben to stare after her open mouthed.

*Did she really just tell me I called Rothean back from the dead?* he wondered, but did not have time to sort it out before Borj, Rothean, and about a hundred cheering, shouting people he didn't know all tried to jam into the hut at once.

~ * ~

Ben felt able to travel within a couple more days, but Rema would have none of it.

"Besides being kicked in the head you lost much blood," she said. "You must rest a few more days at least. You need to eat and drink properly, not just the little I could force down you."

"Nora said time was short," he protested.

"Short or long, it will do no good for you to collapse halfway across the barren land," Borj said.

"Yes indeed, Speaker," Rothean agreed. "You may be able to raise the dead, but none of us can, so it will be better to lose a few days here."

Ben looked silently at the three of them. They and the others he had talked to here all insisted he had called Rothean back from the dead, and they would brook no denial from him so he stopped denying it. He still did not believe it, but he stopped denying it. No one called dead men back to life."

Later the four returned to the same discussion they had been having before the ambush. "Perhaps you were right, Speaker," Borj said. "Perhaps we do not need an army. The gates of Manek flew open at a word from Rothean. Perhaps the gates of the home of the gods will do the same at a word from you."

"And if they won't?"

"Then you will do something else," Rothean said with a surety which made Ben's attention snap to focus upon him. The look of total faith in the blue eyes was so strong Ben felt it drill into his chest, and it scared him. Before, these had reckoned he could speak the Peace to the gods. Now it was beyond reckoning. They all believed he could command life and death! The gods should be no trouble at all!

Ben paled when this new burden of their belief was dropped upon him and his hand trembled.

Rema saw the changes in him and changed from worshipper to protective nurse. "Enough for now," she said in her commanding healer's voice. "The Speaker needs to rest, or we will never go on to the Home."

Borj and Rothean left, leaving Rema to fuss over her patient. She checked for fever and asked if he was hungry or thirsty then tucked him firmly under the blanket before going herself. When he was sure she wasn't coming back, he pulled his arms out from beneath the covers. After a little he found himself staring at the Voyager's Mark on his left arm. *If only I hadn't met Mardian. What am I going to do? They think I am a god now. They think I can just tell Aris and Tarsa to get down off their mountain and stop all this.*

The thoughts ran round and round, and with each re-play the terror of them grew until he was shaking and sweating. For the first time in weeks he truly wished for a drink. A drop or two of bottled oblivion would have been a great help then the thought was gone. He glanced at the Voyager's Mark again, but the tattoo was no help. No flash, no change, no movement came to help him, but after a moment of staring at it an idea came into his mind. *Maybe if we go with an army, Aris and Tarsa will throw open their door rather than resist.*

It was more a wry hope than an idea, but suddenly he felt better. *An army. At least with an army we won't be ambushed anymore. Maybe...*

A week later the Speakers left Manek at the head of what had been a troop of Lady Tarsa's cavalry. It was a small army, but an army none the less.

## Chapter Seventeen

As with everything else Ben Fordham had touched in the world of the gods, his idea of riding at the head of an army quickly got out of hand. No longer did the defense force consist of a single troop of cavalry. It grew with each town and garrison as it moved toward Amlek. The Speakers stopped no battles and did not speak the Peace many times. The Army of Peace tried to avoid confrontation of any kind, but when rumor of their march spread out from their path, fortresses and walled cities threw open their gates and sent their garrisons to join the hoard moving north toward Amlek.

"I do not understand this," Ben said over and over. These cannot all be Speakers! They cannot! What are they doing?"

"Following you, my Lord," Rothean said.

"Yeah? Why?"

"You are the Speaker--him who raises the dead! You are more a god than the gods." Rothean answered, a mixture of humor and awe in his voice.

"The servants of the gods are not trying to capture Speakers any more. From what I have heard from those who have joined us, not one Speaker has died since we left

Manek," Borj added.

"I think from before that, Borj," Rothean said. "I think from the time I was called back to life."

Ben glanced at the red-bearded warrior, but did not bother trying to deny what Rothean believed. It wouldn't have done any good anyway.

"The gods are afraid," Borj said.

Rema said, "I do not care why the killing has stopped. I am just glad it has."

"It doesn't make sense!" Ben insisted. "Are Tarsa and Aris going to just let us walk up to the Home? Are we going to knock on the door and say 'Hey we're here. Peace be with you,' and it is all going to be over?"

"It will not be so easy, my Lord Speaker," Troop Captain Calan said with a sardonic lift of his eyebrow. He was a dapper little man with a wolfish smile, a drooping mustache, and a forceful personality. He had been the garrison commander at Manek and as the Army of Peace grew, he had become its general. No one was quite sure how or why, but everyone obeyed him in things concerning the march so Ben and the others deferred to him in all things military.

"What do you mean, Calan?" Rema asked.

In answer Calan said, "I was born in Amlek. I know the barren land." He pointed east. "There is no wall more high or strong than the ground we must cover to reach the Home. No one, and I mean no one, has ever gone as deep into the barren land as you say we must and returned to tell the tale."

"Do you mean it is impossible?" Ben asked.

Calan shrugged. "To say, 'Peace be with you, put up

your sword,' and have battles stop, or to say, 'Your power is ended oh gods, and have the words shake the Temple of Dark at Cynar to the ground, or to say 'Live,' and have the dead returned to life...what more is impossible?"

Once more Ben felt the crushing weight of their faith sitting firmly upon his shoulders. He shivered beneath it and Rema was instantly alert. "Are you well, my Lord?"

"Please don't call me that, Rema," he said for the thousandth time, knowing it would do no good. "I'm all right. It's just the cold wind. How can it be so cold on the edge of a desert?"

"In summer the barren land is a blazing, wind tormented hell," Calan said. "In winter it is a freezing, wind tormented hell. Either season you will be blistered by sun, scoured to the bone by windblown grit, and dried like trail meat. As I said, there is no higher wall or stronger defense in all the world so far as I know."

"How are we going to feed and water all these people and horses?" Fordham asked.

"We will strip Amlek of every drop of water in its wells and every crumb of food in its store houses," Calan said.

*Just like a conquering army,* Ben thought. "And if it isn't enough?" he asked.

"Then something else will arise," Calan said, grinning.

Ben almost groaned aloud.

Amlek was a city which lay between two deserts. It lay in a narrow strip of fertile plain between the barren land to the east and the sea to the west. It had been a city filled with servants of the Dark who had lived mostly by piracy. Now it was a city which did not know who it served. Word had passed that no one should oppose the army of Speakers lest they become Speakers themselves, yet the instinct of the people of Amlek was to fall on the Speaker and his followers and strip them to the bone. That instinct withered to nothing though when Amlek saw the size of the army advancing on it.

When the army reached Amlek, the gates were thrown open without the least resistance. The army spread itself around the city and settled down to rest until they were told where to go from here. Amlek's elder council greeted the Speaker, and a fine house was turned over to him without his asking. Ben did not know whether the Elders amiability came from the fact he was the Speaker or from the fact an army was lapping at the gates like an incoming tide.

The army worried Ben almost more than the awe struck worshipful way everyone looked at him. He could not see how such a mass of humanity could be brought across the desert without many deaths. Calan was right. There was no need for the gods to send armies against the army of Speakers. The barren land would do the resisting for them.

Over evening tea Ben said as much to Borj, Rothean, Rema, and Calan. "There is enough blood on my hands," he said. "I don't want to try to lead this army to the Home."

They all studied the words in silence. "It will be hard to leave any behind," Borj said.

"It was hard enough to send people away before, my Lord," Rothean agreed. "Now that these have followed with thought of Speaking the Peace to the gods..."

"If we try to march these people across the desert, hundreds of them are going to die!" Ben snapped then felt bad when all their heads bowed beneath his displeasure, but he knew he was right and knew they must believe him. "Am I right or not, Calan?"

Calan miserably nodded his agreement. "You are right, my Lord. Even if we do strip Amlek to its bones of water and supplies, we will not have enough to reach half way."

"Then we must not try it."

"My Lord..." Rothean began.

"Don't 'my Lord' me! I will not have any more people dead because of me! Don't give me that 'You can do anything' look either. I keep trying to tell you I am only human no matter what you think!"

The four sat for a long time with heads bowed under Ben's glare. "Well, say something," he said at last.

Calan said, "They will not stay behind, my Lord."

"Then I'll command them! If I'm everybody's 'Lord' I should get some good out of it!"

Borj shrugged his doubts. "Some will probably do as you command," he said, "but not all. Those who are Speakers want to protect you. Many of those who aren't Speakers want to see you fail or perhaps help you to fail."

"Some will follow no matter what," Rothean agreed.

"And they will die in the desert," Ben said.

"Therefore," Calan began, the wolfish grin playing about the corners of his mouth, "I think the only way to leave them is for us to sneak away."

"It could be difficult," Rema said. "The Speaker's

every breath is noted."

"And the instant it is discovered I am gone everyone will know where and they will start out after us," Ben said, massaging his temples.

"And we can't just walk away from here with what we can carry," Borj added. "Even the four of us will need a pack train of supplies to cross the barren land."

"Five," Calan said.

"No!" Ben said at once.

"My Lord, you need me," Calan insisted. "You will never live to reach the Home without me. I know the barren land, and I know people in Amlek who can quietly arrange supplies for us."

Ben ran his eyes over the little troop captain's grinning countenance and felt his stomach sink. He had seen this kind of determined grin before. On Othway's face. "All right then," he said, "how do we keep the people from following us when you lead us across the desert, Calan?"

"Nothing simpler, my Lord. Some rogue servant of the Dark will try to assassinate you and nearly succeed. You will be laid up recovering and unable to see anyone save we faithful few who will be closeted with you."

All stared at Calan's grinning face for a long time before Ben asked, "Will it work?"

"For a time I think," Borj said.

"Long enough to give us a good head start at least," Calan said.

"When the ruse falls apart, some will still try to follow," Rothean said.

All nodded their agreement, but Borj, still the

practical soldier said, "If you are to

Speak the Peace to the gods, Speaker, some may still be hurt. This way will limit the number, I think."

So it was done. The next day news of the assassination attempt circulated. The Army of Peace and the population of Amlek gasped in horror and settled in to await the outcome.

Well after midnight two days later Borj led Ben and Rema through the pitch black, sleeping streets of Amlek and up onto the city wall. A basket large enough for a man to sit in waited there. A rope was attached to the basket and looped around a tripod frame set up so as to be able to lower the basket down the outside of the city wall.

"We couldn't just walk out the front gate?" Ben asked.

"All gates are guarded, Speaker," Borj explained. "Two heart beats after we passed the guards everyone in Amlek would know you were abroad, so...," he indicated the basket. "climb in, My Lord. Rothean is below."

Ben did as he was told and Borj's tree-thick arms and iron back lowered him slowly into Rothean's waiting grasp. Rema followed shortly then the rope end was dropped and Rothean and Ben brought Borj down.

Well away from the city walls the four found Calan waiting with riding horses and a dozen pack animals. Without many words they mounted. Calan found his direction from the stars and led out. They were well into the barren land before the sun touched the horizon.

Traveling was not too difficult at first. There was a path of sorts, but before noon it had played out and they took their direction strictly from Calan's experience.

The dry cold was the most difficult part. Again, Fordham wondered how a desert could be so cold. And the wind! It found its way into the tiniest opening in their clothes. He had been in the Mojave Desert of California. The wind hardly ever stopped there either and the winter was cold, but nothing like the piercing, slashing cold of the barren land. He imagined this must be what Antarctica felt like.

Before long the wind had sucked much of the moisture from their bodies. Their lips were cracked and dry and their eyes were crusted with blowing sand and salt from evaporated tears. It was so cold and dry their exhalations did not steam. The barren land stole the very moisture from their breaths the instant it was free from their bodies.

Night came with a suddenness Ben could hardly believe. There was no lingering twilight here. One moment it was light and the next minute it was dark, as though a heavy curtain had been drawn across the sun to leave clear star-spattered sky above them and impenetrable dark on the ground.

They camped in a scooped out hollow on the sheltered side of a sand dune and huddled around a fire made of some scraggly brush. "Tomorrow morning we will pick up the horse droppings and carry them with us," Calan said.

The others looked at him with wonder and distaste. He smiled lopsidedly. "Do not worry; they will be dry and hard by tomorrow morning. They will make a warm fire tomorrow night."

"Must we use dung?" Rothean asked. "Even dry it smells and smokes."

"We will use it rather than go without a fire. Soon there will be nothing to burn save what we have brought. Two of the pack horses carry nothing but wood, and it will not last forever. Smoke and smell notwithstanding, we will burn dung. We are now on water ration. We drink only three times a day from now on, so enjoy your tea tonight. We will drink nothing more until morning."

"Is it truly so barren?" Rema asked.

Calan nodded, and Rothean said, "The map we copied from the hollow mountain shows nothing between Amlek and a well about half way across."

"I reached the well once," Calan said. "Seeking a stored treasure." He laughed ruefully. "The trip almost killed me and the water is half way." He shook his head.

"Should we just turn around and forget this?" Ben asked.

They looked into the fire and thought about it for a time. Rema said, "Nora said the doom is set and if we did not carry it out, it would be brought about some other way."

"Does that mean yes or no?" Ben asked.

No one answered him. "Let's sleep on it and decide in the morning," he said finally. Nods agreed with him and after a little they rolled into sleeping robes.

Rema molded herself to Bens back and put her arm over him. "Peace is better, my Lord," she whispered in his ear. "The sooner it is spoken to the gods the better."

"And if the barren lands kills us before we can speak?" he answered.

"Then the doom will go on in another way, and it will no longer be our concern."

*Yeah,* he thought. *We'll be too dead to care.*

The five did not discuss whether or not to go on in the morning. They picked up the dry horse dung, drank the mouthfuls of water Calan allowed them, and moved off in the direction of the rising sun.

By noon all were sun-burned despite the weeks of trail tan they all wore. The sun and its desiccating brother the wind would have blistered them until the flesh peeled from their bones if Rema had not produced an oily salve which they smeared on their faces and hands.

They trudged on with bowed heads and bent backs, walking as much as they could to spare the horses, but still the animals suffered. After days of short rations and low water, Borj's horse reached the point of not being able to carry the soldier's bear like weight. They walked more, but they could hear the rattle in the horse's breathing even above the roar of the wind. At last Borj said, "He can go no farther. His chest is filled with water. He is drowning even as he dies of thirst, and there is nothing we can do. Best we end his life here before he comes to the truly painful stage."

We can also use the fresh meat," Rothean said.

Ben was horrified, but when he looked at the others, they did not seem to find anything wrong with eating an animal they had been riding, so he kept the horror to himself.

Calan and Borj butchered the horse while the other three scooped out their sheltering hollow on the lee side of a dune and unloaded the other animals. They built a small fire of their hoarded wood with no horse dung added then roasted strips of horse meat. At first Ben was not hungry, but the smell of the roasting meat changed his mind.

The wind rose more as they ate, blowing the flames of the fire almost straight out despite being sheltered behind a dune. “It will be colder tonight,” Rema said.

Calan nodded. “I am more worried about the wind though,” he said. “If it lifts the sand too much, we can lose ourselves if we try to move through it or be buried alive if we don’t move.”

“Or blown away,” Ben said. He thought he was joking, but the look on Calan’s face told him it was no joke.

“I have seen the wind so strong it can blow loaded pack horses off their feet.”

“Let us hope it doesn’t blow so hard while we are outside,” Rema said.

The next morning they awoke to find themselves covered with blown sand, but when they dug out they found the wind more calm than it had thus far been. The day seemed warmer, but that proved to be false. In fact it was colder and soon all of them were feeling the effects. Their feet and hands seemed to go numb moments after they had massaged circulation back into them. Rema began making checks on all of them to make sure the numbness did not turn into frost bite.

The next day two pack horses succumbed to the cold and the short rations. The travelers redistributed the supplies among the other horses, but knew they would have to abandon some if any more horses died. They could not determine with any accuracy how far they were from the well marked on the map, but they all hoped it was not too far. They had brought much water and had rationed it carefully, but humans and horses needed a lot of water to stay alive so water was running low. The humans cut their ration to twice a day, leaving the houses ration the same as it was. Thirst became a demon that never left off torturing them.

The wind began to increase again three days later, and by noon they could hardly see the person riding beside them. "This is going to be a bad blow," Calan said.

"What can we do?" Fordham asked.

Calan shrugged. "I think we must dig in and wait it out."

All agreed and they dug in on the sheltered side of a dune. They dug in together, covering themselves with sleeping robes and sat like naughty children hiding under the bed covers, gnawed on dry trail meat, and sipped their water ration.

The hiss of sand against the coverings was beyond hypnotic, and soon they all lay down. They tried not to sleep for fear the sand would cover them so completely they wouldn't be able to breath, but weariness and cold and the monotonous sound of the blowing sand lulled them into unconsciousness.

Minutes or perhaps hours later Ben came awake. He couldn't determine what had wakened him at first, but then he knew. The sound of the wind had changed. It seemed louder. It had backed and changed direction. The miniscule shelter the dune had provided was gone, and the wind that had covered them with sand before was now stripping the sand away.

In moments all the sand which had piled up on them was stripped away and the wind was pounding on them--tearing at their sleeping robes as though they were the last leaves on an autumn blighted tree.

That was when they heard Tarsa laugh.

The cruel, tearing sound made Ben's insides turn to water, and even as he recognized the sound for what it was, he felt the wind increase and force its fingers beneath him. It lifted him and flipped him over then lifted him still higher into the dust clouded air, tumbling him over and over like a swimmer caught in an ocean breaker. He was flying through the air like a loose balloon, barely able to breathe, disoriented by being spun and twisted, unable to tell sky from earth.

At last Tarsa tired of her game and the wind began to diminish. Ben slammed through the thin top of a sand dune. It smashed what little breath he had left out of his lungs, and consciousness faded out as he tumbled down the back side of the dune.

~ * ~

The crash of silence brought him awake. He could hardly move because of the battering the wind had given him and because of the sand piled over him, but he managed to wriggle free and take a breath of the cold, clean air. It was night. A thousand stars gleamed against the total black of the sky, but they gave light only for themselves leaving none to ease the dark on the ground.

"Rema?" he called weakly, his throat tortured by dust and thirst. "Rothean? Calan?" There was no answer. *They might be miles away or dead and buried under the sand,* a tiny voice whispered in his mind. He shoved the thought away and called out again. His words seemed to run a few inches out from his mouth and evaporate in the frigid stillness of the night. The cold seeped through his cloak and made his joints ache, and the dry air made his throat feel raw.

"Speaker, your life is mine..."

Ben spun to face the voice.

Tarsa stood atop the dune above him. Her silhouette blotted out the stars. She was in her huge size, the god-like appearance she and Aris had used when Ben had seen them together in the clouds at Bakar. Her horns were huge and curved, and the starlight glinted off them as though they were covered with silver.

Ben tried to say something, tried to speak the Peace or speak the question "*Where are the others?*" but nothing came out of his mouth. Fear and thirst and the calling for the others had stripped him of his voice.

"I would rather have pulled you to pieces at my leisure, Speaker," Tarsa said, "or watched you squirm on a pole, but Aris has somehow warded you against me so these lovely dunes will have to serve." She laughed. It was a deep contralto sound which stretched out its claws and scored his heart with joyful anticipation of his pain. "It will be a slow dying," she said. "Perhaps the carrion birds will come to help you enjoy it. That would be jolly. I'm sure they will savor Rema's sweet flesh." Her slashing laugh came again then she was gone. Stars rushed in to fill the void of her going.

~ * ~

Ben was near death at dawn. It was only a question of whether cold or thirst would kill him first, but something in him would not simply sit down in the sand and wait for death. He had no idea where he was, where the others were, or which direction the well lay, but he had started this journey to speak the peace to the gods in their very dwelling, and now he determined if he could not actually do it he would die trying. He started trudging toward the rising sun.

Ben was on the edge of sanity. The cold and exhaustion made his mind drift. He thought of the Pillars at the beginning of the trail up to the Valley of Seers. *"All hope abandon..."* he thought. *"I'm in the middle of Hell, and I still don't have sense enough to abandon hope."*

At one point he reached the top of a dune and turned to look back over his trail. He was astonished to see his tracks stretching back so far. *"Long way,"* he thought then laughed bitterly in his mind. *"Tarsa is using the calm to torture me. If the wind was blowing my tracks would disappear, but with no wind I can see my tracks stretching from one faceless dune to another and know they mean nothing. I'll never get anywhere. No progress, only useless movement."* But stubbornness would not allow him to quit all the same. "I'm alive!" he tried to scream at the sky, but it came out only as an indecipherable whisper. "I'm alive..."

By noon he was almost finished. Days of short water rations and hours of no water rations plus the beating the wind had given him had almost done for him. All the moisture was sucked out of him. His tongue was like dry sticky sandpaper and the membranes of is nose hurt from the dry air flowing over them. He rubbed his nose and the movement ruptured one of the desiccated blood vessels and gave him a bloody nose. The flow didn't last long. It froze to his skin and flaked off when he touched it. *"I'm being freeze dried one drop of blood at a time,*" he thought then moved on.

He stopped every few paces to rest, mostly when he fell down. When his knees became too wobbly to stand any more, he crawled.

Presently he found himself lying face down in the sand and realized he had been there for a while because his cheek had gone numb where it touched the cold dune. His strength was gone. He couldn't rise even to his knees anymore.

In his mind he could hear a cacophony of voices from both his lives. Rema and Maggie, Othway, his father, whose voices somehow mixed with Tarsa's. "*It is the end Speaker, and it wasn't even your fight!*"

"Ben Fordham?" the voice came again, and a hand touched his back.

Fordham scrapped his face against the sand turning toward the sound. Scalding bright light stabbed into his eyes for a moment before a touch on his temple darkened his vision.

"I am glad you are still alive, Speaker," Aris said.

*Must be a hallucination. "Why would Aris be here? He wants me dead.*

"Drink some of this," the God of Light said, cradling Ben's body and holding a cup to his wind-parched lips with his own shining hand. Ben sipped, thinking, *If I'm seeing desert ghosts, at least they are kind ones.*

The cup held a mixture of water and wine. It stung Ben's cracked lips, and the liquid disappeared from his mouth without his having swallowed, absorbed by his swollen tongue.

"Easy Speaker, only a little at first. I will carry you away from here when you are a little stronger."

~ * ~

It was a very posh prison to which the God of Light brought Ben--all polished basalt and marble with couches and cushions and fantastically carved tables--but a prison all the same, deep in the bowels of the Home. Ben first thought it was still part of some hallucination, but after a dozen or so cups of water he could separate reality from unreality, and noticed there were no windows. The only access was a doorway leading into a passage.

"Rest Speaker," Aris said, not unkindly. "I will return when you are stronger. Have patience and rest."

"Why did you save me?" Ben asked, his voice still sounding creaky.

"I will explain later. Now I must go to Lady Tarsa. I will do nothing to provoke you. There is not even a door in the opening to stop you, but do not be foolish enough to wander away. You might meet Lady Tarsa or some of her servants which would serve neither you nor this world."

"And I might speak the Peace to her or whoever else I meet before they can silence me," he croaked defiantly.

"Perhaps," Aris said.

"What about the others?"

"They are well."

Ben did not believe him, but felt he did not really have much choice except to pretend he did, at least until he felt strong enough or moved enough to speak the peace to

Aris. Still, he could not stop himself from saying, "I'd like to see them."

"When you, and they, have recovered a bit more."

Ben studied the veiled god for a moment. "All right," he said. "I'll wait a while to see them, but you had best not be lying."

Aris did not answer, just turned and vanished. A moment later a man came in through the door. He had a mop of silvery white hair, and an air of haughty command. He was dressed in a short toga-like robe, and needed only wings sprouting from his shoulders blades to pass for an angel.

"Would you like to bathe, Speaker?" he asked with no air of solicitousness. He made it clear by the wrinkle of his nose that a bath was in order. "And fresh clothes also," he added.

Ben was so surprised to meet another human in the Home of the gods he lost what little voice had returned to him. He could only stare.

The servant ignored Ben's surprise and repeated his question as though talking to a child, or a dog.

Ben swallowed, his mouth still cottony with dehydration, and said, "Yes please, but first, more water. I am still very thirsty."

"I will bring water and wine."

Ben was much tempted by the thought of wine, but he put the thought aside. "Never mind the wine, but bring lots of water and food. Hot food if you please."

The man hesitated long enough to see if there was going to be anything else then tilted his head in place of a true bow and headed for the door.

With malicious intent Ben said, “Peace be with you, servant of Aris.”

The servant stiffened as though he had been struck between the shoulder blades, but to his credit he did not run or cry out. He turned back to Ben.

“Am I changed now, Speaker?” he asked. “Am I a speaker of peace too?”

Ben smiled and regretted it the instant after for it stretched his lips and burst open the desert dried cracks. The taste of blood was coppery on his tongue. “No,” he said. “You are not under the power of the Peace. It was only a wish, not a command.”

The servant stared at Ben for a long moment, disdain and distaste clear in his eyes, before he bowed with a bob of his head which managed to convey a haughty anger and contempt before he went to do as he was bidden.

## Chapter Eighteen

Rothean dug out of the sand and looked around. The wind which had rolled him across the sand like a tumble weed and finally buried him had calmed and most of the dust had settled out of the air, but the night was still black with only the fitful light of the stars to break it up. He thought about trying to find the others, but realized it would be impossible in the dark so he burrowed back into the sand for warmth and tried to sleep. He only succeeded a little, between bouts of worry about whether or not the others were still alive. He thought he could remember hearing a bone chilling laugh carried on the wind, but he shoved the thought away with all his might.

The morning was calm, clear, and cold. There was no sign of any of the others. He had no idea how far the wind had carried him or the others. He did not think he had been rolled far, but there was no way to tell. Judging by his bruises and aching muscles it might have been miles. He shook himself trying to get some of the sand inside his clothes out while considering what to do next. After a little he scrambled up the tallest dune he could see and looked around a moment then gave a whoop of joy. Westward, atop another dune,

Calan was doing the same thing as Rothean, and his reaction was about the same as Rothean's. They ran down their separate dunes, up and down the lower dunes between them and met with much pounding of backs and brotherly hugs atop one of the hills of sand.

"I found half of the pack animals," Calan said when they stopped congratulating themselves on being alive. "Or rather they found me. They were surrounding the place I was buried when I poked my head up."

"The Speaker? Did you see him?"

Calan looked down then nodded, not wanting to puncture the joy they had felt a moment before. "I saw him disappear into the air, going up like a rock thrown from a catapult."

"Which way? We must try to find him," Rothean said.

"There will be no finding him I fear. Lady Tarsa has him."

"What? How?"

"Did you not hear the laughter? The storm was not a common blow. Lady Tarsa stirred the wind and used it to carry off the Speaker. That is why you and I are still alive. She was so interested in the Speaker she merely brushed us aside."

"We must look for him!" Rothean said. "I must look for him! He may still be alive! He came for me when I was dead, how can I not look for him when there is any chance he may still be alive."

Calan gripped Rothean's wrist to restrain him. "And he might be with Lady Tarsa in the Home, or he might be miles away, dead and buried in the sand. We have no way of knowing."

"Hello!" Rema shouted and waved her arms from the top of another dune. She was a speck against the aching blue sky. It took the three of them half an hour to get together.

"A couple of horses over there," she said and waved toward where she had come from. "There were three dead ones too. Pack animals all of them. Where is the Speaker?"

Both men looked at their boots then Calan inhaled a deep breath and told her.

Rema listened, her face wooden with tightly controlled emotion. "We must look for him," she said at last, wrapping her arms together and holding them protectively across her middle. "We must."

Rothean suddenly lifted his face up toward the sky and sniffed. "Do you smell that?" he asked.

Calan and Rema both imitated the red-bearded warrior. "Smoke," Calan said and began turning slowly around. In the direction Rothean and Rema had come from a thread of smoke rose and drifted toward them.

"The Speaker?" Rema asked, full of hope. The other two hurried to nod their agreement that it might be, but all knew it probably was not.

Calan said, "I will go get the horses I found, and you two pick up those Rema found then we will go to the fire."

"The dead ones had a lot of supplies still in their packs and scattered beside them," Rema said. "If the wind comes up, it could bury it all so we won't ever be able to find it again."

"I don't think we'll have to worry about wind for a while," Rothean said and pointed with his chin a little higher than they had been looking. Carrion birds circled on the cold air. "All we will have to do for a day or so is look for the birds. They'll pick out every carcass around."

~ * ~

Borj was sitting by a small fire patiently toasting strips of dark red horse meat impaled on the end of his dagger when the others came around the dune. Two riding horses, unsaddled, stood quietly a little way off, their reins tied to their saddles which lay on the ground.

"What, no tea?" Rothean asked, grinning.

Borj shrugged and did not rise. "The dead horse I found was loaded with wood and nothing else so...," he lifted the dagger and its burden a little. "Is the Speaker with you?"

"We were hoping he was with you," Calan said.

Borj shook his head.

"We must look for him," Rothean said, more controlled than earlier but still adamant.

"No," Borj said with the cool practicality of the professional soldier. "We have no idea even where to begin. Instead we should sit here by this little fire and cook ourselves some horse meat and wait for him to smell the smoke like you did. If he has not shown up in a while, then we can discuss what comes next."

"What if he is hurt?" Rema asked.

Borj looked straight into Rema's golden eyes and said, "We all know he is either dead already or Lady Tarsa has him. He may have spoken the peace to her, but I don't think so. We would have felt it if that were so. I think he is dead, Rema."

A thunderous silence rushed in to fill the air when Borj finished. The four looked from face to face and knew what he had said was true. None of them wanted it to be so, but they knew it was. Still they shoved the thought aside and continued to hope. Even Borj.

They rested out the day then the night in the place Borj had built the little fire and took stock of the situation. They had some water, but not enough to keep them alive for long. They had trail meat, hard bread, and parched grain for themselves and some horse grain. They had a horse load of fire-wood. They had several dead horses to cut meat from, but those would not last long. Already carrion birds were wheeling above and landing to tear at the frozen carcasses.

"I figured we were about a day from the well before the blow," Calan said.

"How far are we now?" Borj asked.

Calan shrugged. "One way or another we are closer to the well than to Amlek."

"Can you find the well?" Rothean asked.

"I think so." He lifted his face toward the sky. "There are the stars which have guided us so far. If we continue we should strike the well--I think."

"And if we get there, then what?" Rema asked despair and sorrow mixed in her voice.

Borj answered without a moment's hesitation, "I will continue on to the Home. The Speaker set out to speak the Peace to the gods, and I will try to finish it for him."

The other three looked at one another in the wavering red light of the fire and knew they were going on too.

~ * ~

Ben did not know how long he had been sleeping when the God of Light woke him, but thought it must have been quite a while because he felt rested. Even the gritty residue of the barren land had washed out of his eyes as he slept.

"How do you feel?" Aris asked.

Ben kept his back to Aris' glare as he put on the silken robes he had been given. "I can't believe you really care," he said, turning and holding his arm over his eyes against the dazzle which escaped the heavy veils the God of Light wore.

Aris reached out a blazing bright hand, but Ben pulled back from him.

"Come, come Speaker, don't be childish. Let me darken your eyes."

Ben reluctantly allowed Aris to touch his temple. "I really do care, Speaker. Much more than you can know."

"Sure you do," Ben said bitterly.

"You are alive and comfortable here...," the god said, seating himself on a divan cushion across the room from Ben--as though afraid of him.

Ben laughed. "I'm imprisoned here, and you left the others out there to die, didn't you? That's how much you care." He did not know if this was true, but he had to assume it was since he would have been dead if not for Aris having come for him. He wondered why he did not find this assumption maddening enough to cause him to speak the Peace to Aris, but there was no desire. It was almost as though he were caught in some sort of Limbo between sorrow for Rema, Borj, Rothean, and Calan, and gratitude for Aris having saved his life.

"I told you before, your friends are not dead..."

Ben's heart jumped with a pain of hope that twisted in his chest, but he quickly lost the hope. Aris had lied before and was probably lying now.

"...And you are not locked in," the god continued.

"I wonder whether I should believe you." Ben said, trying to fend off the gratitude which kept trickling into his heart. "I never thought of a god as being able to lie until I met you. I've learned a lot."

"They truly are alive," Aris said with a great show of patience.

"Alive like all those Speakers you servants stuck up on poles? And you know, now I think about it, it might have been better than letting them dry up and freeze out there. It would have been quicker. Maybe like Othway? Or is he alive too? Maybe it was just my imagination and he is going to come bouncing in here any second now." Ben said, trying to work himself up to the anger he had felt at Cynar, but for some reason it would not come. He felt bitter hatred for Aris and Tarsa but the rage was cold and passive. It was as though the very size of his hatred made it unwieldy.

"The balance had to be preserved," Aris said. "It still must be preserved, in spite of you or Lady Tarsa or all the Speakers you have created. It is the most important thing in this world.

"The Balance," Ben said with an acid chuckle. "The Balance is gone and you know it."

"Not so, Speaker!" Aris denied.

"The Balance has been broken since Tarsa sent Borj and the others to pick me up from the cave when this thing...," he stuck out his left arm with the Voyagers mark on it "...brought me here, and you know it."

Aris shook his sun-bright head. "Not so. At first you had no effect on the Balance at all. You were not even on the scale. You were an out-worlder of no importance."

"Then why did Rothean and the others bother to save me from Tarsa? Seems like an awful chance to take for a man of no importance."

"Because it was in the nature of their service to me to preserve your life. Even one of no importance. But more, it was their joy to take something, anything, from Lady Tarsa. You were not significant. Lady Tarsa's not having you was."

He paused to stare at Ben for a moment then said, "It would have been better if they had let Tarsa have you...or that we should have abandoned you in the caverns as Marrad and Randau counseled, but Rema would not hear of it. She argued that you should live, and I let her persuade me! I even fooled myself into believing I might be able to use you in the Balance!" The God of Light laughed. It was a mocking sound, full of regret.

"And then I spoke the Peace, and all of a sudden I was important."

"Yes. Yes indeed. You became a heavy factor--are still a heavy factor, but it didn't happen all at once. One or two lives don't make much difference on the great scale, but in my arrogance I thought I saw a way to use you to tip the scale a little more toward the light. You see, Lady Tarsa had won several victories before you arrived, and the Balance was tipping rather far over toward the dark. She of course would never try to correct the Balance. It is not in her nature. She is dark. She desires chaos, the end of all things, and she would have continued until she achieved chaos. I could not allow that. Chaos and destruction are not in my nature."

A slashing, cynical laugh Ben hardly recognized as his own escaped when he heard that. All the blood and pain and exhaustion and fear of his experience in the world of the gods burst forth like a stream of acid. "No--Of course not!" he said. "You're the wonderful god of order and light who considered whether of not to let Tarsa have me because it was in your benevolent nature. You're so much for life you let your servants amuse themselves by poling thousands of Speakers."

"The Balance had to be preserved!" Aris snapped in answer.

Ben laughed again and shook his head in disbelief. "And now your precious Balance is smashed to pieces! You and your world are finished. All we have to do now is wait for the Over-God to come in and sweep up the mess."

Aris held his answer back and looked pensively at the Speaker for a long time. "That should be so Ben Fordham," he said at last, "but somehow it isn't. There is some kind of new Balance."

"Speakers on one side and gods on the other?"

"No. Not Speakers. You. Nor are you balanced against us. You are balanced with us."

"Same thing, different words."

"No! Not the same. Lady Tarsa and I are still in the

Balance, but your weight is somehow on both sides. You and your Peace are both Light and Dark. That is why I saved you from the barren land. You are the Balance now, and if you are removed, the scale will tip too much."

"You must think I am an idiot or something," Ben said. "There is no Balance anymore. In the Valley of Seers Nora told me the doom of the world was set, and there was no avoiding it, even if I stayed in the Valley; even if I never tried to come here to speak the Peace."

"And what is this doom, Speaker? If this doom is set and the Balance is truly broken, why has the Over-God not returned to 'sweep up the mess' as you said?"

Ben had no answer.

"It is because you are both Light and Dark, Speaker. You are on both sides of the scale."

"No," Ben denied again. "No! That would make me some kind of duel god and I'm not. I am just a man like any you had killed for the sake of your precious Balance."

Aris shook his head. "You are not the same as them Ben Fordham. They served one god or the other until they began to serve you. Now both servants of Light and servants of Dark serve you as they once served Tarsa and me. And you serve no one save yourself, like Tarsa and I. Like a god."

"I am not a god!"

"Perhaps not when you first arrived, but you certainly are now. How else can you speak the Peace, and collapse temples with a word of command, or call back the dead? I *am* a god and I have no such power."

Ben opened his mouth, but, with a force like being struck down with the Peace, he suddenly understood. He was indeed both Light and Dark, and what seemed to him things of light had often resulted in darkness, and what seemed things of darkness resulted in light. Would he have ever spoken the Peace for the first time if Othway and his partner had not attacked them with murderous intent on the road to Rayhan? Would the Peace ever have spread so fast if not for the blood spilled on the plain of Bakar? Would the power to call life back from death have ever come if Rothean had not died? Fordham had already spent many sleepless nights considering how his good deeds had brought nothing but death and pain, now Aris confirmed that nothing Ben had done was either all good or all evil.

And yet...

"It can't be Aris," Ben said, his voice rising. "It can't. I can't command life out of death whenever I want to or I would have called all the others back to life! I can't speak the Peace whenever I want to. You proved that with your test at Bakar. I'm proving it again by sitting here wishing I could destroy you with the Peace, but I can't do it. I am not a god! I am not!" Ben was shaking his head in violent negation, trying to convince himself, but knowing all his denials did not make what Aris said any the less true. He truly was the mixed god--the out-world god upon whom the Balance of this world now depended.

At last Ben settled himself enough to ask, "If I am a god, why did Tarsa try to kill me? How could she kill me if I am a god?"

"And are you dead?" Aris asked with an ironic twist.

"Not for lack of Tarsa's having tried. I'm alive because you warded me against her then came to get me when you decided it was the way to preserve the Balance."

"I did not ward you against her," Aris said thoughtfully. "Which is another reason to believe you are a god. You were protected from her. And you are right to believe the Balance is why I saved you. If I had let you die, the Balance would have been broken beyond all repair. I had to save you to save the world, though she wanted you dead. She is the Goddess of Dark. The Goddess of Chaos. She wants the end of the world. It is in her nature to want destruction."

Fordham blinked and thought a moment before asking, "The others--wouldn't saving them from Tarsa have helped save the world?"

Aris shrugged.

"You did lie, didn't you? You didn't pick them up. You didn't even look for them, did you?"

Aris said nothing and confirmed what Ben said by his silence.

"Why? Why didn't you pick them up too? Why did you wait until I was almost dead? Do you get some kind of joy out of human suffering?"

"I get no joy from your pain or theirs," Aris said. "I took so long to pick you up because I did not know what she had done. Then it took time to search for you."

"Search for me? What kind of god are you, who doesn't know what goes on in your own world?" Ben demanded, unwilling to let the God of Light get away with the deaths of Rema, Borj, Rothean and Calan. He had let them die because they had no significance against his precious Balance.

"I am a god of limits!" Aris said, frustration in his tone. "I am not the Over-God who sees all things and understands all things. I am only the God of Light, Balance for the Goddess of Darkness. I only know what the Over-God allows me to know, for which you had best be thankful, for it means Lady Tarsa is limited too. She does not know that you are still alive, but she knows your end will bring the Great End, and when the Great End does not happen she will figure out why and she will be furious."

"And she will begin to think you might have had something to do with it," Ben finished for him.

"Yes."

Ben thought for a time, even considering simply seeking out the Goddess of Dark in a sort of suicide attempt that would destroy everything once and for all, but at last he discarded the idea. "Will she begin looking here at the Home?" he asked.

"I don't know. Probably. No matter what, she will not give up until she finds you and ends you."

"I am protected from her, or so you said. And if she attacks me I can speak the Peace."

"Can you? Have you the power to speak your Peace to a god? You have not spoken it to me. You said you could not."

*Nora had said the strength of all would be needed*, Ben thought, *but then again Aris said he did not ward against Tarsa, which must mean I have some power alone.*

"I don't know," Ben said at last, "but I think Tarsa believes I can. I think that was my protection out there."

"Yet you did not speak when she attacked you with

the wind."

Now it was Ben's turn to shrug.

Aris gazed at him speculatively. "Perhaps you can, and perhaps you cannot, but I do not think it would be a thing worth testing. Either way the meeting would bring on the ending, so you and the Balance will be better served if you stay out of sight."

"And if I decided to leave, are going to try to stop me? Do *you* think I can speak the Peace to a god?" Ben asked with a vinegar smile. "And how long can I stay hidden? Days? Years? You know, whether I am a god or not, I'm still mortal. Even if you keep me hidden for years, someday I'm going to die, and when I do, your damned Balance is finished. So you're done for no matter what. The Seers Nora and Arna said the doom of the world was sealed already and wanted only the working out."

Aris stared at the Speaker for a long moment. "Perhaps you are right, but I cannot deal with that yet. I have other problems. Stay here in safety for now while I deal with them." In a blink he was gone.

~ * ~

The horses smelled the water before the well came in sight, and it was hard to hold them from running to it. Then it was harder still to get them to drink slowly so as not to bloat themselves. Calan's guess about the location of the well had been surprisingly good considering he had been less than sure of their beginning location, and it was a good thing too since the water they had managed to save after the blow was gone.

They had kept a small, smoky fire burning for two days as they ranged out to recover what was left of the horses and supplies, hoping the smell or sight of the smoke might be a beacon to draw Ben Fordham to them, but when the Speaker did not turn up, they all knew in their hearts he was probably dead, though they avoided saying it.

"How much farther?" Rema asked Calan as they rested, wrapped tight against the cold.

He shrugged and grinned through his up turned mustache. "I wish I knew. This is the farthest anyone has ever come so far as I know. It the map is right we have several more days--about as many as we have traveled so far."

"Only without the three day waste of time, we hope," Rothean said.

They all agreed.

"What are we going to do when we get there," Rema asked.

"We are going to speak the Peace," Borj said, as if it were so obvious it could not be over looked.

"That is not what I meant, and you know it, Borj."

Borj answered the sharp tone with a rueful smile. "I don't know, Rema. We are hardly going to lay siege to the Home, and I doubt a siege, even if we had ten thousand, would do much good. The gods would simply ignore us to death. So I think we must take some direct action. If the gate to the place is wood, we can always try to burn our way in, but to say what we will do with any surety is impossible. We will do what we can do when we see what is possible."

They looked at one another, not satisfied, but

knowing the former soldier of the Dark was right.

"So then we go tomorrow at first light," Rothean said. They all knew what he was thinking or rather what he hoped. He hoped the Speaker was still alive and only held captive in the Home. They all hoped it, but they all knew it was a vague hope at best. If the Speaker were alive, he would have spoken the Peace to the gods already and they would not still be freezing in the midst of the barren land.

Calan said, "We will have to see how the horses are tomorrow. They need rest and to drink more than they can be allowed to drink in a short time. Better to delay a day or even two than to get halfway and have them collapse."

"Delay is..." Rothean began to protest but Borj cut him off.

"Delay is not problem at all, Rothean. The Home has been there since the making of the world and will be there until the end of the world. Nora said the doom of the world was set and could not be changed, but it might not need us to work it out. Personally I want to be present at the end, even if the end is delayed by a few days to rest and water the horses."

Rothean did not like what he heard and showed it in his eyes. "What if Mother Tarsa is watching and sends another wind storm?"

"And what if water suddenly begins gushing up from the desert in such floods we cannot pass?" Borj said with more sharpness than he had intended, dropping silent tension over the four.

After a moment Borj said, "I am sorry Rothean. I'm tired and my temper is short, but I should not have snapped.

Still, what if Lady Tarsa is watching, or Lord Aris? There is nothing we can do about them save deal with whatever they send against us when it comes."

"Borj is right," Rema agreed. "We can only do what we can do."

Rothean did not like what they were saying, but, like it or not, he could not disagree so he nodded his accord after a little and stared into the fire thinking thoughts of revenge on the gods. Revenge for the death of Ben Fordham. Revenge in the Peace which would destroy the world.

## Chapter Nineteen

Time passed, but Ben did not know how much. He had no way to measure save the meals the servant, whose name was Egar, brought him, and his periods of sleep. But those were not accurate measures. He ate and slept what he thought was about a week's worth, but he knew eating and sleeping could be manipulated. He tried to talk to Egar, to ask if there were other humans beside the two of them in the Home, but the man mostly kept mum, speaking only enough to accomplish his business. He seemed by turns fearful and angry with Ben.

"It would be nice if you would talk with me, Egar," Ben said the next time the servant brought him food.

"Lord Aris instructed me to serve you but not to answer questions, Lord Speaker," he answered with an edge to it.

"Then how about taking me for a walk?" Ben shot back with an edge of his own.

"No, Lord Speaker," the other answered and turned to go.

"Why not? I'm bored and I need to stretch my legs. A little exercise, you know? Something to keep the cholesterol moving through my veins. Wouldn't want them to clog up and maybe give me a heart attack. I could die, and it would be good bye world."

"Or we might meet Lady Tarsa," the servant said, "And then it would be good bye world."

"Ah, I understand. Thank you, Egar."

"For what, Lord Speaker?"

"For the friendly information."

The man's face turned a little red.

"Don't worry," Ben said. "I won't tell Aris."

"I told you nothing you did not already know," he said stiffly.

"All right, have it your way then, but I still won't tell Aris."

Egar raked his eyes up and down the Speaker, trying to decide if this was serious. After a little he turned and left.

A few days later Egar caught Ben in the hall.

"Speaker," he shouted, his face mottled with anger. He stopped to gain control of his temper then continued with cold command. "It is not good for you to be out here. Lady Tarsa..."

Fordham almost ignored Egar just to see how vexed he would get, but after a moment the servant changed from haughty to fear-strickened so he relented. After that Egar was a bit chattier, and a bit less angry, but not more forth coming with information.

Some days later an earthquake like jolt followed by a tremor shook Ben awake. With instincts trained by a Los Angeles up-bringing he was on his feet and headed for the door before he was fully awake. Two steps from his bed the lights went out and he skidded to a halt.

The darkness was more frightening than the trembling earth because it was the first time during his stay in the Home of the gods there was darkness. In the palace of the God of Light the very walls reflected Aris' brightness, but now Ben's cell was as dark as the depths of the earth.

Another shock rattled the building, and the floor quivered. Ben was on the edge of panic expecting the roof to pancake down upon him any second and not knowing which way to run. "Egar!" he screamed, his voice rising as his panic rose.

After a moment Egar answered. "Here, Speaker. I am coming as fast as I can!"

"Do you have a light?"

A brightening yellow glow from the hall answered him as Egar rushed through the door carrying an oil lamp.

"We must get out of here," Ben said, calmed a little by the light.

"No, Speaker. All is well. Lord Aris has everything under control," Egar said. He pulled a candle from somewhere in his robe and lit it from the lamp flame then did a double take on Ben who was naked and unaware of it.

"What do you mean 'under control'? It's an earthquake! The floor is still shaking! Now let's get out of here before the whole place comes down on us." Ben started for the door, but Egar stepped in front of him.

"Speaker, you must not!" He commanded, but not too steadily. "All is well. The floor will stop shaking soon and the light will return. Have patience."

"Patience? What the hell is going on?"

"All is well," Egar insisted and, at the moment, the floor did indeed stop shaking. "I will prepare a bath for you--since you seem to be dressed for it," he said with a sneer.

"Bath? Egar, I don't take baths in the middle of an earthquake!"

"It will compose you for sleep."

"I don't sleep either! Now just point me to the way out of here," Ben said, grabbing the candle from Egar, "then you can have *yourself* a nice bath!" He pushed past the servant and headed out the door.

"No, Speaker!" Egar said, panic wiping the command from his voice. "You must not!" he grabbed Ben by the arm without thinking and tried to pull him back. When what he had done got through to his panic-stricken consciousness his mouth dropped open and he let go then glared at his offending hand as though it were not part of his body.

Ben stopped.

"I am sorry, Speaker, I did not mean to do you violence, only stop you from leaving." All color was gone from his face.

Ben did not understand the reaction at first then knowledged dawned on him. Egar expected to be struck with the Peace. Suddenly, he felt sorry for the man. Egar was a jailer and an officious ass, but he didn't deserve to be scared to death. Ben put his hand on Egar's shoulder. "It's all right. You didn't hurt me. Don't worry."

The servant smiled his relief, but the smile was wiped off an instant later when Ben headed out the door into the hall.

"No, Speaker, you mustn't!" Egar said, following

him. "Lord Aris will be angry...and...and you are naked."

Ben stopped and looked down at himself, noticing for the first time he was indeed naked. He turned back to Egar and found the man so full of anxiety he was hopping from foot to foot in a sort of worry dance. It was so comical looking Ben almost laughed. "What? Will Aris be offended at me running around naked?" he asked, but didn't get the smile he expected. Instead Egar looked even more fearful.

"And what will Aris do if you lose me, Egar? Have you poled?

Egar looked at the floor and didn't answer, but the fear sweat was a sheen on his face and arms. He didn't look comical anymore.

Ben took a deep breath and said, "All right, I'll come back..." Egar's head snapped up and joy replaced the fear in his face. "...but I'll only stay if you tell me what the hell just happened with this earthquake."

Egar's face fell again. "I cannot, Speaker."

"All right then, I don't need clothes anyway," he said and turned to walk away.

"No," Egar squeaked.

Ben turned back and said, "So?"

Egar hesitated another moment then said, "It was no earthquake."

"That is no news."

The light came back on. Around the hall nothing looked broken or out of place. "If it was not an earthquake, what was it?"

"Please go back into your chamber."

"Not until you get on with some explaining."

"I will explain. I will--but only if you are in your chamber."

Ben glanced down at the candle flame. It seemed feeble against the light now flooding the corridor so he blew it out. "All right, but if I don't like what you tell me, I'll be on my way again."

"Yes, Yes," Egar said nodding and gesturing up the hall toward the door to the cell.

When they were back in the cell, Egar said, "I will bring wine," and started for the door.

"Hold it!" Ben said and stepped into the door opening to block it. "No wine, no water, no food, no bath, no nothing until you tell me what I want to know. Sit down."

Egar sat on the edge of the divan cushion and drew a deep breath. "It is because Lord Aris and Lady Tarsa are in contention," he said.

"And...?"

He shrugged and looked a little sullen. "That is all I know. When Lady Tarsa is wroth, she and Lord Aris contend. When they do, the light goes out for a little while and the Home shakes. It usually does not last long."

Ben studied him and waited for more, but when nothing more was forth coming he asked, "And does Lady Tarsa get "wroth" often?"

Egar shrugged again. "More, lately."

"Um hum," Ben grunted. *So, Tarsa is angry. And there's no question at all why. She knows I'm still alive, and she knows Aris had something to do with it."*

"Now may I bring wine, Speaker?"

Ben looked at the servant wondering if there was

anymore to be gained from him, and decided there was not. "Yes, if you want to bring wine or whatever go ahead."

Egar looked relieved and thanked the Speaker for his good sense with several bows as he got out.

Ben s mind was still ticking. The next question was did Tarsa know he was in the Home, and if so would she come visiting soon? He thought not or she would be there already, but how long could Aris keep him hidden right under Tarsa's nose.

Egar returned with the wine and poured a cupful.

"Pour yourself some too and sit down," Ben said.

Egar shook his head. "I cannot. I must go now."

"Why? Stay and talk with me a while longer. You made such a good start?"

"I cannot, Speaker. I must go now if you are in no need." He looked worried and anxious again with no sign of his usual haughtiness.

Ben thought about blocking his path again, but decided against it. He sipped the wine and said, "All right then go, and don't worry. I won't say anything to Aris about our little talk, and I won't try to leave again."

The hint of a triumphant smile crossed the man's lips and was gone.

"At least not yet," Ben added, and Egar flinched. "If I get lonesome though," he continued with a shrug, "you can't ever tell what I might decide to do. I may go looking for company. It would be nice if you would come back and visit once in a while. We can talk some more."

Egar nodded noncommittally and walked out.

The light stayed on and there were no more tremors,

for which Ben was glad, but he decided he was tired of being a god and subject to gods, and tried to think of some way to get on to the end of the doom Nora had promised.

~ * ~

The Speakers remained two days at the well, encouraging the horses to drink all they could hold, and drinking all they could themselves then started east leading two horses as well as those they rode and the pack horses.

The traveling was remarkably easy. The barren land was still brutally dry and cold, but the sky remained blue and the wind remained calm. The main problem became to protect their already sun and wind burned skin and abused eyes from the unrelenting brightness. They even had to devise shades for the horses' eyes lest they go blind from the glare.

At evening, six days after they left the well, they camped, ate some dry trail rations, drank tea as hot as they could swallow to stave off the cold, then rolled into their sleeping robes for the night. They lay jammed together so as not to waste even the tiniest bit of body heat.

After a little while, when the glow from the fire light had died down, Rothean sat up and pointed slightly north of the direction they had been traveling. "What is that, Calan?" he asked.

"What is what?" Calan asked from the depths of his sleep robe. He did not sit up.

"That." Rothean pointed toward the place where the starry sky and the dark desert met.

"How should I know?" Calan grumped, still not sitting up. "Probably a star or something. Go to sleep."

Rema sat up and looked where Rothean pointed. "It is very bright," she said. "Not like a star, and it seems too low."

Rothean agreed. "Not like the light of a fire or a lamp either. It isn't yellow enough."

Now Borj sat up and looked. "Could it be the Home?" he asked, more thinking aloud than expecting an answer.

Calan sat up quickly then, and they all looked at the light in silence for a while. Calan stroked and twisted his moustache ends thoughtfully. "It could be. It really could be," he said at last.

"I think it is," Borj said. "And I think we should turn toward it tomorrow."

Calan looked at the former soldier of the Dark. "And what if it isn't the Home?"

"How much worse off are we if it is not?" Rema asked, rhetorically.

Calan grunted. "You are right. All in favor of turning toward the light tomorrow say so now."

As one they agreed.

After a few more moments staring at the light, they lay down feeling a strange calm when there should have been excitement. They were all asleep before the stars wheeled much further.

The light grew steadily brighter over the next three days, even to the point of being visible in daylight. On the evening of the third day they were sitting around their small fire sipping hot tea and looking at the light when suddenly it winked out. They all gasped in surprise and stared at the place where it had been, then turned to one another with the question, *What happened?* In each face. After a little the light came back. They watched for a little while more then turned in.

Two days later they reached a mountain which jutted up abruptly from the desert floor as though it had been pried from a mountain range and plunked down there. Light poured from it to make the evening as bright as day. Carved into the living stone of the mountain top they could see squat ugly demon pillars of Tarsa's dwelling. Atop that, like a crown upon the brow of the mountain, was the shining palace of the God of Light.

"Now what?" Calan asked as the four stood with heads tipped back, looking up the sheer cliff to the Home of the gods.

"Now we rest and think," Borj said without taking his eyes off the seemingly smooth wall. "We study this mountain until we study out a way to climb it."

"Umm," Calan grunted. "We better study it out soon, and hope there is water up there or somewhere near. We will begin to get thirsty by and by."

~ * ~

Egar was even more closed mouthed and sullen than usual when he brought Ben's supper a few days after the earthquake. He would not even look into Fordham's face, but there was a boiling sort of intensity radiating from him.

"What's the problem, Egar? Is Aris giving you grief? I know it isn't me. I've been a good boy," Ben said lightly. "I'm still lonesome though. You haven't come back to chat like you promised."

"I did not promise, Speaker," he said, still avoiding Ben's eyes.

Ben sensed something important was on the man's mind, and when Egar finished laying the repast on the table and tried to get out, he found Ben leaning indolently across the door opening.

"Let me by, Lord Speaker," he said like a man barely in control of his temper.

"Make me," Ben said crossing his arms and putting a nasty twist in his voice.

Egar breathed in, and breathed out, and held his temper. "You know I cannot," he said. "Lord Aris has commanded me not provoke you in any way."

"And yet you are provoking me! Why Egar, I am so vexed with you I just may speak the Peace to you right now."

Egar glared. There was anger in his eyes--the sort of anger that makes men reckless. "Go ahead, Speaker! Do it if you can! You might as well. It is only a matter of time until you do anyway. You or your Army of Peace which destroys the Balance and the world! Or one of those thrice damned fools who tried to climb..." Egar stopped short with his mouth open, and the color drained from his face.

Ben blinked and shook his head, trying to understand what Egar had been going to say. After a moment he grabbed the servant by the shoulders and lifted him until they were eye to eye. "What were you going to say?" Ben demanded.

"Who tried to climb what? What happened to them?"

Egar's mouth worked open and shut, but no sound came out. After a moment he shucked himself out of Ben's grasp, pushed him out of the way, and ran down the corridor.

Ben looked after the fleeing man and tried to make some sense of what had just happened. *It has to be Rema and at least some of the others. Aris left them out there to die, but they didn't die! They came on without me! They tried to climb up here to speak the Peace to the gods!*

After a few moments of standing like a statue in the hall he turned and began shouting, "Aris! Where are they? Show yourself you misbegotten son of a bitch!"

Nothing happened.

"That's it! I'm through waiting. If you won't come to me, I'll find you!" He started off at a jog in the direction Egar had fled, shouting for Aris every few steps.

Aris' eye scalding brightness blinked into solidity in the corridor ahead of Ben. The light was so blinding he had to stop and throw his arms up to shield his eyes from the pain of it.

"Please Speaker," Aris said, a hint of real pleading in his voice. "Lady Tarsa..."

"To hell with Lady Tarsa, and with you," Ben screamed. "What have you done with Rema and the others?"

"I told you before, they are well."

The pain of the God of Light's brilliance was almost enough to drive Fordham to his knees, but he was defiant. "You lied! You left them out in the desert, but they didn't die like you intended. They made it here! Now where are they?"

Aris hesitated, probably wondering how dangerous

this situation was; wondering how angry this god from another world be in order to Speak the Peace? At last he opted for truth. "They are here," he said. "They were trying to climb up, so I brought them up rather than chance their reaching here on their own. They are safe."

"I want to see them."

"Soon..."

"Now!"

Aris hesitated. "And if I refuse?"

"Then I will go bashing down the halls of this place screaming at the top of my lungs until I find them myself," Ben said. His words were muffled by his arms still held up to shield his eyes but the determination came through clearly.

"Come here, Speaker. Let me darken your eyes so I may see your face as we talk."

Ben was in sufficient pain not to refuse. He allowed the God of Light to touch his temple and the blinding glare diminished. The headache it had given him still pounded as though his skull would burst, but it began to lessen almost immediately.

"Now then," Aris began.

"No!" Ben said and shook his finger side to side in negation. "No, *now then.* No sweet reasonableness, no nothing! Take me to them or bring them to me right now or get out of the way so I can get on with finding them myself."

"Lady Tarsa..."

"...Is no problem at all anymore."

"She could..."

"What? Kill me? If she couldn't do it in the barren land she can't do it here, and even if she tries, I'll speak the

Peace and it will all be over but the shouting!"

"The Balance..."

"Where are they?"

Aris stared at the Speaker for a half dozen heart beats then said, "Very well. Come here."

Ben took a tentative step forward, but stopped.

"Come, come, Speaker. The longer I am absent from Tarsa's presence, the more likely she is to realize you are here."

Ben stepped to the god and felt the shining arms come up to embrace him. In an instant the arms opened. Aris disappeared, and Ben found himself in a chamber much like his own. Rema, Borj, Rothean, and Calan stood close together around a marble block table. He barely had time to recognize them when an earth shaking jolt threw them all to the floor. Darkness crashed down upon them like an avalanche.

Rema screamed.

"It's all right," Ben shouted over the rumbling groan of the earthquake. "It will stop in a minute."

"You are here!" the flesh tearing sound of Tarsa's voice overrode the other noise. "Now you are mine!"

A coldness more piercing, more deathly, than the cold of the barren land engulfed them, squeezing everything but acid terror out of them. They lay on the floor, legs drawn up, arms covering heads, utterly helpless, trying to keep from slipping over into mindless, screaming horror.

Light exploded around them. It was as though they were inside a nuclear detonation.

"You cannot!" Aris shouted, and the terror which

gripped the Speakers receded. The malevolence which had been so hungry for them suddenly turned its focus toward the God of Light.

Tarsa and Aris faced one another, not touching, but battling all the same. The atmosphere crackled with electricity as each attempted to exert power over the other, but failed.

The Speakers, released from Tarsa's grip managed to sit up. Fordham crawled to the others and they huddled together in the flimsy protection of the marble table. Fear and fascination drew their eyes to the gods, but there was no surge of anger or need to command the gods to Peace. The connection was so far beyond their humanity they could hardly comprehend it.

"I will have him, husband," Tarsa hissed.

"You will not. I will not allow you to destroy the world!"

"The world," she laughed scornfully. "Your precious Balance is crumbling, husband. The armies of the out world toy which you stole from me are conquering your world. Let me have him that I may enjoy him before all is ended!"

"If you could not harm him in the barren land..."

"Because you warded him against me..."

"No, I did not. He is a god!"

"He is a morsel to be swallowed!"

"He commands life and death!"

"I command life and death! At my behest are battles joined!"

Aris screamed in an agony of frustration and leapt with claw shaped hands at his god-wife's throat.

The battle was like the crashing together of planets.

The power of it washed over the awe-struck Speakers like ejected magma from the cataclysm. As one the five shot to their feet commanding with one voice, "PEACE BE WITH YOU!"

The vast and aching silence of the universe fell upon them and lasted an eon, or a moment.

A voice so mighty it was felt in the very marrow of the bones spoke. "THE BALANCE IS ENDED! NOW IS JUDGMENT PROCLAIMED!"

## Chapter Twenty

The Place of Judgment was a hewn stone amphitheater of gigantic proportion. At one end of the half circle stood a throne, not less than ten stories tall and hewn from a single block of white marble. At the other end, opposite the throne, the amphitheater opened to a plain which stretched beyond the ability of sight. Standing upon the plain shoulder to shoulder, side by side in ordered rows stretching from horizon to horizon, were the people of the world. In the front row, just outside the reach of the theater stood Rema, Borj, Rothean, and Calan. On their left stood the Seer Nora. On their right the Seer Arna. All those on the plain stood looking up.

Ben, feeling like an ant, stood in the center of the amphitheater before the throne. He turned slowly around trying to determine where he was, but there was nothing familiar at all. The place seemed to exist in the midst of nothing--adrift in the blackness of space. Above the amphitheater and plain was the yawning eternity of the universe all spattered with stars. He looked toward the plain and called out to Rema and the others, but they did not respond nor even look at him.

"Ben Fordham," the same voice which had proclaimed the judgment called.

Fordham turned back to the throne. It was no longer empty. The Over-God had come to judge the world and Ben Fordham.

The awe of being in the presence of the Creator almost stole Fordham's breath. The Over-God was like pictures which had been put into his head by Sunday school teachers and preachers from his childhood. This creator was a huge old man with flowing white beard and hair, but there was no air of decrepitude, only an air of ancient, unending power. He was dressed in long flowing white robes which swept the floor before the throne. He looked neither angry nor benign. It was more as though he were--relieved.

Ben began to wonder again about his sanity; to doubt this was real. It was too much like some conventional dream with its own skewed kind of sense.

"Very good, Ben Fordham," the Over-God said, smiling. "You have found me out. I am not this," he passed his hand over himself. "I chose this only because it was what you thought to see. I am not confined or shaped except within the strictures of your thoughts."

"Are you real?"

The Over-God smiled again. "Yes."

Ben stared at the being on the throne then realized what he was doing and looked away. "What should I call you?" he asked.

"No matter. Sir will do. There is no need for formality. If you feel like bowing and scraping go ahead, but it is of no consequence to me."

Ben hesitated a second then said, "Thank you, sir."

"Very well then, with all that out of the way let's get down to business." He leaned his cheek on his hand, elbow upon the arm of the throne. "This is the end of the world, you know?"

The tone puzzled Ben a little. The Over-God seemed to be taking this rather lightly. "Yes Sir," he answered. "Aris, I mean Lord Aris, said if the Balance was tipped too far, the end of the world would come. I guess this means the Balance is well and truly broken, doesn't it?"

"It does," the Over-God said with a nod. "You and your Speakers have seen to that."

Ben suddenly felt the guilt of all the blood shed, all the lives lost, all the pain, and now the very end of the world. "I'm sorry, Sir...," he stammered

"No, No, No, don't be sorry. It is the way it was all supposed to go. I'm relieved the whole mess is finished and came out right at the end."

Ben shook his head, not sure he had heard what he though he had. "It was supposed to happen?" He did not know whether to be outraged or relieved.

"Of course. That is the doom my servant Nora told you about."

"There was never any question of how it was to turn out?"

"I didn't say that. There were several times when things could have gone differently. You might have been killed, or you might not have had your quirk about peace, or you might have decided to just wander around the world for a while, and things would have been much different as they have been before. Things never quite turned out right until you."

Ben thought about it for a time. "You mean there have been others like me?"

"Oh yes. I prepared many."

"Prepared?"

"Yes. You were told about them when you first arrived in the cave, remember? Borj and Sko commented how you seemed different than the others. They--the others--never affected the world though. They just landed here, existed for a while then disappeared into history without so much as a ripple."

"You prepared many others?"

"Yes. Many. And I am happy there were no more needed than there were. There were a lot of possible choices before I got to you."

"Got to me? You mean you brought me here, not Tarsa?"

"Well, it was Tarsa, but it was done at my behest."

"You mean Mardian works for you?"

"After a fashion. Mardian works--worked for Tarsa, who existed at my behest, so in a way Mardian worked for me, but he did not know it. You understand?"

"No, I don't. What do you mean you prepared me and many others?"

"I used the other world to sort of--incubate you and the others."

"So that's why I never felt like I fit there," Ben said. "And the reason for the nightmares I had as a kid."

"Yes, exactly."

"But I don't fit here either!"

"True. Still, it had to be that way, you understand, to achieve my ends."

Ben had been feeling a growing sense of anger at this being who claimed to be the Over-God. "Yes, I understand!" he began. "I don't like it, but I understand. You're just like Aris and Tarsa. You want what you want and you don't care who gets hurt. You're worse than Tarsa! At least she had the excuse of being the Goddess of Dark. You expect her to be evil."

"Wait, wait, wait, don't get all upset! Think about it a little. First off, you are mistaking dark for evil, and it isn't necessarily so. The demarcation is nothing as clear as all that. Evil can be light too. Didn't Aris have a great deal to do with evil by your definition?"

"Doesn't matter! First you 'incubate' me then you steal me from the life I managed to make there. You had Mardian snatch me here to amuse you! What kind of God does that? An evil one!"

"Ah. Your life before. And a fine life it was too. Full of wonderfulness and joy. Just where would you be if I hadn't *snatched* you, as you said? You were a man out of place in his own world, and the mad man with the hammer very nearly *snatched you* out of that world before I could get to you. Not so?"

Fordham was stopped by the truth of that, but he had been pushed and prodded and shoved into places and situations not of his own making for so long he could not stand to have it happen anymore without at least some token struggle. "It was still my life, no matter how I got there" he said, thinking how much like a spoiled child he sounded. "I was born in it, and if I was going to die, I should have died in it."

The Over-God stroked his flowing beard and said, "Perhaps so, but what a waste it would have been. As things stood you would probably have died of cirrhosis of the liver in a few years if you didn't fall under a bus or get your skull split for the change in your pocket. Instead you were brought here to change a world."

"To change a world…Right!" Ben said scornfully. "The world changed all right--from a place of blood and death to no place at all! You decided to have the whole thing over and POP it's done. Well, it isn't right and it isn't fair!" Tears rose in Fordham's eyes and threatened to choke off his voice, but he refused to let them fall. "What about all the people who died? What about Othway and all those poor suffering bastards on the poles outside Cynar? I changed the world for them all right. I'll bet they're just as happy as Hell you brought me here to change their world! And all those lives are on my head because you wouldn't leave me alone in the gutter."

"Easy, Speaker, take it easy. Not to worry. All that was just flesh, and it was not your fault. It was mine."

"Just flesh! Maybe it was just flesh to you, but you weren't the one who saw Othway hanging there in agony with the pole through his guts. You weren't there to see the carnage at Bakar or smell the stink of death in that little village where all the corpses were in the square..."

"Nohar..."

Ben stopped his ranting for a moment and looked up.

The being on the throne suddenly seemed sad.

"The village was called Nohar. You could not remember the name. I cannot forget it."

Ben frowned.

"You are wrong, Ben Fordham. I saw all the horror and felt all the pain of each and every one of my creatures, but unlike you who think it was your fault, *I know* it was mine. You spoke the peace and caused the Balance to swing, but I created the balance and all the pain which came from it. That is why I had to bring you here."

Fordham stared into the Over-God's face and shook his head. "How could you create such a place? You didn't even give the people a choice in what they were doing before I got here. No matter which god they served they had to go on killing one another to keep the Balance. They couldn't even say 'No more,' because that's not the way you built the world."

"Not so," the Over-God said.

"What do you mean, 'Not so?' Before I came..."

"You once considered how Rema became a Speaker."

"Don't try to change the subject!"

"I am not. You considered it on the road to the Valley of Seers. Why was Rema a Speaker?"

"Rema?"

"Yes, Rema. How did gentle Rema who was a healer, who had never done violence to anyone in her life, how was she able to speak the Peace? She was no warrior. How could she be changed by your command?"

Ben blinked, then looked down and raked his top

teeth over his lower lip seeking an answer. He remembered wondering why in the haze between nightmares. He did not find an answer then nor did he find one now."

"She was the same as she had always been," the Over-God went on. "She was a healer, sickened by the violence. How could she speak the Peace? And Calan. He was a soldier of the dark, yet he became a Speaker without having been commanded to it. He decided Peace, and to serve you, was better. Without benefit of your command, he had the power to speak the Peace..."

"Borj or Rothean or someone commanded Calan."

"No. He opened the gates at Rothean's request, not at his command. The Peace was there all the time. It has always been. People needed only to seize it. All they had to do was put away their worship of blood thirsty gods and seize the peace."

Fordham thought about what he had heard before asking, "Then why did you bring me here?"

"They had not learned it could be done so. I brought you to show them it could be."

"Couldn't you have just told them without me?"

"What do you think the Seers have been doing since time began?"

"The pain and the blood and the death? Why didn't you create a perfect world?"

"I did! The world was perfect, and some pain and some dying were all part of it. Those things must be if a world is to be alive, otherwise it is just a thing with no being. All living is a balance between joy and pain. For every good there is a bad; for every joy there is a pain. Subtract either and the thing is no longer alive."

"You are powerful! You are the Over-God! Why can you make a living thing without pain?"

The Over-God leaned back in his throne and laced his fingers together before his lips, considering how to answer Fordham. At last he sat up and put his hands in his lap. "I am not sure you will understand what I am going to tell you, but I will try if you will try."

There was such gravity in what the mighty being on the throne said Fordham found himself wondering if he really wanted to hear what was coming. He had a feeling the explanation might shatter him like glass, but he thought, *I have come this far, I might as well go all the way.*

"All right, sir, I will try to understand, but please take it slowly and make it simple."

"No worry on that part. The simplicity is what is so hard to understand. So, here it is. There is no beginning, and no ending, only continuing. The universes--and there are an infinite number of them--the universes exist. They have always been and they will always be. They were not created nor will they end. They will change and grow and shrink in the void, but they always are."

"That's Einstein--and Buddha."

"Yes, but they had only a tiny hold on the idea. In your universe there are those who think all started with a gigantic collision of all matter. In a way they are right, but it is the same thing I just said. The universes just are, and they always will be in one form or another."

"And you, Sir? Are you Forever?"

"As I recall a man in your world once asked God who

he really was, and God answered, 'I AM.' That is my answer to you. I AM."

"In church we used to say "Who is, was, and ever shall be..."

"Yes, just like the universes."

"Where does that leave people?" Ben asked. "Does all this cosmic '*beingness*' make them hurt less or bleed less when they are cut?"

"No, but as I told you, that is all part of the universes. The beings change and grow and shrink with the universes, but they always are and so is joy and contentment."

"But you are the Over-God! Can't you change things?"

"I can re-arrange things a little, but never change the essence of them. Like your understanding of the speech of this world. I re-arranged your mind a little, but I didn't change it."

Ben, trying to fathom all he had been told, glanced down and his eyes fell on the Voyager's Mark. The tattoo was still there, but it was different now. The drawing no longer glowed or pulsed, and the depictions of the gods were blacked out. There was no life in it anymore. It was only a rather primitive tattoo, not even as good as many others he had seen. "What happened here," he asked. "My Voyager's Mark is all changed."

"That place is no longer. It is changed."

Ben looked at his arm then back to the face of the Over-God. "You destroyed it," Ben said bitterly. "You told me nothing was ever destroyed, but you destroyed this," he held up his arm.

The Over-God lifted his hands in exasperation and shook his mighty head. "You are a vexatious soul, Ben Fordham," he said, but not unkindly. "And you don't listen very well. Did I say destroyed?"

"You said this place," Fordham shook his arm again, "no longer exists."

"No, I said it no longer is. The universe is rearranged a little--not destroyed or uncreated, just re-arranged."

"What about Aris and Tarsa? I don't see them out there anywhere," he pointed back toward the plain where all the people of the world which no longer was stood. "Are they re-arranged too?"

"Yes."

"And the dead? Are they 're-arranged?'"

"Yes."

"Are they alive again some where else?"

The Over-God smiled a small secret smile. "Were you not listening when I said 'the universe is.'"

"Doesn't answer my question."

"Further than I have said, I will not say."

"I thought you were omniscient?"

"I did not say I do not know, I said I will not say further."

"It's the same dodge preachers used on earth! Humans can't understand God. He is incomprehensible." Ben sneered. "It was a low trick from them and a low trick from you. I would have expected better from the Over-God."

The being on the throne shrugged. "I was afraid you could not understand, and indeed you have not."

"It is still the same dodge," Fordham said stubbornly.

"If you say so, but it is the best I can do for you. Like it or don't like it, what is, is."

"I don't like it, but I guess I don't have a choice."

"True, you don't have a choice."

Ben drew a deep breath, let it out, and after a little asked, "What comes next?"

"Ah, indeed. What does come next?"

"You're going to send me home, aren't you?"

"Yes."

"Well, that's pretty god-like I must say. Snatch me out of the gutter/incubator, ship me here, use me and abuse me, and when the job is done, zip zap shabam, and back I go. Nice touch. Very--*omnipotent.*"

The Over-God laughed and the amphitheater shook with the echoes of it. There was no bitterness or scorn or cruelty in it, only amusement such as a parent is amused by a precocious child. "You are a marvelous piece of work, Ben Fordham. Marvelous."

"Thank you too much!"

The Over-God cocked his head to the side and asked, "What have you lost by being here, Ben Fordham?"

"We've been over that."

"Precisely. You have lost nothing really. You are better off now than when you arrived. You are sober and sharp and you have been a god. If I return you to the Golden Gopher where you started, you come out ahead. You start with more than when you left, and you will be free to go on in any manner you wish."

"Free." Ben snorted. "What is free when you can pull

or push me where you want?"

The Over-God shrugged.

"Besides, I don't want to go back there. I didn't belong there in the first place. There is nothing there for me. When I first woke up chained to a wall I would have given anything, one of my arms or eyes, to go back, but now--I don't want to go back to being a drunk who doesn't fit. And Rema. What about Rema? I love her and she loves me. I want to be with her for the rest of my life."

"Yes, there is Rema, and all the others. What about them? A god should look out for his creatures, or so you implied a little while ago."

"Yes, a god should, but I'm not a god," Ben protested. "I'm just a man. I've told everyone all along that I am just a man."

"They didn't believe you."

"I don't care. Their belief doesn't make me a god."

"You are wrong. You were a god, at least as much as Tarsa or Aris. You changed the world. When you spoke the peace to Aris and Tarsa every person there," he pointed to the plain, "became what they could have been all along. A Speaker."

"I had no choice!"

"Ah, we return to choice."

"Yes, choice. A god should have choices. I had no choice. So far as I can tell, I still have no choice."

"And if you did, what would you do?"

"I'd...I'd take Rema back to my world with me."

"And live happily ever after? What about all the others?"

Ben stopped short and looked into the eyes of the being on the throne--into the eyes his own mental picture had given the Over-God. "You are laughing at me, aren't you?" he said angrily. "You are sitting up there playing with me like a cat with a mouse, aren't you?"

"No, Ben Fordham, I am not. I am only trying to show you the impossibility of what you are saying."

"Why? Why is it impossible?"

"How would your world react to a few hundred thousand new humans who simply popped out of nowhere?"

Ben thought about it for a moment before saying, "You're right."

"So this choice is no choice. Try again."

"I can't! I can't choose! That is a choice up to a real god, not a kidnapped misfit," he cried.

"Yes. Therefore, I will choose."

"And you will send me home." It was not a question.

"Yes."

Fordham rubbed his hand over his face, ordering his mind to acceptance of what could not be changed. "Can I at least say good bye?" he asked.

"Yes."

With that Fordham found himself standing at the edge of the amphitheater facing the humanity covered plain. As he cast his eyes over them, a sound like a wind rippling over water came to him. It took a moment for him to realize it was the sound of breath from all the people on the plain. The breathing in and breathing out of the entire world as they came awake.

"Speaker," someone called out. "What has

happened?"

"Yes, my Lord," Rema said. "What has happened? What is this place?"

Ben smiled sadly at hearing Rema call him *Lord,* though he had told her so many times not to. "I am still not a god, Rema. I am only a man who loves you," he lifted his eyes to all of them. "Who loves you all," he said.

"I am sorry Ben Fordham...," she began, but he held up his hand to stop her.

"It doesn't matter anymore," he said.

"What is this place, Speaker?" Borj asked.

"It is the Place of Judgment," he answered. He didn't speak loudly, but all the people on the plain heard him and there was a huge gasp. "The Over-God called us here after we five spoke the Peace to the gods."

"And the doom, Speaker? Is it worked out?" Nora asked.

Ben turned back to the Over-God, already knowing the answer to Nora's question. The being on the throne nodded and with the nod a sigh rose from the plain.

"Are we ended then?" several voices asked.

"It matters not at all," Rothean answered them before Fordham could. "If we are ended, we are ended in Peace."

Ben found tears flowing down his face and said, "Yes, Peace."

"Then all is well," they agreed.

"Better a little time of Peace than eternal war," Calan said

Ben looked over the plain for a time then said, "You have been the fulfillment of my life." He dropped his eyes to the front row. "Borj, you kept me sane on the first day. I didn't think it was kindness then..."

The former soldier of the Dark grinned his wolfish grin. "Nor did I, Speaker, but after Bakar I was glad you were still alive."

"That was because of Rothean," Ben said.

The red-bearded warrior of the Light said, "you returned the favor amply, Speaker, and because you did...," he tilted his head at Calan "...he joined us."

Ben shook his head. "I had little to do with that. Calan became a Speaker by choice rather than command."

"It was not a difficult choice, Speaker," Calan answered. "A choice of life over death."

Ben wondered if it were true since he could feel the eyes of the Over-God on his back, but he said nothing.

After a moment he turned back to Rema. The pain in his heart was almost unbearable as he looked at her lovely face, and felt the magnetic depth of her golden eyes. "I love you, Rema" he said. "And if I had a choice, I would spend eternity with you, but it seems I have no such choice."

"Then this must be enough, my Lord. My Love," her eyes shown with tears, but they did not fall.

Seeing her twisted his heart, but there was nothing he could do about it so he looked away. After a little he looked over the plain of humanity. "Before the gates of Bakar," he began, "and at Tarsa's temple in Cynar I told you all to go and speak the Peace to everyone you met. You did and our speaking has brought us to this place. For good or ill there is nothing more to be done now save speak the words back to you, therefore, PEACE BE WITH YOU ALL, FOREVER."

And they were gone.

~ * ~

Ben Fordham opened his eyes and looked around. He couldn't figure out where he was. Nothing seemed familiar. The walls of the room were light green, except for the parts that were glass. Sunlight streamed through a window on his right, but his position made it impossible to see out the window. There was a white ceiling with metal drapery tracks above him. The drapes were pulled back out of the way. The place would not quite come into focus. He squeezed his eyes shut again and tried to shake his head to clear his vision, but found it more difficult to do than it should have been. His head seemed heavy and there were things attached to it. The little movement he made gave him pain--not much, but some.

"Ben," a feminine voice edged with anxiety said, and a familiar face came into his range of vision.

Ben squeezed his eyes shut again then opened them. The face was still there, the golden eyes filled with concern.

"Oh please, God. Ben, don't you recognize me?"

"Rema?" he asked, his voice nasal sounding because of the tube clipped beneath his nose.

Tears of joy and relief sprang to her eyes and flowed down her face. 'Yes, baby! Yes! It's me, it's me." She lifted his hand to her lips and kissed it.

"How...? What happened? The Over-God..."

Rema's brows drew down and some of the worry returned to her eyes.

A sound of rubber-soled foot steps came, and another familiar face entered his range of vision. Nora. She wore a white lab coat and a stethoscope hanging around her neck. "Mr. Fordham," she began, "I'm glad to see you are awake. We were beginning to wonder if you'd ever come back to us. Do you know where you are?"

Ben blinked several times, trying to sort out what was going on. "Home?" he asked

"Maybe soon," Nora said, "For right now you're in Angels of Mercy hospital."

"Los Angeles?"

"Santa Monica. I'm Dr. Heleen Nora."

"Doctor..." he began, still confused.

"It's all right if you don't remember everything yet. It'll get clearer as time goes by," Dr. Nora said, peering into his eyes. She used a tiny pocket flashlight to check his pupils then shifted her gaze higher and gingerly touched the front of his head just above the hair line.

"I remember..."Ben stopped, suddenly not wanting to go on with what he had been going to say. "How did I get here?" he asked.

"The easy answer...," Nora began, not turning her attention away from her examination "...is you got here by ambulance, but I assume you want a little more in depth explanation." She began checking his reflexes. "I'll leave that to your wife and friends though."

"My wife? Maggie is here?"

The doctor looked at Rema who looked worried, and shrugged. "Well," Nora said, "I actually meant this wife here, but if you have more than one you can work it out between you later." She smiled crookedly and to Rema added, "I'd wait until the skull fracture heals before you discuss that. No sport in killing a man who's already been as close to the next world as your husband has been. Besides, the baby might need a father even if he is a bigamist."

"Baby?" Ben asked.

"You don't remember?" Rema said as tears began to fall again.

The doctor turned to her and patted her shoulder. "Don't worry about it, Mrs. Fordham. Some short term memory loss is not at all odd in cases like this. It looks as though he is doing fine, but now we need to let him rest. OK?"

Rema sniffed back tears and said, "OK."

The doctor turned back to Ben. "I'll be back in a while to check you over again. Meantime rest. And you might say a little prayer of thanks you're as thick skulled as you are." She smiled reassuringly and went out.

Rema kissed him carefully and whispered, "I love you," then went out.

When he was alone Ben tried to puzzle out what was going on. It was as though the life he remembered--both the lives he remembered had never been. He remembered being hit with the hammer in that other life, and apparently that was why he was in this hospital in this world now, but what had happened to the world between the first one and this one? Or was this one, that one? Was all the rest just some dream? Some hallucination? Maybe induced by a clout on the skull with a framing hammer.

Still, it had seemed so real!

"Doc said we could look in," a voice said from the door. It was Rothean, looking not much different than the last time Ben had seen him except now he wore a flannel work shirt and jeans instead of leather and bronze armor. Borj and Calan stood behind him. With some minor variations they were dressed the same as Rothean.

"You OK?" Borj asked.

Fordham hesitated, but finally said, "I guess. Things are still pretty fuzzy though."

"I don't wonder," Calan said. "If Johnny and Emile hadn't pulled that crazy son of a bitch off you, you'd be shaking hands with Saint Pete right now."

"Yeah, I guess so. Thank them for me, will ya?"

The three looked at one another with slight puzzlement on their faces, but decided to let it pass.

"No sweat, Fordham," Rothean said.

"Maybe you'll do the same for us someday," Borj added.

Ben blinked and added this new information to the things he needed to consider.

"We gotta go," Calan said after another moment. "The doc said not to stay long. We'll be back later."

"Yeah, OK. And thanks again."

All three grinned and lifted hands in good bye gestures as they turned away.

Fordham lifted his own left hand and his eyes fell on the primitive black line tattoo which stretched from his elbow to his wrist.

A rustle caught his attention and he looked up.

A smiling man with long white hair and flowing

beard, dressed in floor sweeping white robes stood framed in the doorway. "Welcome home, Speaker," he said.

"Home? But...," Ben began. The other stopped him with a lift of the hand.

"PEACE BE WITH YOU," he said, and disappeared.

THE END

## About the Author

G. Lloyd Helm has been writing for 30 years, having published poetry in a wide variety of magazines and newspapers including "The New York Poetry Anthology," "Stars and Stripes News," "The Los Angeles Times," "The Antelope Valley Press," and "The Antelope Valley Anthologies," among others.

...Has published short stories and memoirs both in the US and in England in such journals as "Pligrimage" which published the memoir "Football" in Spring 2005, and a second memoir "4 April, 1968" in the winter of 2008. He has published short stories in "Citadel" the literary magazine of Los Angeles City College," "Delivered Magazine," which is based in London, "Short Story Library," The University of S. Illinois' "Eureka Literary Magazine," "Tales as like as not," and London's "Black Gate Magazine." Recently published "Even Up" a Civil War Ghost story and a Poesque Short story called "Molly and Me and Baby makes three." at www.ruthlesspeoples.com English on line magazine, and the short story "A Lovely Elephant" in Delivered, an English fiction journal.

...Has published three novels in the F&SF field,

1) OTHER DOORS, From MousePrints Publishing, and
2) DESIGN from Publish America.
3) WORLD WITHOUT END from Rogue Phoenix Press, www.roguephoenixpress.com .

Helm is also a publisher of and contributor to "The Antelope Valley Anthologies" which are collections of poetry, short stories, and essays from the residents of

Southern California's Antelope Valley. These have been published for the last six years the most recent of which THE RAVEN AND THE WRITING DESK will be released 28 October, 2008.

...Is a former leader of the Palmdale Playhouse "Writers' Roundtable" and current facilitator of "The Unknown Writers of the Antelope Valley workshop."

# Also Available
## by G. L. Helm
## at Rogue Phoenix Press

*World Without End*

When an author writes a story, creates a world and the creatures in it, does the literary world actually come into being in some parallel universe? Joshua Gordon, creative writing professor and writer of pulp fiction thinks so and is in fact so convinced it is true that when he is diagnosed with a terminal illness he sets out to find a protege who he can convince to take over as the creator god of the world. He finds that protege in the person of John Fisher.

www.ingramcontent.com/pod-product-compliance
Lightning Source LLC
LaVergne TN
LVHW010602100826
845148LV00014B/2814

* 9 7 8 1 6 2 4 2 0 0 2 4 3 *